D0895008

THE PICNIC AT SAKKARA

THE PICNIC AT SAKKARA

P. H. NEWBY

FABER AND FABER
24 Russell Square
London

First published in mcmlv
by Jonathan Cape
First published in this edition mcmlxvi
by Faber and Faber Limited
24 Russell Square London W.C.1
Printed in Great Britain
by Latimer Trend & Co Ltd Whitstable

5

1

THE NOTE OF AMBITION

Sɪᴘᴘɪɴɢ ʜɪs ʟᴇᴍᴏɴ ᴀɴᴅ ʙᴀʀʟᴇʏ ᴡᴀᴛᴇʀ, His Excellency confessed to a secret ambition; he wished to serve his country. Although there were richer men in the world, in India, for example, no one enjoyed His Excellency's special combination of wealth and patriotism; no one, that is to say, had a power for good equal to his own. Naturally, he had to beware of rogues — of hangers-on, of confidence men, of jewel thieves, of charity organizers, of beautiful but dissolute women who might compromise him. On the other hand, he must not be afraid to take a risk. At times he must be prepared to take risks which, to the ordinary person, would seem absurd. That would only be due to the ordinary person's lack of imagination and ability to see a man's character in his face.

'I'll tell you what I mean,' he said, still speaking in French although this was supposed to be his English lesson. 'When we were at Luxor, the Princess and I, the year must have been 1942, we were evacuated, you see? This scientist had a kind of hut in the grounds of the hotel. We saw him only at meals, a little man with big nostrils like a horse. Nobody knew what he was up to. He was a Belgian. Perhaps he was working on Perpetual Motion. That was my idea. Now, if he had come to me and taken me into his confidence I should have listened sympathetically. For the sake of Egypt I should have invested in him. I would have built him a laboratory and the country would have benefited. But what did he do? He disappeared.

He disappeared into the Sudan and for all I know that is where he is still working.'

His Excellency said he was reminded of another scientist he had known in Paris. On that occasion the scientist had asked for money, but not before a perfectly satisfactory demonstration had been arranged. 'A little clockwork engine went round and round on some rails. I call it clockwork, but who am I to know what it was? The engine never stopped. We sat and watched it for two hours. There were two newspaper men, a science professor from the Lycée Henri IV, and it was a complete mystery. What made the engine go? The scientist wanted ten thousand pounds to let me examine the engine. He would sell his secret for ten thousand pounds. He said it was the greatest invention since steam. But I didn't give him ten thousand pounds. I went away, but I've always regretted it. The Gestapo must have got him in the end.'

The big German wolfhound rose from his settee and stood barking in the warm November sunshine. Only now had he become aware of the presence of his master's English tutor, a man he detested, and his blue body shook with angry barks.

'Tais-toi, Tipou!' said His Excellency sharply, and the hound slunk back to his cushions.

Perry, who had fought down his impulse to yell with alarm, re-seated himself on a gilt and plush chair and for some time — until the Princess herself entered the room some thirty minutes later — did not allow his eyes to leave the dog except to gaze into the brown, deliciously soft eyes of the Pasha himself, or to glance at the document he had placed on the Pasha's desk. A dusty palm frond tapped against the window. There was silence in the Palace.

It embarrassed him to speak French. In the first place, he spoke it badly; in the second place he presented himself two afternoons a week at the Palace to give His Excellency English

8

lessons and Perry's conscience was troubled when His Excellency took up all the time chattering in French, saying that he wanted a friend, not an English teacher, that in spite of his wealth, and his position, and his ambition, he was a lonely man, and so on.

'As His Excellency will see if you — ' or should it be *he*? Perry wondered wildly — 'if he reads my report, the students need a lot more than a canteen. In my view that is.'

'But M. Perry, what have we here?'

'I've discovered there is a canteen of sorts already; at least there is in the Faculty of Arts and I'm sure the other faculties have them. The trouble is much deeper than that.'

'This is English thoroughness,' said His Excellency, smiling. 'It is not the Germans who are thorough, no. It is English thoroughness that makes you speak in this way.'

Interrupting himself in the act of picking up Perry's document His Excellency made a gesture intended to bring the various objects standing on his desk to Perry's attention — the black telephone with a dial, the red telephone without a dial, the rock crystal paper knife, the jade screen, the tray of Roman gold coins — 'From this desk, M. Perry, many of the affairs of Egypt are directed. And how many men walking the streets of Cairo know anything about it? A great deal of the greatest good is done quietly, even secretly. That telephone communicates directly with His Majesty.'

He allowed the tips of his fingers to rest on the red telephone. 'But if the students go to sleep in lectures at the end of every month because they've spent their monthly income and go without food, that is serious. It is serious for Egypt. What finer gesture could the Princess and I make than building a large canteen where all can feed for a few piastres a week?'

'What the university needs is a range of hostels,' said Perry looking at the blue dog which lay, snout out, one eye shut and the other implacably hostile.

'You mean like the new buildings at Al Azhar?' said the Pasha.

Perry thought of the buff battlements that had been reared among the minarets of the Old City to house students of the Moslem university. 'Yes, like that, but bigger,' he said.

'I think the Azhar hostel cost a million pounds.'

'Then the Fouad University hostels must cost two millions.' Speaking quietly, because of an obscure idea that his faulty French would be less noticeable in that way, Perry said he was ashamed that he had taught at the university for so long without exploring the living conditions of the students. What he had seen had appalled him.

'Two million pounds! Did you say two million pounds? That is a great deal of money. The war just over, all sorts of plans for reconstruction, making good our losses, salvaging from the ruin, well, I ask you, where is two million pounds coming from? But I'm glad, anyway, that you have seen how your students live, M. Perry. Now confess! You wouldn't have gone, would you, if I hadn't sent you? It was my idea. The students, you see, are our future. We must see that they lack nothing. But two million pounds! Let me put it another way. It is out of the question that I should provide this money.'

Perry said nothing for some moments. When he had entered the Pasha's study half an hour before he had no intention of urging him to spend a couple of million pounds on students' hostels; he had certainly been shocked by the Gizeh tenements where the students lived but he could have sworn the idea of a hostel had not entered his head until he heard himself say, 'What the university needs . . .' Now the proposal had been made he experienced a dizzy rush of enthusiasm. Two million pounds? Who said two million? It might turn out to be as little as a million and a half. And what was a million and a half pounds?

'They would call it the Tureiya Pasha Hostel.'

'Quite out of the question,' said His Excellency, smiling at the thought. 'Oh dear! I see that you have written your report in English. When I show it to Her Highness she will say. "What does it all mean?" and I shall say, "I don't know, it is in English," and she will say, "What do you take English lessons for?" and I shall say, "I take English lessons because I like M. Perry. He is the only man in Egypt I can talk freely with." But, it is true, M. Perry. I am a bad pupil. I am not a credit to you.' To cheer himself up the Pasha attempted a few phrases in English. 'Good day. Good morning. Will you be so good as to show me some fancy socks, some ties, some shirts.'

At this moment the Princess herself entered the room, followed by the English butler wheeling a tea-trolley. With a great show of gallantry the Pasha rose and darted round his desk to kiss the withered skin of her left hand. There was an unmistakable extravagance in his manner which Perry put down to the fact that the Princess was of the Blood Royal, that she had been married twice before, that her present husband, the Pasha, was twenty-five years her junior and not royal — he was merely of noble blood, even if that blood was Turkish. In spite of all this, the Pasha seemed to be saying to the Princess, I love you dearly.

Keeping the Pasha between him and the blue wolfhound who had now risen to his feet once more, Perry put his heels together and bowed in the Princess's direction. The Pasha he liked, but the Princess had won his admiration; she was about seventy, had a noticeably long, bird-like neck which had once been beautiful and now had to be disguised with pearls. Her nose was fine — indeed, it made such a beautiful arch that she always insisted on being photographed in profile and then she appeared to have a truly Roman dignity. In real life she was too *petite* for real dignity; what is more, she had the vivacity of a girl of twenty. Brown eyes sparkled out of her thin face and patches of white gathered around the nostrils, making her red cheeks garish. She always had some project on hand. At the moment it was the launching of a feminist magazine to be printed in Arabic, French and English. Perry had already translated the Princess's first editorial from French into English.

'Good afternoon, Mr. Perry,' she said in English, with a good accent. 'Can you imagine my husband buying his own socks, ties and shirts? Don't, I beg you, teach him shop English. I want him to read English poetry. He is a practical man. There is not enough fantasy in his life.' After this they all spoke in French.

Mr. Swain, the butler, who had a Tyneside accent even after thirty years in Egypt, made a polite observation to Perry about the weather. Although he was small, in no way fat, there was an over-ripe fleshiness about the man which Perry found distasteful; he suggested a jockey who has been unable to keep his weight down and taken to drink. 'A nice, sunny day, sir,' said Mr. Swain as though they were in England and not in Egypt where most days were nice and sunny. Perry thought Swain did it on purpose because he despised his employers and wanted to strike a common note with a fellow-countryman. Perry nodded politely and turned to listen to what the Princess was saying.

'If the magazine is going to succeed it must have a popular appeal. Not a bit of good printing a lot of articles about the rights of women. M. Perry, I don't even think we ought to print your translation of that article by Mrs. Pankhurst. I've written a short story instead. Naturally it is set in Ancient Egypt, the sixteenth dynasty this time. That's where I feel at home. That's where my imagination flourishes. Besides, I don't think we all realize what rights women had in Ancient Egypt. In some ways they were much better off than they are now. They were mistresses in their own homes. They could sell it all up if they wanted to. They could turn their husbands out of doors. But my story isn't about that. It's the story of the Pharaoh's concubine. What is this?' She picked up Perry's report and held it level with her eyes. 'Is this a contribution?'

Now, it is most unlikely that Perry would have presumed to take his report out of the Princess's hands without her permission; and as she clearly intended to examine the document it seemed equally improbable that she would grant that permission. Nevertheless, Perry found himself standing in front of the Princess with the report in his hands and with a sense of having made a quite dreadful, an unforgivable, mistake. The Princess stared at him in surprise. The hand which had held the report was still raised in front of her. But surely, Perry thought desperately, she can't see to read without her glasses. She was screwing up her eyes. She must, without doubt, have made a gesture of impatience and passed the report to him —having seen it was in English — to read aloud. But in that case why was she standing there with one hand still upraised? And why had the white patches around her nostrils become larger? In the face of His Excellency, too, there was a change. Normally, his neatly trimmed moustache and somewhat prominent cheek-bones gave him the appearance of a popular French actor of the silent films — Perry could never remember his name — but now the aristocratic face rounded, became baby-like, even balloon-like, and the brown eyes looked unblinkingly at the face of his wife. The blue dog sat up, scratched himself noisily, and grinned round the room.

Perry was so astonished at his own behaviour, and so humiliated, that he began to apologize in English. But his words and his agitation made no impression. The rouge on the Princess's cheeks floated on her pallor, like brick-dust on milk. The Pasha stared. The air washed noisily in and out of the dog's mouth. To himself Perry applied solemn and silent obscenities. Only the dog seemed at ease. They had all dropped into a pocket of time where ordinary chronology did not operate and where motion was arrested. However, Mr. Swain came into the room with his eyes down, coughing quietly to himself and Perry — who had not previously noticed Swain's absence — was released from his spell and immediately began tearing the report up into small pieces. Mr. Swain offered more tea all round but retired in distress when he saw that the cups had not been touched.

'Your Highness,' said Perry, 'this report of mine is really all nonsense. I must do it again and have it properly translated into French for you.' He had reduced the dozen or so typed quarto sheets to pieces of paper about the size of playing cards and they were flowing out of his hands and fluttering to the floor; he looked round for a waste-paper basket and could not see one. He tried to put the pieces of paper into his pockets. After some moments he became aware that his feet were surrounded by litter. He foolishly picked up one of the fragments and said, 'You see, it just doesn't do justice to the situation.'

The dog snuffled through the papers and the Pasha spoke. 'But M. Perry, this is extraordinary! I have never seen anything like it. Highness!' he appealed to his wife, 'have you seen anything like it? You are very curious, M. Perry.' He was completely at a loss. At heart, he wanted to be angry; but his curiosity was too strong for him. Perhaps the English Professor was mad; perhaps he had been mad all the time and this tearing up of the report was the first open sign. The Pasha could imagine himself telling the story. 'I once had an English professor who was mad. He revealed his insanity little by little but, of course, I knew the signs. I kept him about me. I wanted to study him. At times, when the moon was at the full, he was actually dangerous.'

'Your Highness,' said Perry, 'I do apologize most sincerely. I can't imagine what came over me.'

The Princess had already recovered her poise. 'You have made my husband's study look like a rose garden after a high wind, Mr. Perry,' she said gently in English and Perry was only dissuaded from the extravagance of kneeling at her feet — he was so delighted by the implied forgiveness — for fear of making an even bigger fool of himself.

'Anyway, if it was a report I'm glad you tore it up. I seem to spend my life reading reports, and they're arranged under As and Bs and Cs, and ones and twos and threes; how can it mean anything? What was this report about?'

The Pasha put a hand on Perry's shoulder and spoke with a cordiality that mystified him. 'My dear, M. Perry and I were preparing a surprise for you. It was a report on the living conditions of university students.' Although he was addressing his wife the Pasha looked at Perry; he was examining him closely, particularly the whites of the eyes.

'A surprise? That's pleasant. But how can you surprise me about the students? They live like pigs.'

Perry waited until the Pasha had finished explaining about the proposed canteen and then said that, with Her Highness's permission, he wished to make a more exhaustive report on the student quarter at Gizeh; a superficial report like the one he had already drawn up would probably do harm rather than good. People would say, 'But is this all? There are more urgent problems, hospitals, for example.' It was a question not only of gathering information, but also one of marshalling arguments. For example, although he had been into many of the rooms occupied by students he had come across no books. It rather looked as though they possessed no books.

'But what has this to do with me, M. Perry?' asked the Princess. 'I'm not the Minister of Education.'

'Highness,' said the Pasha, startled into sententiousness by the implied rebuke. 'You are the Conscience of Egypt. This is well known.'

'Yes, oh dear, it doesn't sound attractive, does it? A Conscience.'

'Well then, a Fairy Godmother. Journalists often write about you as a Fairy Godmother.'

'And that sounds infinitely worse. A Godmother is an old woman, isn't she, Mr. Perry? True, I am old. Do you know how old I am? Seventy. Now, don't put on that incredulous look because you think it will flatter me. I shall soon be dead, and what will reports matter to me then?' For the Princess this was the most delightful of all turns for a conversation to take. She rejoiced in her husband's confusion, for example. She knew how much he hated the mention of death. And as for poor Mr. Perry, he was being forced into the making of some consolingly complimentary remark and, clearly, he could think of nothing to say.

She touched one of the bell-pushes on her husband's desk and a girl of about eighteen appeared, wearing a voluminous blue garment with gold piping so cut that her figure was disguised. Only her head and hands could be seen. The Princess addressed her in Turkish. The girl bowed and withdrew.

'Very well, Mr. Perry,' said the Princess in a tone of dismissal, 'go off and make your report and make it as full of information and as argumentative as you like. But remember, whatever your opinions may be you must express them with moderation. There is no knowing who will read the report. Perhaps the King will read it. Who knows? Perhaps the King will be pleased to take an interest in this matter. Have the report prepared in Arabic and French, and we shall see what we shall see.' The girl in the blue gown padded into the room and handed her mistress a large brown envelope. The Princess now rose to her feet and her husband and Perry rose with her. 'Here is something of greater urgency. I'd be glad if you would translate my story into English before the end of the week because they are waiting for it at the press.' Momentarily she paused to look at the pieces of paper that littered the floor; and then, lifting her chin like a cat in response to tickling, she walked out of the room.

'If His Majesty interests himself in this, M. Perry,' said the Pasha as soon as they were alone, 'the hostels will be built. If he does not, the hostels will not be built. You understand, this has nothing whatsoever to do with the welfare of students. That is a secondary matter. I tell you this so that you will not have false illusions. However,' he caught himself up, realizing his indiscretion, 'you mustn't bother your head about politics. Such matters can safely be left to me. Her Highness can be counted upon to act with all nobility. I think she likes you. I like you too. We are good friends.' He laughed aloud and shook Perry by the hand. 'You can always speak to me as frankly as you like. I am a man of the world. My family once sent me to work for a time in a bank. In two years I was Managing Director. Behind all this talk there is a firm resolve, you understand me? To serve Egypt.'

Perry descended the wide sweep of stairs on tip toe; otherwise his footsteps on the marble would have rung out disconcertingly. He paused, as he always paused, to look at the enormous tapestry of Louis XVI charging out of a dark wood on horseback, and touched, with the tips of his fingers, the cold back of a jade buffalo which comfortably slept on a block of porphyry. He wondered, as he always wondered, whether anyone watched

17

from behind a screen. Seemingly, he was alone in the main hall of the Palace. Because the Princess and the Pasha were both keen collectors he was surrounded by treasures — pictures, porcelain, statuary — and it seemed inconceivable that they were unprotected. But, as always, he was permitted to leave the Palace alone and when he stood in the glare of the court-yard he automatically looked up at the façade of the building — a copy of some Florentine palace, he had been told — before making for the gates. Two impressive Sudanese guards in blue robes and white turbans rose out of the shadows and chuckled at him.

Perry did not know whether he admired the Princess because she reminded him vaguely of his grandmother or whether it was because of her rank and her withered beauty; or her liveliness, or the dark, oriental splendour of her past. She had been brought up at the court of the last Sultan of Turkey. Possibly her attraction for Perry was due to a combination of all these.

As he waited for his wife to come home from one of the in-numerable functions she had succeeded in busying herself with since her arrival in the country a few weeks before, Perry thought of the Princess as a wife and decided the quality he liked best in her was her unsentimental forcefulness. Take this short story she had written, for example. It was the story of a concubine falling in love with a prisoner who worked in a chain gang outside the palace of the Pharaoh. Seeing that a guard was about to execute the prisoner because he had dropped to the ground in exhaustion, the concubine had jumped out of the window and run towards the chain gang, calling on the guard to stop.

Now came the interesting twist. 'With uplifted sword,' the Princess had written, 'the guard waited. He smiled because he thought that the little favourite of the Pharaoh wished to give herself the pleasure of executing the prisoner with her own

18

hand.' In a European story this would have been an imaginative flourish. The Princess thought it a commonplace; she made the point casually, without emphasis. And this, thought Perry, was an expression of some part of the Princess's nature that strongly appealed to him.

Political demonstrations of one sort or another were a daily occurrence at that time and, on the whole, Perry enjoyed them. The thousands of tarbooshes outside the university were like a swarm of red bees. Cheer-leaders waved their arms on the steps of the Faculty of Law; the air was stabbed with cries of, 'One valley, one king, one religion', and with reasonable luck the students would declare themselves on strike. But it had to be a big strike to bring the English Department out; Perry's students had a dogged seriousness about their work that kept them in the lecture room when everyone else was out in the sunshine, listening to speeches, eating nuts or, perhaps, quietly sleeping among the bushes of the nearby Botanical Gardens.

This had happened only yesterday, when Perry was lecturing on *Othello*. He could not understand why they were so quiet and so still. The faces looked down at him; in the front row were the Coptic girls, all pallid and plump; a couple of rodent-faced youths from Saudi Arabia sat in a row by themselves, their tarbooshes set rakishly; and behind, was the main body of men students, quite worn out by their efforts to suppress yawns.

But when Perry began discussing what he said was the moment of supreme irony in the play a student in the back row laughed out loud.

'What's the matter, Muawiya? What's funny about that? Iago and Othello are kneeling together and praying.'

The other students took up the laughter. They were genuinely amused.

'Sir,' said Muawiya, 'don't you see that Iago is tricking Othello?'

'Of course.' Perry was puzzled. 'It's a play about intrigue.'

'But Othello is such a fool.'

'What do you think of Iago?'

'Ah!' said Muawiya with evident admiration, 'He is a clever man.'

The laughter ceased. The lecture room was so quiet Perry could hear the bell on a passing camel. The chanting from the forecourt of the university had fallen silent too. Perry peered up at Muawiya — the room was an amphitheatre — wondering how such a man had succeeded in registering himself in the Faculty. He was at least twenty-five. The rest of the students in this first year class were no more than eighteen or nineteen.

'Do you mean to tell me you *admire* Iago?' said Perry.

'No, no,' said one of the women students. 'It is impossible for anyone to be as wicked as Iago. He is unreal.'

'It is very possible.' Muawiya sang these words out. He added something in Arabic which Perry did not catch and there was a new gust of laughter in the room.

Perry had an idea. 'Do you think that Desdemona was really unfaithful to Othello?'

'No, no, of course not,' said the women students in a ragged, shocked, chorus.

'Yes, with Cassio,' Muawiya shouted, 'Shakespeare spoiled the play by not letting Iago seduce her. That would have been perfect.'

Without warning, the door was thrown violently open and a gang of excited students rushed in. Perry had seen none of them before; obviously they were from some other Faculty, probably the Faculty of Law which was where most of the trouble started. They ignored Perry. A young man in a well-cut, English style suit stood at Perry's side on the dais, haranguing the class in Arabic; very pink for an Egyptian, Perry thought him, red-lipped, plump as a baby. His black tarboosh tassel was agitated. He beat on Perry's desk with his fist. It was as much as he could do to make himself heard above the shouts of his companions who were rushing up and down the gangways inciting the class to come out and join a demonstration.

'Sir,' said one of the visitors in Perry's ear, 'we demand the unity of the Nile Valley and the immediate withdrawal of all British troops.'

Perry looked at him in surprise; the youth had spoken courteously and now stood waiting with a confident smile on his face. 'The blood of our murdered fellow-students cries out for liberty,' he went on.

'If you and your friends don't leave immediately I shall take all your names and report you to the Dean. How dare you come bursting into my lecture like this?' Perry was now addressing everyone in the room. But it was impossible to speak over this tumult. Perry felt a fool because he knew his face was as red as a sunset; he always coloured up when he was at all put out.

'Hooligans!' he shouted, only to see the word taken down in a notebook by one of the Saudi Arabians. He and his companion sat in silent indifference, waiting for the lecture to continue.

Muawiya's deep voice began vibrating from the heights of the amphitheatre and all other voices at once sounded puny. He was standing on a chair with an arm rhetorically extended towards the pink-faced leader of the agitators. He fanned his fingers out and averted his head. 'You are rude people,' he intoned in English, 'it is very uncivilized of you! It is not nice! What our English professor will think of you I don't know!'

The agitators jeered so Muawiya dropped from his chair and clumped down the gangway towards them; his heavy face was blue with three or four days growth of beard and curiously distended, mask-like, intimidating. The Arabic came welling up. He made straight for the pink-faced youth and would probably have caught him by the throat if another student had not intervened, a member of the class this time, a tall, respectable-looking boy in glasses who stood in front of Muawiya with a delicately raised hand, the tips of the fingers and thumb just touching one another. The gesture made an appeal to reason. The respectable-looking boy moved his hand backwards and forwards in front of his mouth, touching his lips occasionally, as though drawing from an unwilling or unworthy mouth the appropriate words of conciliation.

'Sir!' said one of the Saudi Arabian students in Perry's ear, 'What is the etymology of this word "hooligan"?'

'Muawiya, sit down!' Perry was further than ever from the centre of the disturbance. More students were entering the lecture room all the time — some through the windows — and Perry could only have held his position at the front of the dais by using more vigour than he felt disposed to. He was ignored. The demonstrators excluded him by the pressure of their number. In some unaccountable way Perry found himself at the door and here, for the first time, he wondered what his colleagues were doing. Surely his was not the only lecture to be broken up?

But when Perry reached the Common Room he found it unoccupied save for one of the attendants, a fat old buffoon in a felt skull cap and dirty *gallabieh*, asleep in Perry's favourite chair. Clearly, Perry was the only Englishman on the premises that morning; his more experienced colleagues had seen which way the wind was blowing and sensibly decided to stay at home. Perry woke the old man gently and sent him off to make a cup of coffee.

'Oh, and see if you can get me a newspaper,' Perry called

after him. He went to the door and shouted down the corridor. 'In English.' Because undoubtedly his best plan was to wait in here until the excitement subsided and then, in an hour's time say, make for home. Even he realized that lectures were over for the day. Through the window he could see the deserted steps of the university library and the dark, cool, cavern of the main entrance made absurdly theatrical by all the noises off — the rhythmical chanting, the tapping of a drum.

When Perry heard the door open he assumed it was the man with the coffee and did not turn round.

'I am very glad to find you here, sir,' said Muawiya's thick voice and Perry turned to see the student with his back heroically against the door, his stiff collar flapping free of its front stud, his eyes unusually large, unusually bulging. 'You must hide. You must run and save yourself. Abdul Aziz is saying that it is twenty years since we shot an English professor.'

'Who is Abdul Aziz?'

'He is my friend, the gentleman I was talking to at the end of your excellent lecture. Sir, you spoke jewels, during that lecture! I thought Abdul Aziz did not come in at the right moment.'

'You mean he's the ringleader of that gang?'

'Ah, but he is an old friend. His brother worked with me on the railway. That is why I know what is in his mind. When he says, "It is twenty years since we — the students, that is — last shot an English professor," I know that he is excited. He is not himself. There are packing cases of rifles buried in the football ground and Abdul Aziz is taking his friends out to dig them up.'

The sandals of the *farrash* could be heard slip-slopping down the corridor; when the old man knocked at the door, belching importantly to announce his identity, Muawiya said excitedly, 'Perhaps this is a trick!'

23

'Oh, don't talk like a fool, man. Stand away from that door and let my coffee come in.'

'With your permission, sir, I will stand guard at the window.'

Perry drank the tiny cup of coffee in one gulp. 'No, be off with you! If they're going to shoot me, well, they'll shoot me. Your being here won't make a scrap of difference. What's it got to do with you, anyway? I mean, why should you want to protect me?'

Muawiya ushered the *farrash* out of the room and once again placed his back against the door. 'These are children,' he said contemptuously. 'They do not understand men like you and me. What do they know about culture? When I am a graduate I shall go to England for my doctorate. Besides all this, I am a poet. At the end of the war I was working on the railway and I wanted to come to the university but the government would not let me because railway is a reserved occupation. One day I saw the Prime Minister on the station. Nahas Pasha!' Muawiya had stood up. He was re-enacting the scene. His lips were drawn back to reveal a pair of brilliantly clean artificial teeth. Suddenly he knelt down. 'I threw myself at the feet of Nahas Pasha and recited my poetry. He walked along. I held on to his trousers. Men kicked me and spat at me. I said my poetry.' Muawiya stood up and dusted his trousers. 'Nahas told one of his secretaries to take my name and that is why I am at the university today. Sir! I can hear the students coming back from the football pitch. You must climb over the railings. To think,' he said by way of afterthought, 'that a man like me had to work on the railway. It was so vulgar. Sir, you have no idea!'

'I must tell you frankly,' said Perry, 'that I don't believe that story about the Prime Minister. Anyway, I'm not leaving this building in your company to climb over any railings.'

He opened the newspaper left by the *farrash* and read the

account of yesterday's disturbances and what had been anticipated for today. Apparently the students were planning to
march to the Palace. Well, it made his present situation more
real, Perry thought. No happening seemed real until it was
read about. Waiting for a gang of law students to arrive with
rifles he could even anticipate the moment when his execu-
tioners raised their rifles to their shoulders only to discover they
did not know how to fire them, or that they had no ammuni-
tion, or that the mechanism had rusted. Something would
certainly go wrong.

'You have insulted me, sir.'

Looking up, Perry saw that Muawiya's eyes had returned to
their normal size; indeed, they now appeared unusually small.
They were set in dark sockets — as though the flesh surrounding
the eyes were now charged with black, angry blood.

'Insulted you? What are you talking about? Another thing.
Iago, let me tell you, is a villain. He is the blackest villain in
English literature. Othello has his weak points, that I grant
you. He has his tragic flaw. But his character is noble. Desdemona is pure beyond criticism. To say, as you said just now,
that she went to bed with Cassio is absurd. Now, Muawiya,
will you go? And before I see you again may I hope that you
will have studied your *Othello* a little more carefully?'

To his surprise, Perry now found himself standing in an
empty room. Still rigid with anger — and crimson in the face
as he well knew — he looked at the closed door. Perhaps, he
thought too late, Muawiya was pulling his leg. In any case it
was perfectly absurd to lose one's temper with a student over a
silly misunderstanding of Shakespeare when there were university professors in England who had won their jobs with theories
scarcely less crack-brained than Muawiya's.

The distant excitement sounded more subdued. If the young
idiots were indeed digging up crates of rifles now was the time

to break and run. In the corridors no one was to be seen, not even the old fellow who had brought the coffee. Notices stirred on the board. Perry passed the room where he had been lecturing and saw that it was deserted; even the Saudi Arabian students had packed up. Though where they had all gone *to*, Perry thought, was another matter. He peered around. Surely, they had not all gone to the football ground, women as well! Why, even in matters like this, could they not be sensible? One rifle, one cartridge, was enough for the job in hand. But no! Nothing would satisfy them but the grandiose.

Emerging from the main entrance of the Department building he was momentarily dazzled by the brilliant light. It struck at him from the marble steps, from the pillars, from the sky. Heat and glare brought him to a stop and even made him close his eyes. When he opened them he saw that an enormous crowd of students, thousands of them it seemed, stood in wait. Their presence was impressive. They were silent. All wore the red tarboosh; all were watching him. He was reminded of a story he had once read in a science fiction magazine; Martians, it seemed, revealed their passions by the changing colour of their skulls. Red, for anger, for example.

Very well! They were angry with him. He was angry with them. Instead of retreating into the building, his first impulse, he walked slowly down the steps, myopically wiping his glasses with a handkerchief. He was going to pretend the crowd was not there. He liked to boast he was as blind as a bat without his glasses; this was an exaggeration but now that he held the glasses in his hand he was certainly very short-sighted. In this way he hoped to find it easier to ignore the crowd.

'Excuse me!' he said when he became aware of shapes blocking his path. He put out a hand. His fingers closed on a tarboosh tassel. This could only mean that he had not yet reached the bottom of the steps; so he pressed on, until the sun was quite

shut out and he could hear breathing close to him and
around him. By slipping his spectacles into his breast poc[
he had both hands free for groping; and he went through t
crowd, calling, 'Excuse me, gentlemen', smiling and noddii
now that he realized the students' uncertainty. When he ha
arrived at the centre of the crowd he heard voices at the frin
calling for blood. But hands were patting Perry on the bac[
There was a nauseating reek of chewed pistachio nuts an[
garlic. 'Move along there', Perry called out in his atrociou
Arabic, assuming the manner of a conductor on one of the Cair[
buses. 'Will the learned masters make room?' The crowd
ejected him, so to speak, in a spasm of laughter. Perry stood in
the sun again, the students roaring at him good-naturedly. He
put his spectacles on and he was abruptly confronted with
tarbooshes, white faces, brown faces, scarred Sudanese faces,
moustaches, negroid nostrils and Mediterranean lips — the
countenance of young Egypt.

At the main gates he paused to look back. The crowd had
forgotten him already. A frenzied orator, mounted on the
shoulders of a friend, was working himself up to a synthetic
crisis, waving his arms so violently that his support had to
be supported in turn. Perry felt the sweat cooling on his body.
He had seen no rifles. But that did not mean Muawiya had
necessarily been wrong. Probably it was an entirely different
group of students who had gone off to the football ground.
Now that he had escaped from the university premises, though,
the immediate task was to find a place where he could sit in
the shade and recover. The experience in that crowd had been
most unpleasant. With so many people breathing on him it
would be a miracle if he escaped an infection. Even now he
seemed to be breathing a garlic and pistachio atmosphere; he
would not feel clean until he had had a soaking in a bath scented
with his favourite pine bath salts; and even pine bath salts, he

thought, would not rid him of the most clinging odour of all:
the patronizing contempt of the crowd. He was angry with
himself for having made them laugh. Gordon of Khartoum
would not have behaved in that way! Through the trees that
bounded the Zoological Gardens, a place he had not visited for
some time, came the bellowing of some penned animal. There
was an island in a lake, he remembered, where you could sit
under awnings and drink coffee.

Walking in the shade of a eucalyptus grove Perry listened to
the bellowing from the Zoo and thought of the prison governor
in a film he had once seen. Confronted by a mob of rioting
convicts the governor had not retreated. He had walked steadily forward, looking neither to right nor left. He had marched
through that mob of dangerous men and when he came out the
other side, unharmed, there was complete silence! How different, Perry thought in disgust, had been his own performance at
the university and he began to re-live the experience more
heroically. He was so lost in fantasy, head down, hands behind
his back that not until he was brought to a halt by colliding with
a figure planted squarely in his path did he look up and realize
that he was in the hands of yet another gang of demonstrators.
Some of them, like the youth who straddled before him, wore
lengths of white cloth round their tarbooshes and there were
even a few turbans in the Sudanese style. Perry saw, too, that
nearly all wore *gallabiehs*. If appearances were anything to go
by these young men were a more dangerous proposition than
anything Perry had run into so far: they were students from Al
Azhar come over to Gizeh probably to ginger up the less
fanatical students of the European-style university where
Perry taught. They carried green banners and long staves. A
hand jerked at Perry's tie. He tried to step back and learned,
from a howl, that he had trodden on somebody's naked foot.

'I beg your pardon,' he said in English.

Then he became aware of an odd circumstance. Angry faces were shouting at him in Arabic but he could not understand a word. Normally he could understand the gist of anything said to him in Arabic — certainly he ought to understand the threats and insults they were throwing at him now — but the words baffled him. He remained still, protecting his head with a raised arm, trying to resist striking out at the nearest faces. Some had the set ferocious expressions of the provincial fanatic; some were laughing, others were merely shouting mouths. But what were they shouting? What was the language?

A stave fell shrewdly on his raised arm, chilling it from shoulder to fingers. Using his good arm to wrest the stave from his attacker Perry accidentally knocked his own spectacles off and trod on them; and because he could not see he could smell all the better. He could smell the sweat souring on their bodies and the curiously goat-like stink to the dust raised by their stamping feet. Yet Perry had the stave. He whirled it with his left arm and began to shout his satisfaction when he heard it buzz in the air. But he did not manage to hit anyone. He struck this way and that but no one yelled and the stave buzzed, and he shouted, and they shouted back in their un-Arabic, and the dust rose until he had to stop and lean on his stave, helpless with sneezing.

'Damn you!' he said. 'Damn you all!' For the first time that day he was really frightened and he began to trot, striking out wildly with the stave and shouting, 'Help! Help!'

'Sir,' said a familiar voice in thick English. 'Here! This way!'

'Which way? I can't see you. I've broken my glasses.'

'Oh sir, run!' said the guttural voice and Perry blundered off in what he judged to be the speaker's direction, taking cuts right and left at his assailants who still, however, kept a distance. Muawiya — by this time Perry had recognized the voice — continued to call excitedly, even merrily. They were right under the wall surrounding the Zoological Gardens and the animal Perry had heard earlier recommenced its bellowing. To Perry's confused mind it seemed that the beast had joined in the hunt. He was surrounded by bushes. Most striking of all was a new smell, a smell of rotting leaves and Perry was about to run into the deeper shade from where the smell seemed to come when he tripped and fell. It may have been one of those decorative hoops with which they edged the paths; or it may have been a foot stuck out. Even then, with his nose in a pile of leaves so moist they might have come from an English autumn, Perry considered the matter. He was, however, lifted by the neck of his jacket and dragged to the dark heart of a large shrub with leaves pricklier than a holly.

'You are not English,' Muawiya hissed into his ear. 'You are a Frenchman. Understand. Ici on parle français. But yes!' And rolling over on to his back Perry could look mistily up into Muawiya's eyes which were wide with conspiracy.

'Did you drag me in here?'

'Yes, sir. I am saving your life.'

'I thought it was a panther.'

Muawiya was already arguing with the crowd. He stood in front of the one gap in the foliage that gave access to the heart of this ferocious bush and declared with great solemnity that the European was not an Englishman, he was a Frenchman and an old friend. Perry had sufficiently recovered to be pleased he could understand Muawiya who went on to say that Egypt owed a great debt of gratitude to France. In the first place it had been the French who first revealed to the world the wonders of Ancient Egypt. Champollion had deciphered the hieroglyphics and he was a Frenchman. De Lesseps had cut the Suez Canal and he was a Frenchman.

'The Canal for Egypt!' shouted the students from Al Azhar

and this time Perry could understand their Arabic perfectly well. Muawiya went on talking for some time. He made a speech of his own. He pointed out British injustices they had never heard of before — did they, good patriots that they were, realize that the Cairo police were clothed in cast-off British Army uniforms? The speech continued so long that Perry had time to recover the use of his arm. He opened and closed his right hand to stimulate the circulation but dared make no other move for fear of reminding his persecutors of his existence. Ants crawled over him. The animal in the Zoo went on bellowing, other animals started up, jungle birds screamed; but Perry's thoughts were divided between the cost of a new pair of spectacles and the curious language the students had used when he had first run into them. After his exertions he may even have slept a while.

'Sir,' said Muawiya, touching him gently on the shoulder. 'I have indeed saved your life. You owe me your life. But it is nothing. You insulted me, sir, but it is nothing.'

Perry lay on his back, gazing up quietly through the spiked foliage. 'Have they gone?'

'I lied for you. I told them you were a Frenchman.'

'Have they gone?'

Muawiya helped him out of the shrubbery and Perry stood swinging his right arm in a dazed kind of way, saying, 'Why couldn't I understand them? You say they were speaking Arabic. Why did it sound so queer? It was gibberish.'

'All Egyptians speak the very best Arabic, sir. It was not gibberish. I think you must go into the Zoological Gardens. You will be safe there. Besides, sir, they are among the most beautiful in the world. The late Mr. Theodore Roosevelt, the American hunter, said they were the most beautiful in the world. All animals are there, even a polar bear.'

Perry could see quite well enough to walk without any

assistance but Muawiya gripped him by the right elbow and steered him along so vigorously Perry would have protested if he had not thought the student would consider him unaware of his danger, and so not sufficiently grateful for the way he had been rescued. The encounter had been ugly. Muawiya was probably right when he claimed to have saved his life; yet, frightening as the violence had been, the most frightening part of the experience had been the words the students had uttered and his realization he could not understand. No, that in itself was not frightening! He was afraid because of the suspicion that he understood perfectly well and rejected the knowledge.

'Muawiya,' he said when they had paid their piastres, entered the Zoological Gardens and were staring at a group of heavily-built storks. 'Have you ever read Freud?'

'I love him very much. I love all English literature. I think you would like to sit down now and have a good rest.'

Perry led the way round the enclosure until he was at the point nearest the birds. From what he had been able to make out they had an air of striking melancholy and he wished to confirm the impression. Yes, there they were, dressed in severe black and grey. Their beaks were so large the birds rested them moodily on their breasts. They stood about on one leg in the sun with their eyes shut, radiating such gloom that Perry cheered up a little. He even thanked Muawiya for the way he had come to his assistance. He took his jacket off and rolled up his shirt sleeve.

'It is nothing,' said Muawiya in a loud voice.

The stave had left a purple mark immediately above Perry's elbow and the arm throbbed, but Muawiya was right. No real damage had been done. Perry bent his arm several times and thought he could hear the elbow joint squeaking. It was the first time that morning he had enjoyed sufficient quiet to detect the squeaking of a joint; the bellowing animal was silent; so were the birds. The whole Zoo was hushed and Perry looked at Muawiya to see why he said nothing either. His eyes were closed.

In the outburst that followed the eyes were not opened. The shoulders were thrown back, the arms were rigid and held slightly forward with the hands open, palms uppermost. 'I am a religious man and I would not tell lies. It is not according to Islam to tell lies. You have insulted me and now I ask you to apologize. If you don't apologize I shall not come to your classes any more, though you are the best professor. It is to your advantage to keep me as your student. I work, I am a poet, and I shall be a credit to you. For both our sakes you must apologize.'

'What for?'

Muawiya opened his eyes in astonishment. 'You must think that Egyptians have no feelings, sir. I told you that I caught hold of the Prime Minister's trousers and — '

'Oh that! Yes, I remember. All right. I apologize.'

Perry was surprised to see Muawiya's anger.

'Is it so unimportant to you? That is not a good apology.'

Turning to walk away, he revealed that his coat was split at the back and a slim triangle of shirt was shining in the sun.

'You must let me buy you a new coat,' Perry called out but Muawiya clearly did not understand the significance of the remark. He kept on his way. And although Perry would have liked to hurry after him and make peace he was suddenly overpoweringly tired. He thought this was largely due to having no spectacles because when he arrived home some time later by taxi and put on his spare pair he immediately felt refreshed. Yet the real fatigue, he thought, was not physical at all. He had received a real, if minor, spiritual check. Until he realized how thoroughly he enjoyed tearing the Pasha's report into small pieces he quite thought his dejection was due to the

33

ease with which Muawiya had been able to persuade the Al Azharites that he was a Frenchman. For Perry considered himself unmistakably English.

However, when he was tearing up the Pasha's report —

'Eager as always, the Royal Huntsman outstripped his followers. The dust rose from the hooves of his noble horse. But, alas! At the very moment the Young Pharaoh was preparing to discharge his arrow the horse stumbled and, standing up in his golden stirrups as he was, holding the extended bow, the Monarch was thrown to the ground. The lion turned with a savage roar. Dazedly Amenhotep struggled to his feet and thought, "Alas! dear heart, my little slave-girl, Poter-hes-met — if I die who will there be to supervise the building of your tomb when you are dead?"'

Perry had just reached the lion hunt in his translation of the Princess's novel when the telephone rang. As he picked up the receiver his wife came to the door of her room and hovered in case the call should be for her. She was holding a fountain pen, and he assumed with some irritation that she was writing to her lover.

'Yes, Monsieur Perry speaking. I'll hold the line.' He put a hand over the mouthpiece. 'It's all right, darling. It's for me. The Palace. I expect the Pasha wants to cut his lesson.'

'Ah, bon jour, Excellence.' For some moments he listened intently. He quickly realized, with relief, that the Pasha was not cutting his next lesson after all: the Pasha paid strictly by the lesson and his secretary kept count. 'In *Al Ahram*, you say? There's nothing in the English paper. I thought they couldn't publish anything like that because of the censorship. No, I'm all right, arm a bit bruised and I lost my glasses, of course, but it could have been worse. One of my students told them I was French.' He listened again. 'Oh, that's absurd! Just one blow on the arm. I was dragged under a bush.' The conversation continued in these terms for some time until it occurred to Perry to wonder how the newspaper had acquired the story. 'I beg your pardon,' he said. The Pasha said the Princess was interesting herself in the case and would probably insist on replacing his glasses. He wanted to know why Perry had not mentioned the incident the day before, when, as he said, they had met for their usual lesson.

'We were on other subjects, Excellency.'

The Pasha laughed heartily at this and Perry remembered, with shame, the way he had taken the report out of the Princess's hands and torn it up. 'You want to build a hostel for the students, M. Perry. And what do they do? They beat you with a stick.' He stopped laughing abruptly. 'No, but it is serious. I will send you a case of best navel oranges at once.'

Perry replaced the receiver and saw that his wife was still standing at the door of her room. He had omitted to tell her about the happenings of the day before yesterday, too. But then she could not expect to enjoy his confidence. After a separation forced on them by the war she had joined him only a month before. She was not staying, she said. As soon as she had made arrangements about the divorce she was returning to England to marry a man with a Scottish name Perry could not remember. Mackinder or Mackenzie or Macmillan, or something of the sort. When Perry asked her why she had bothered to come all the way to Egypt, at his expense, to give him news of this kind she said she liked him and could not bear to think of him suffering. She wanted to break the news gently.

'What's all that about?' she said.

Perry explained briefly and she made him take his jacket off and roll up his sleeve. He acquiesced, because when all was taken into account, he liked her, too.

'What awful brutes they must be.' She stared at the bruise

35

so intently and paused so long before speaking that Perry knew she would make trouble. He could read the signs. Even more ominous than her deliberation was the quietness of her voice. 'Why didn't you tell me about this before?'

She was eight years younger than Perry but she could make him feel like her young brother. For this there were physical reasons; she could give him a couple of inches and fourteen pounds. She had, too, an unusually large face for the size of her head. The ears were set far back, giving more room for the countenance. Her eyes were grey and widely separated. The nose was quite straight. She had the appearance, he felt, of a wiser person than himself and it seemed natural to imagine that wisdom had something to do with age.

'When all is said and done,' she remarked, 'we're still married. It isn't as though the divorce had gone through yet. Why do you have to be so secretive? Have the police made an arrest?'

'An arrest? Good heavens, we're not in England! Where are you off to now?' Normally he would not have questioned her comings and goings but she was in such an obvious passion that Perry momentarily feared she might have some plan to go out and molest the first Egyptian she came across. He could tell by her pallor that she was angry. Strands from the dark coiffure appeared untidily on the nape of her neck and he looked at them hungrily. For Perry these loose strands had irresistible appeal. 'Oh, my priestess!' he thought to himself. 'Oh, my darling priestess!'

'Have you reported this to the British Consul? No, I thought not! I call it downright unpatriotic of you! If these hooligans think they can beat up a British citizen with impunity there's no knowing where they'll stop. Well, I shall go and report it myself and, what's more, see that a protest is made.'

'Mary, my dear.' Perry spoke patiently. 'If you go to the

Consulate I shall ring them up while you're on the way and say you've had a touch of the sun.'

'You'll do what?' She had been fiddling about inside her room but at Perry's words she reappeared at the door with lipstick poised in front of her open mouth. 'But they might have killed you. You said so yourself.'

This was true. Perry had been unable to resist the desire to impress her by the dangers he had survived. 'Well, they might and they mightn't. Even if they had killed me they wouldn't have meant it personally. This is politics. You don't understand politics, Mary.'

'Politics be damned! When a man's murdered he's murdered personally and his wife is made a widow personally. If you were killed in a riot James and I couldn't possibly get married. I'd have inherited all your property. Don't you see, you'd have created an impossible situation. I've got to talk to someone sensible about this. If you won't let me go to the Consul will you come along and see Grimbley with me? Surely you'll want to tell him?'

Grimbley was Perry's professor. 'In an hour's time I'm catching a train to Zagazig to give my lecture. No, I won't come to see Grimbley. Who said he was sensible, anyway? He'd probably start laughing and you know what that sounds like. If it's my will that's bothering you I'll draw one up when I come back from Zagazig tomorrow. I'll leave my bits and pieces to Gertrude.'

'Gertrude has quite enough to go on with and you know perfectly well how shocked she'd be. Inheriting from her brother when her brother had left a widow! She'd insist on handing it all over. It would be incredibly embarrassing. James and I would have to go and see her. Can you imagine it?'

Perry was dressing for his monthly trip to the British Institute at Zagazig where he gave lectures on such subjects as 'Images of Corruption in the novels of Charles Dickens', 'The Decline of the Epic' and 'The Renaissance Conventions of The Rape of Lucrece'. He was working his way into a clean shirt. 'Mary,' he was going to say, 'do you seriously imagine that I care if I *do* create a situation embarrassing for you and this What-you-m'call-him?' But when his head popped out of the neck of the shirt Mary had gone. Perry finished dressing and went downstairs to cross-examine the porter. According to this pock-faced old Sudani the lady had gone off in a taxi, saying, 'Shubra, Shubra', to the driver. To do Mary justice, Perry thought, she would not work herself into this state out of mere self-interest. This talk of being a widow and inheriting his property was a mere smoke-screen. She was, in many ways, absurdly altruistic and if, as seemed to be the case, she had gone to see Grimbley it was entirely out of regard to him. She wanted him to go on living. She thought it was in his own interest.

In times of tension Shubra was one of the most dangerous parts of Cairo for a European to wander in alone. The quarter stretched amorphously north of Cairo Main Station. Having tried the discipline of Roman Catholicism and the austerities of the Greek Orthodox Church, Professor Waldo Grimbley said he had at last found a sense of security in Islam and had rented the top floor of a mud brick house on the very limits of Shubra where, from his lattice, he could look out over the berseem fields. It was a good mile beyond the tram terminus but that did not mean, Perry thought with annoyance, that one took a taxi all the way from the centre of Cairo. One took a horse-drawn gharry from the terminus and so saved a pound.

He would have telephoned Grimbley to give warning of his wife's approach but Grimbley was trying to lead the life of a well-to-do Egyptian of a hundred years ago and had no telephone. Perry was tempted to go off to Zagazig in the usual way but realized he would not be easy in his mind until he knew of Mary's safe arrival at Waldo's house. The city was reasonably quiet after the effervescence of the day before yesterday but an Englishwoman riding alone in a taxi through the wilds of Shubra could easily spark off the sense of fun for which the suburb was known. Perry did not think they would do her any harm but the citizens might turn her out of the taxi and make her walk. He had no alternative but to hire another taxi and set off in pursuit. He took his pyjamas and lecture notes with him because once assured of Mary's safety he would make a dash for the station.

'Oh, Mr. Macmillan, or Mackinder, or Mackenzie, why am I doing all this for you?' he thought sadly as the taxi joggled him northwards. Whatever the Scotsman's name it seemed reasonable to suppose that he was responsible for a new vein of impetuosity in Mary's character. In the twelve months or so, which was the extent of their married life before Perry had to leave England for this Egyptian job, she had been a reserved girl of twenty-eight who liked playing the piano to herself in the evenings. Now, a mere four years later, the sight of a large weal on her husband's arm was enough to stir her to immediate and extravagant action. Possibly she was being gnawed by remorse. Perhaps she was eager to snatch at any opportunity to show how ashamed she was of her conduct. But no! Her solicitude was expressed too vehemently. It was more likely she wanted an excuse to visit Waldo.

While new glasses were being made for him Perry wore his second best pair and it had become increasingly obvious that his eyes had outgrown them. At first he had noticed no difference. Then, the previous evening he developed a headache. As he now descended from the taxi before Waldo Grimbley's house the ground appeared so far away it was inconceivable he could touch it with his feet. The buzz of flies and the animal reek that rose from the shadows added to his slight dizziness and when he asked the taxi driver to wait — he was only going to be a moment, he said — the man seemed to waver in the gritty wind. A pink buffalo rubbing its chin on a mud brick wall was so remote Perry might have been surveying it through the wrong end of a telescope. But he could, and did, touch its wet muzzle.

The porter revealed himself in the dark of the entrance by the gleam of his white clothes. Perry was about to question the man, who had not stirred from his bench, when he heard Waldo calling down the stairs in a tone of such annoyance that Perry could only imagine his wife had interrupted him in some religious observance. Dressed in a handsome muslin caftan, striped in grey and rose, he appeared abruptly in the sunlight of his own threshold. 'This will make a scandal in the neighbourhood,' he said. 'You know very well I never receive women alone.'

'Then she *is* here,' said Perry in relief. He was tempted to climb back into the taxi but Waldo was plainly agitated. He had even taken the briar pipe from between his teeth.

'I tell you frankly I'd have turned her away if she hadn't already dismissed her taxi. But you can take her home. Tell her she must never do this again. It will be the talk of Shubra.'

Perry did not take Waldo's religious professions with the seriousness of some of his colleagues so he made no immediate comment. Waldo might dress the part and might even live the life of a good Moslem — Perry did not know — but in face and manner he was never anyone else but an Englishman of a fairly common type and his neighbours probably thought of him as a harmless lunatic. The black briar pipe was rarely out of his mouth. Careful daily shaving conferred a blue tint to his bony jaw. Hair grew from his ears and from the nostrils of an

40

inordinately large nose. His conversation was at its happiest when it had the jaunty tone of high-class autobiography. He ran into old school-fellows under the most surprising circumstances. At one time, he said, he had been intended for a cavalry regiment.

'Waldo, you simply must lend me a pair of your reading glasses.' They had climbed the stairs and were panting at each other on the landing. 'My best pair are broken and the pair I've got on give me a most terrible giddiness. You remember how you lent me your reading glasses once and I said how comfortable I felt in them?'

Waldo began a mess-room barking. 'Take 'em and welcome, old man, provided you take your wife out of my *mandarah*.'

The simply furnished room which Waldo apparently called his *mandarah* was occupied not only by Mary who was calmly sitting on a low divan but also by Abdul, a smiling youth in a blue cotton gown and with a band of some white material round his tarboosh. Abdul was known to Perry because, as Waldo's servant, he frequently appeared at the university to carry a book. He bowed and went off to prepare coffee. In spite of Waldo's anxiety to drive them off the premises he could not now avoid offering the customary Moslem hospitality. First of all he produced the reading glasses and handed them over to Perry with a grunt. Putting them on, Perry felt his head clear and saw that Mary was looking straight ahead in precisely the same attitude as when he had entered the room.

'Waldo is quite livid, you turning up like this. Aren't you, Waldo?'

As was indicated by Waldo's restlessness he was, in fact, going through a struggle. First of all he kicked off his slippers and squatted on the divan in the corner; then, he jumped to his feet and padded up and down the room, talking quickly, but never once looking at his two guests. The struggle was between

Waldo the Moslem and Waldo the would-be cavalry officer, the one still recovering from the shock of Mary's unescorted arrival, the other a self-possessed gallant. Out of the conflict emerged Waldo the professor with views on the place of the classics in a university curriculum. He talked, quite irrelevantly, of university politics; there was a move in the Classics Department to teach Latin and Greek through the medium of Arabic. And it was all vanity, said Waldo. It was simply a trick to oust the European lecturers and substitute Egyptians; he was boring on the subject until Abdul brought the coffee in.

'I've about twenty minutes to catch my train,' said Perry when they had swallowed the mouthful which was all the cups contained. 'There's a taxi waiting outside, Mary. He can drop me at the station and take you on home.'

The coffee ritual had mellowed Mary. She even asked Waldo the names and functions of the various pieces of furniture in the room. Then she apologized for the way she had burst in upon him. 'Fond as I am of Edgar, there are times when he maddens me. If I hadn't rushed out of the flat this morning I should have scratched his face for him.'

'Oh come,' said Waldo genially. She had put him in a good mood with her questions about the furniture. He had known all the names. 'But I'm sorry to hear you were mixed up in that rumpus the other day,' he said to Perry. 'Of course, you were a fool to go. You know, Mrs. Perry, they don't mean any real harm. It's their sense of humour that saves them. Make them laugh and everything is all right.'

Mary set her cup down with a clatter. 'That's like the advice they give you when bathing in shark-infested waters. Hold the shark's tail out of the water and he's helpless! I suppose Edgar made them laugh the day before yesterday! I suppose it was the way he crawled under the bush that did it! That's why they only beat him and didn't kill him. I don't know why you stay in the country. If they were paying you decently it would be a different matter. You're just educating them up to bite the hand that's fed them. No, I'm not being old-fashioned. I'm upset that Edgar — who is a good, simple man — should be beaten up by a gang of hooligans who aren't fit to lick his boots. Tell me, Professor Grimbley, what is the good of education in a country like this?'

'I don't know what you're talking about,' said Waldo. He was growing exasperated once more. 'Education is education, everyone knows that. Everybody knows education is a good thing. Let me tell you something else! English teaching in this country is of the greatest importance. If they weren't learning English they'd be learning Russian, and then where should we be?'

'I'm not a good, simple man,' said Perry.

'Oh yes you are,' said Mary, 'otherwise you wouldn't be such a fool as to develop a conscience about the students' living conditions?'

'What's this?' demanded Waldo.

When Perry explained, with some pride, that he proposed carrying out an investigation into the students' tenements at Gizeh and presenting a report to his pupil Tureiya Pasha in the reasonable hope that it would find its way to the King himself, who might then interest himself in building hostels — when Perry explained all this, with a modest playing down of his good standing in the illustrious circles he had mentioned, Waldo snatched his pipe out of his mouth and jumped to his feet. He was alarmed and horrified.

'I forbid you to do anything of the sort, Perry.'

'Good,' said Mary.

Waldo hitched up the skirt of his caftan and set one san-dalled foot on the iron charcoal burner. 'Do you realize what sort of a genie you could let out of the bottle? You'll have university administration down on you like a ton of bricks. It's none of your business. It's none of our business. Teach 'em how to read and write English by all means, but everything else is politics. When you were at Oxford what would you have thought if the Reader in Japanese made a report on the students' living conditions and got somebody like Lord Nuffield, we'll say, to send it to the King. First of all you'd think the Reader in Japanese was a fool, then you'd think it was none of his business, and then I expect somebody or other would turn his rooms upside down. Here, it is enormously more serious, and you know why, just as well as I do. Forget it, Edgar, for heaven's sake. Now your wife's come out why not have a good time? Frankly, I don't suppose our students will put in an appearance until after Christmas.'

Waldo was so disturbed that he spoke reasonably. But his attempt at calculated inconsequence was a failure. 'I expect you find Cairo quite a change after England, Mrs. Perry.'

'Mary and I are parting,' Perry interrupted. 'She's divorcing me, or something. Or I'm divorcing her.'

'Oh,' said Waldo, staring at her with more interest than he had shown previously. She flushed. The abrupt revelation had taken her by surprise. Her mouth opened but she said nothing.

Through the lattice window Perry could hear the taxi driver and the porter quietly chatting. From the berseem fields came a monotonous jangling, caused perhaps by a bell on some animal's neck. A sherbet seller walked past the house clashing cymbals. The murmuring of voices, the intermittent jangling from the fields and the now muted clash of the cymbals, came to Perry's ears with an undisguised melancholy.

'No, Waldo. I don't accept that parallel with Oxford.' He spoke sadly because he did not want to argue and yet it was impossible to agree. Waldo's attitude surprised him. He would have thought him more independent. 'I can see this is a situation where I shall have to follow my own conscience.'

'Conscience?' Waldo laughed. 'Have you thought why the Palace should consider you so useful?'

'The Palace?'

'Certainly. The Palace, the court, Tureiya Pasha and the old Princess. Why should they employ an Englishman to stir up trouble?'

Perry thought about this. 'I shall still have to consult my conscience. One thing I can say. I shall need a lot of convincing I'm not doing the right thing. Come on, Mary. I really must go and catch that train.'

On the way to the station Mr. and Mrs. Perry said little to one another. This was mainly because the taxi made so much noise they would have needed to shout. But when they were waiting for a loaded camel to swing across the road Mary looked at her husband curiously and said, 'You know dear, I don't think you should have told him about us. It was very embarrassing. I can't understand why you should blurt it out like that.'

Neither could Perry and he tried to ignore her remark. 'Waldo is quite disgusting, going native. Mary, remember that what I am saying is no generalization. It's true only of myself. But ever since I arrived in this country I've been walking the back of a knife. Extraordinarily hard to keep a balance. I can't be neutral. I can't be passive. Either I hate the country or I like it very much. Either I loathe my students or I admire them. If I don't feed my admiration and — yes, love if you like — I could easily fill up with hate.'

The way clear once more, the taxi roared fiercely along the tram lines and as they went along Perry pointed out details of interest, an elaborate minaret, or a string of lamps outside a dilapidated house. He became quite hoarse from shouting.

❧ 2 ❧
❧

THE NOTE OF DECEPTION

AFTER BREAKFAST MARY STILL FELT DEPRESSED so she went
back to bed with a large clam shell reposing between her
breasts to serve as an ash tray. When she had smoked this nearly
full of butts and ash the telephone rang. She lay and listened.
Edgar was in Zagazig and probably would not arrive home
before lunchtime, Hassan was shopping, and Mrs. Curtis, their
resident landlady, was out of the flat and off to her hairdressing establishment every morning by nine o'clock. Mary
had for so long been listening to the usual sounds of a Cairo
morning, the swish and clatter of the trams and the nasal
passion of the radio from the laundry basement in the block
opposite, that the throb of the telephone was almost cheering.
Instead of feeling gloomy she now became sulky. She was alone
in the flat. Unless she went to the telephone it would, in a
moment, stop ringing. That would be tiresome. For the rest of
the day she would catch herself wondering who it had been.
Nevertheless, she did not move. With eyes closed she thought of
Egyptian nationalism, the liberal outlook in international
affairs; she thought of education, divorce, the cost of a first-
class passage between Alexandria and Tilbury; and she thought
of her own life and why, in getting upset over Edgar's injury,
she had succeeded in making such a fool of herself.

She was able to think about all these matters in so short a
space of time because they were, to her, different aspects of a
single subject: her life with Edgar.

46

Within half an hour of her disembarkation at Port Said she had realized that during their separation Edgar had changed in some way or other. She could not put her finger on it but the change seemed to be for the better. Not certain whether all the amenities of life could be found outside Europe, and prepared to take no risks, she had packed an unusually large supply of sanitary towels. Edgar stood at her side while the customs official, a young man for such work she thought, went through her luggage; when he began opening up the packages in obvious ignorance of their nature Edgar asked whether he was married. He put the question in a tone of such con-spiratorial masculinity that the youthful inspector flushed and closed his eyes with embarrassment. The rest of the luggage went through without examination. But Edgar was not embarrassed, that was the point. And the man she had known four years ago, still a junior lecturer in spite of his age, would have preserved greater delicacy. He would have turned his head away.

Perhaps she came nearest a description of Edgar's evolution when she wrote in a letter to her mother that he had become more direct, more frank in his manner. His general conversa-tion was as boring as it had always been but on that first evening in Egypt she had found the directness of his behaviour irresistible. Immediately they were alone together Edgar had begun to undress her. It was early in the evening. They had not even dined and taxis were still driving up to the hotel with passengers who had been only a little slower to disembark than Mary herself. However, he had been so sweet since she had come ashore that she hadn't the heart to repulse him. In the middle of his love-making she began to giggle — a giggle of simple pleasure — and Edgar said sharply, 'What's the matter, Mary? What's the matter?' This made her giggle all the more, because he spoke so urgently. He clearly thought he was in a situation where things could *be* the matter; he was demanding that she should answer, 'I am hysterical', or, 'My foot's gone to sleep' when, of course, there was nothing to say at all. How serious he was! He was just like the letters he wrote! She giggled so much that he couldn't kiss her. She turned her head away and when he went off to the bathroom, padding across the linoleum like a big duck, she could feel his anxiety coming back to her in waves.

Their room was not part of the hotel proper. It was a kind of cabin on the flat roof of the hotel which had been put there, together with half a dozen others, to house part of the staff. The hotel having prospered the cabins had been fitted up to receive guests. As a result, Mary could walk up and down the parapet overlooking the front of the hotel with propriety; her dressing gown was sufficient protection against the tepid salt air and daylight had gone. The palm trees along the front were quite black — or quite black, anyway, against what she saw through the fronds here and over the fronds there: the line of mildly phosphorescent surf. Walking up and down she conducted what she considered to be a struggle with her conscience. Had Edgar now to be told about James? Or had Edgar behaved in such a way as to make it unnecessary? Was he as unexciting as she thought he was?

'Mary! Are you there, Mary? Mary!' She saw him come out of the cabin and walk straight towards her. Assuming he had seen her she did not answer but when he continued to call for her in a breathless, impatient, irritated way she realized that he had not put on his glasses and was therefore practically blind in the near-darkness. Even then she waited. She stood and watched his uncertain silhouette. Behind him, over there to the east, the moon was rising out of Asia. Behind her lay Africa. She had never left Europe before. It was her first evening in the Levant and here she was with Edgar who was all anxiety

— anxiety to find her and, when he had found her, anxiety to know why she had giggled!

'Are you sure you're all right?' he inquired when they were back in the cabin once more and he was wearing his glasses. 'I've sent for a pot of tea. I thought you'd like that.'

After love-making, she remembered, Edgar had always insisted on a cup of tea. Without any doubt at all she was now on the point of scandalizing Edgar in a way she knew to be unforgivable and which nevertheless she was unable to avoid.

'I meant to tell you, Edgar,' she heard her own voice declaring, somewhat theatrically. 'Just before leaving England I became engaged.'

Edgar frowned. By this time he too was wearing his dressing gown; it was much too short for him. Perhaps it was not his dressing gown at all, she thought, because it appeared to be too big round the middle. He bunched it over his stomach like a boxer about to duck into the ring. Instead, he sat on his bed and waved his hand, smiling, not understanding at all. 'What d'you mean? D'you mean some sort of musical engagement?' This was a natural supposition, because for the last two years she had been a pianist attached to an itinerant ballet company.

'To think,' she said, 'that in spite of what I promised James I let you do what you did.'

Edgar stared at her so fixedly through his perfectly round, steel-rimmed glasses that she began to cry in spite of herself. She sat on the bed beside him and cried through her fingers until a knock came at the door and Edgar said, 'Come in,' with a voice that sounded, she thought, surprisingly calm under the circumstances. The tea had arrived. A white-gowned, red-sashed, tarbooshed servant placed the tray on a table, asked Edgar to sign a chit, and made off again silently. She heard Edgar stirring the contents of the tea pot with a spoon, a habit she detested.

49

'What d'you mean, engaged?' he said. 'And who is James?'

'I ought not to be sharing this room with you.' She had wiped her face and was hunting for the eau-de-cologne. 'I can't tell you how disgusted with myself I am.'

'We shouldn't have got two rooms anyway. The hotel's absolutely full. There are two boats in.'

'What a dreadfully cynical thing to say.'

'Cynical? Why is it cynical? It's obvious.'

'The implications were cynical. I know very well what you meant. How dare you, Edgar! James and I are to be married as soon as our divorce comes through and I won't have you taking advantage of your position in this way!'

'No married woman can be engaged,' said Edgar as though he understood not a word of what she was saying. 'You are a married woman. Therefore you cannot be engaged.'

He poured tea and they sat side by side on the bed drinking it. Mary lit a cigarette. Edgar produced his pipe. A liner in the harbour gave a series of shattering blasts on its siren. In the silence that followed they listened to the washing of the sea on the beach and the occasional whine of a mosquito.

'You cannot be engaged,' Edgar repeated. 'A married woman can have an affaire. Is that what you're trying to tell me, that you're having an affaire?'

'Yes, Edgar.' A monstrous lie, of course. But it seemed too late to retreat.

'Then that throws an entirely different light on the situation,' he said abruptly and began to dress for dinner. Mary knew he was miserable because he spoke so quietly. She also began to dress, wondering how, for the rest of the night, the proprieties were going to be observed between them; and wondering, too, with a pang of horror what James would have said if, by some magic or other, he had been party to her confession. 'You must be out of your mind woman,' in all probability, because that was his favourite remark. As business manager of the Chandos Ballet Troupe he had frequent occasion to use it. But on the present occasion, no! He would find something more forcible to say, for James was certainly not her lover; he had a family somewhere in Fife and was devoted to them. He was a vigorous, out-of-doors man with a fringe of hairs on both cheek bones. Everywhere the ballet company went a bag of golf clubs went too. Photographs of his wife and small children were produced on long train journeys; and when he was not talking about ballet — for which he had a profound love — or his family, or golf, he would speak angrily of his battle with the War Office to return to the active list once more. Before the war he had held a regular commission only to be invalided out because, as he put it, of 'some bug picked up in foreign parts'. Mary adored him and he liked her too but that was as far as the relationship went.

Poor Edgar! She was on the point of confessing when she became aware that he had gone. Even by the time she had finished dressing he had failed to put in an appearance. How like him and how exasperating! Instead of losing his temper and making a scene like any normal creature he had, in all probability, set off on a long walk. Not feeling equal to entering the dining-room alone she ordered a meal over the house telephone. An enormous moon had risen. She walked about the flat roof of the hotel in a mood of exaltation with a leg of roast chicken in one hand and a glass of red wine in the other. Perhaps the mood was, in part, a simple tipsiness. Undoubtedly, too, there was an ingredient of fatigue. But no matter from where the release came, she now felt uplifted. She floated in the evening. Ferdinand de Lesseps, on his statue at the end of the breakwater, appeared to be preparing for a pilgrimage to Asia across the silver winks and dimplings of the water. Mary returned to the cabin for more wine. Soon she would be thirty-three and middle-aged. While it lasted, youth had to be made exciting. And perhaps — in spite of the wine, the moon and a phantom lover — she had now left it too late.

Too late! Too late! The telephone continued to ring out the two words with all the emphasis of mockery. But was it too late? Mary was depressed because she thought she might be pregnant; that was why she had lain in bed smoking. A baby would mean middle age indeed. But if only she could now reach the telephone before it ceased ringing the spell might be broken, Edgar might be transformed into the jealous and passionate beast of her yearnings, quarrels and reconciliations would take place daily, and they would travel across the desert on racing camels to remote and haunted monasteries where Edgar would implore her to forget her lover and stay in Egypt with him!

Smoking all those cigarettes was enough to make anyone feel sick, she thought, so why worry? Once on her feet she shook her head and closed her eyes. All those cigarettes and nothing but coffee and toast could make anyone dizzy. But the telephone seemed to falter in its ringing. She hastily made her way to the hall, snatched the receiver from its hook and was so exultant to hear a man's voice addressing her that she was not even put out by the fact that he was speaking Arabic. The spell was broken! She was not too late! Anything might happen!

'Mush hinna,' she said, believing this to be Arabic for 'not here'. The voice had uttered a word that was recognizably 'Perry'. Encouraged by her reply, the voice flowed rapidly on but Mary was content to remark, 'Mush hinna!' now and again, not really caring who the man was or what he was saying. She had reached the telephone in time, that was all that mattered! Who knows? Perhaps the pregnancy was a false alarm! The deep, Arabic-speaking voice was now replaced by a light voice attempting English. 'This is the palace of Her Highness. Who is that, please?'

'Mrs. Perry,' Mary said.

'Mrs. Perry,' the voice repeated thoughtfully, as though its owner were writing the name down in a notebook. Then, more briskly, 'Please rest at the apparatus'. After a pause the voice announced, 'Her Highness will speak to you personally because it is a matter of greatest importance'.

'Professor Perry is not married!' declared a clearly enunciated old woman's voice in English. The accent was good, the tone firm. 'Who is that speaking to me? I can't hear you! Professor Perry has not mentioned the existence of a wife.'

Mary had never previously been addressed by royalty, even Egyptian royalty, and she found the experience sent a tremor through her. The Princess's remarks amounted to a claim of having heard Mary speak, but this was not true; Mary had not said a word. When she did speak it was to say, 'Your Highness, this is Mrs. Perry speaking. We were married five years ago in London and I've just come out to join him. If you want my husband he is in Zagazig and won't be home till lunchtime.'

Mary could hear the Princess sighing like wind in the wires. 'Welcome to Egypt! I will send you some flowers! Now that you are in Egypt you must not see only Cairo. You must see the provinces. I will lend you a car. Cairo is not Egypt, you understand? The last time I spoke to the Professor on the telephone I found myself speaking to another Englishwoman, an old woman. Her voice was old and cracked like mine. Her voice was not young. You have a young voice. It is like a little fountain in a courtyard. How old are you, did you say? But no, tell me first, who was this other woman?'

'That must have been Mrs. Curtis. She's our landlady.'

'I am bewildered by all these women in the Professor's apartment. He is translating into English a story I have written but, you understand, I must have the manuscript back at once. I do not want him to translate any more of it, not until I have altered the end. You know where my manuscript is? You can find it? Delay is impossible. Will you allow me to send a servant at once to bring it to me? I send him in a car. And please, will you be kind enough to return to the Palace with him and have some lunch with me? No, let me think! You are not dressed. You will want to prepare yourself. It is now eleven o'clock. Will you be ready at twelve o'clock, please, because I should like to work on my story before lunch. Just some finishing strokes. The tomb is not described. I forgot to describe the tomb. The tomb must be there on the last page.' The wiry voice broke off abruptly and the second voice Mary had heard, that of the English-speaking man, took over. He was obviously a secretary and he now formally confirmed the arrangements Her Highness had informally just made. 'It is convenient?' he said at last.

'Yes, oh yes, it's convenient all right,' said Mary. She put the receiver down and made straight for the cold shower.

At Zagazig little had gone right for Perry. His host, the director of the local British Institute, had failed to awaken from his siesta in time to meet the train. Not caring to hire one of the bug-ridden gharries which were lined up outside the station, Perry walked the length of the town and then another half mile along the bank of an irrigation canal before reaching the director's house; and there he discovered that the director, a tall, pale, discouraged-looking man called Ronald Colt, was one of those who did not regard afternoon tea as a meal. Perry was hungry. Because of the confusion before catching the train he had not lunched. But he was too polite to mention this and when the time came for Colt to take him down to the Institute for the lecture he felt quite dizzy with hunger. His subject was

'George Eliot and the Crisis of the Novel'. He was scarcely ten minutes into the lecture when the lights failed and Perry, only momentarily disconcerted, said, 'If you've no objections I'll carry on. I might as well carry on, don't you think so, Mr. Colt?' The blackness pushed at his eyes.

'Why, yes certainly!' said Colt with what Perry thought to be unnecessary heartiness. Judging by the noise, Colt then stood up and stepped into a bucket. 'I'm quite all right. Don't move, anyone,' he said. He laughed reassuringly. 'I expect a fuse has gone. I'll soon fix it.' He made off, clanking, into the darkness.

'Well, if you'll bear with me,' said Perry, 'I'll carry on with what I was saying.' The point he sought to make was that George Eliot's style in *The Mill on the Floss* was remarkable, here and there, for its suppressed sexuality. Yet try as hard as he might he could not believe that he still faced an audience. He could hear nothing but his own voice ringing back from the four walls: not so much as the creak of a chair, a cough, or the usual sigh of approbation. Surely the breathing of thirty-seven men and two women could be heard if one listened intently enough? Perry paused and listened. A silence so pure he trembled to break it! Were they shocked? Perry had merely said there appeared to be textual evidence in the book that George Eliot had once cut a pony's mane with a pair of shears. But an Egyptian audience was unshockable! It was more likely that they had all seized the opportunity to escape; by some extraordinary means they had contrived to withdraw from the room without making any noise and Perry was now speaking to empty chairs. The blackout was so complete he might have been entombed.

Perry went on talking but his suspicion grew. He was alone. Dizzy with hunger and dazzled by the blackness he stretched out one hand tentatively in the direction his audience had once been. His intentions were not at all considered. They could scarcely have been to locate the audience by touch and yet, when the tips of his fingers came to rest on a firm and furry shape he allowed them to wander about inquiringly. The lights snapped on and he found that he was fondling the tarboosh of a man in the front row, who was middle-aged, weighed a good two hundred and eighty pounds, wore a heavy moustache, and now gazed up at Perry with the morbidly melancholy eyes of a whipped hound.

No one had moved. The thirty-seven men and two women were still in their seats looking just as serious as ever. Instead of apologizing to the man in the front row, as perhaps he should, Perry drew back and began gesticulating with his offending hand. Ronald Colt hurried in carrying a metal waste-paper basket, calling, 'It's quite all right. Keep calm. Carry on. But frankly, it's a complete mystery to me. Someone's been playing a joke on us. The fuses were all right.'

The fat man in the front row and Perry were gazing into each other's eyes, flashing at each other messages of accusation and denial.

'A very silly joke, of course,' said Colt, laughing to ingratiate himself with the audience. He sat at Perry's right hand.

'Well, if that's the case it's absolutely disgraceful,' said Perry more to the fat man than to anyone else. 'There might have been a panic.'

Presuming on their intimacy, the fat man leaned forward and said, 'George Eliot was a woman. She was not a man. She was a woman.'

Perry's comment was interrupted by a second failure of the lights and this time there was a rumpus. Chairs fell over as people stood up, there was thick Egyptian shouting, Colt began striking matches and calling for calm, and Perry worked away from the door to be out of the threatened stampede. But the worst did not happen. The lights came on again so abruptly the fat man could be seen with his eyes firmly closed, presumably the better to see in the dark. Silence fell. Actions were arrested in mid-course, feet poised, arms uplifted, mouths agape. Still holding aloft a lighted match, Colt yelped as the flame burned down to his fingers. And from the back of the hall came the sound of a window being flung up.

Framed against the night were the head and shoulders of a young Egyptian who, a moment later, had swung himself into the room itself. He stood with cheeks inflated to keep back the laughter and with arms raised as though to conduct the applause which, he seemed to assume, would follow his entry. His clothes were flashy. The double-breasted suit was in black and white check of such a small pattern that, from a distance, it presented a mottled effect. He wore sharply pointed alligator-hide shoes and a tartan tie. On his head was a well-brushed tarboosh. A white handkerchief foamed from his breast pocket and an ostentatious ring flashed on his right hand. It was some moments before Perry realized that this brilliant creature was none other than his student, Muawiya.

'Sir,' said Muawiya. 'This is my native town. I am honoured to welcome you to my native town. This is where I grew to manhood. Only at the last minute did I hear you were giving a lecture in my native town. What is the subject, may I ask?' He put one alligator-hide shoe over the other and allowed his shoulder to make contact with the wall, laughing extravagantly. If he'd been English Perry would have thought him drunk. As it was, perhaps Muawiya had taken hashish.

'How dare you come into the room through the window,' said Perry. 'Were you responsible for putting those lights out?' The encounter had developed into a straight duel between Muawiya and Perry. Colt had not yet recovered from the shock of seeing an Egyptian enter his Institute by the window and the rest of the audience had come to the lecture in a passive state of mind, anyway, in the hope of being entertained. They were not so quick as Perry to link the lighting failure with Muawiya's sudden appearance.

'You see,' Muawiya remarked to the room in general, 'Mr. Perry is angry with me for something of no importance at all. He is not grateful to me and yet only the other day I saved his life. He would not be here now telling all you ignorant people about English literature if I hadn't saved his life. I risked my life to save his. Now he is angry. Professor Perry, you have not been just to me. When I said Nahas Pasha allowed me to go to the university you called me a liar.'

Perry had the wit to see that he was faced with a situation of more importance than any of the remarks he had prepared so carefully about the repressed sexuality of *The Mill on the Floss*. Muawiya was highly excited, visibly moving out of laughter into rage. The audience, too, were becoming angry. Visits to the British Institute created a prickliness about the state of Egyptian culture and a little grey-headed man began talking loudly to himself, saying that if a man were as ill-educated as a camel he would know better than to come into a room through the window; even a Berber would enter by the door. 'Or a horse,' he said, achieving his climax. 'Even a horse would not jump through a window.'

'I am not a horse!' Muawiya shouted. But he was attacked in Arabic and had to defend himself in Arabic. Everyone now knew that Muawiya had been responsible for switching the lights off and making such fools of them. Many voices spoke at once. The fat man came up to Perry and said, 'I regret this intrusion.' He uttered the words with force and precision, obviously delighted with his command of English. 'This man is no good. This town is no good. I used to live in Manchester. Let someone send for the police.'

A group of the younger men were closing in on Muawiya

with the obvious intention of bustling him out into the street.
Colt was holding the door wide open so that when Muawiya
was shot through he could quickly lock it after him. Perry
stood watching. In a few moments the interruption would be
over and he could proceed with his lecture. There was no need
for him to raise a finger. But just when twelve hands had taken
a grip of the young man Perry decided to intervene. 'I'd like
Mr. Muawiya to stay to my lecture,' he said. 'That is, of course,
if Mr. Muawiya wants to. Do you?'

'Yes,' said Muawiya simply. All the hysteria had gone out
of him. His jacket was up round his ears, he had lost his tie
and the legs of his trousers were sufficiently hoisted to reveal that
he was wearing no socks. In spite of his dishevelment he was
more dignified than at any moment since he had climbed
through the window. The twelve hands fell away from him.
Some even began to brush him down.

For the rest of his stay in Zagazig Muawiya occupied most
of Perry's waking thoughts; even when, as was the case some
minutes later, he was talking about George Eliot again with a
careful avoidance of Muawiya's eye. Where the devil had he
obtained all that finery from? he wondered. Why had he
shaved? Why had he wanted to make such a brilliant impression?

Question time at the end of his talk was always a severe test
for the visiting lecturer at Zagazig. Perry was glad to dodge a
quite irrelevant query about his failure to mention Mr. War-
wick Deeping by turning to Colt and asking where Muawiya
had disappeared to. It was true. Muawiya had gone. Throughout the lecture he had occupied a chair at the end of a row with
his head against the wall and his eyes closed. Perry was quite
certain that the fellow had been taking hashish; he had little
idea what the effects of hashish were but what other explanation
could there be for a repose that was as profound as his previous

excitement had been violent? Colt stood up. Everyone looked at Muawiya's empty chair. No one had seen him leave; though, now they came to consider the matter, it was quite an easy matter for him to leave quietly. He had only to step over an unoccupied chair behind and disappear through a small door which led to the cellar where the ping-pong tables and skittle alley were housed. And there was, naturally, a way out of that hall of culture.

Colt grew mushrooms in a corner of the cellar with spawn imported from England and as soon as he had assured himself the bed had come to no harm ('These young fanatics will go to any length, you'd never believe it') he said, 'What does it matter, anyway? We've got rid of him. Let's go home and have some dinner. Lieutenant Rashid and Doctor Ibrahim are going to eat with us tonight. I always like to get in a couple of the local dignitaries for a bite afterwards. They couldn't manage to come to the lecture, I'm sorry to say.'

Instead of standing at the door like a non-conformist parson to shake hands with everyone as was expected of him Perry walked a few steps townwards in the darkness, hoping to catch sight of his student lurking in some corner. There was no sign of him. A few stars were reflected in the canal. There were lights in some of the windows of the Water Company's office opposite and thirty yards down to the road a standard gas lamp snored in the wind. These and the naked electric bulb over the entrance to the Institute behind him were the only illumination in a singularly dark night. It was hopeless to search for Muawiya and the very hopelessness made Perry angry. He had *not* been angry when Muawiya played the trick with the lights and then climbed through the window like a schoolboy; he had not been angry, even, when Muawiya made the speech about saving his life. But he was wildly angry that he could not find Muawiya now and when he rejoined Colt on the steps of the Institute, he snapped, 'I don't want anyone else for dinner tonight. Can't you make some excuse?'

'What's the matter? Not feeling too good?'

'Is it true what Muawiya said, that this is his home town?'

'Lieutenant Rashid is *just* the man to tell us,' said Colt triumphantly. He slapped Perry on the shoulder. 'I've got a bottle of Scotch at home. You'll feel better after a snifter.'

They walked briskly because of the cold, Colt showing the way with an electric torch. An irrigation pump coughed rhythmically in the darkness. Colt chattered about the lecture and the crowd who had turned up, with a lightness that revealed his determination Perry should not protest once more about Rashid and Ibrahim coming to dinner. He said nothing about Muawiya. Anyone would think, Perry reflected, that it was nothing unusual for a man to enter the Institute by a window and break up a lecture. Perhaps, in Zagazig, it was not unusual.

'Why the hell he should clear off like that I can't understand,' said Perry. 'D'you ever hear of anything so thoughtless? How do we know he hasn't fallen in the canal? In the state he was anything could have happened.'

But they were already at Colt's house. As they climbed the steps to the balcony a suffragi opened the door and said to Colt, 'Very sorry, Mr. Rashid and Mr. Ibrahim are drinking the whisky.'

The light was dazzling after the long walk in the dark; and the noise going on in Colt's lounge was almost stunning. With eyes half shut Perry made his way into the room where a man in the blue uniform of a police lieutenant was holding a glass of whisky and thundering with laughter. His face appeared to be all white, flashing teeth. Then he closed his mouth and the little snub nose appeared, followed by the red-rimmed eyes and a closely cropped fuzz of woolly hair over the neat little skull.

He spoke English deep in the throat as though it were Arabic and Perry found it difficult to understand him. His companion was a middle-aged man in a grey suit who sat quietly smiling to himself. Obviously this was Dr. Ibrahim and when Colt made the introductions he looked at Perry and then at Rashid and then back to Perry once more, as though to say, 'I despise this creature.'

The kitchen door was open and the smell of cooked food caused Perry's stomach muscles to contract. The excitement of the last hour or so had made him forget his hunger but the pangs returned now in the form of nausea. He drank a finger of whisky which Colt offered him and was immediately intoxicated. One moment he was wretched, the next he was overheated and aggressive. He stood to attention. He feared that if anyone so much as touched him he would fall over.

'Mr. Rashid,' he said when the policeman had stopped laughing. 'I've already told Mr. Colt that I prefer to be without company this evening, but since you are here will you kindly do something for me?'

'But of course, sir,' said Rashid eagerly. He thought the remark about being alone was intended as a joke and he began to laugh again, quite elated to discover that Mr. Colt soon joined in, nodding his head and looking at Perry as though warmly appreciative of his witticism. Rashid decided that Perry was a man after his own heart, a hard drinker and jovial.

'Then, Lieutenant Rashid, if you are, as you say, prepared to do something for me will you kindly listen to what I have to say?' Perry spoke with some formality because Rashid had usurped the role of host and put more whisky into his glass which he, Perry, had drunk. 'I did you an injustice when I first heard your name mentioned. I thought you were an army officer. I see you are in the police. Now, will you be so good as to telephone your police station and ask them whether they can locate a young man who is in this town at the moment. His name is Muawiya?'

'Muawiya?' said Rashid in surprise. He had been straddling about the room like a stage Prussian. 'You don't mean Muawiya Khaslat?' The lieutenant was a different man; he even spoke quietly, staring at Perry as though seeing him for the first time.

'As a matter of fact I think that is his name.' If Perry could remember one part of an Egyptian name he considered it sufficient; but he suspected that Muawiya Khaslat was the name inscribed on his lecture roll. 'Yes, d'you know him? He said this was his native town.'

'He is here, now?' demanded Rashid. 'Where is he?'

'That is just what I want you to find out.'

From nowhere the Lieutenant produced a flat cap, placed it on his head and then gave Colt a formal salute. 'You must please forgive me.' He hurried out of the room and did not wait for the suffragi to open the front door. A moment later they heard his footsteps pass the window.

Colt looked quite frightened. The change of atmosphere brought about by the mention of Muawiya's name had been remarkable. Even Dr. Ibrahim seemed interested. Yet when Colt asked him why Rashid should hurry off like that the doctor only smiled, shrugged and breathed in some more whisky. 'Who knows? Perhaps they were at school together. Or perhaps this Muawiya — is that his name? — is a celebrated criminal with a price on his head and the gallant lieutenant is out to make an arrest.' The doctor spoke English really very well. 'Who knows? This is a very funny part of Egypt. I come from the Fayoum where we have different traditions.'

Perry was holding on to a standard lamp for support.

'Excuse me, doctor,' he said solemnly. 'Muawiya is not a criminal. He is a student of mine with a most original theory about Shakespeare's *Othello*.' He then fell forward over a divan, dragging the lamp after him. The suffragi and Dr. Ibrahim carried him off to bed while Colt went into the kitchen to make sure the meat did not burn.

Zagazig railway station was crowded the following morning. Apparently a branch line train had unexpectedly turned up from one of the obscurer reaches of the Delta. A mob of fellaheen invaded the Cairo line platform with large baskets on their heads and when Perry arrived, five minutes before the train was due, he despaired at first of even passing the ticket-collector. The entrance to the platform was choked with black-gowned, black-veiled women who were arguing among themselves while their children screamed and youths tried to sell them hard-boiled eggs and bread for the journey. He stood patiently sweating in the sun, trying to give up all memory of the past and all anticipations of the future; he was so ashamed of getting drunk on a couple of fingers of whisky that he allowed the flies to settle on his face. He had thoughts of mortifying the flesh. The train would arrive and depart without him. Then he would squat in the shade like a peasant and wait for the next one; he would have no pride; any indignity would be suffered without complaint.

'Sir!' said a familiar, fat-tongued voice from out of the mêlée, 'be so good as to enter this way.' With a large, official-looking key, Muawiya was opening what might well have been the station-master's own private gate and waving Perry forward. He was as handsomely dressed as on the evening before and bore no mark of any rough handling. 'Come on, sir. Quickly!'

His eyes were wide with excitement. 'A compartment has been reserved!'

The next few minutes were filled with so much violent

activity that Perry had no time to give himself up to the genuine feeling of relief he experienced at the sight of Muawiya. The train arrived from Ismailia. Perry dodged through the station-master's gate and found himself helping Muawiya to close it in the faces of some determined orange salesmen; would-be travellers began boarding the train and climbing in through the windows even before it had come to a halt and there was a vigorous press of bodies across the platform at right angles to the path Perry was being led by Muawiya. Perry repeatedly found his suitcase trapped on the other side of two men, one of whom then attempted to climb over his arm. 'Beware of pickpockets!' Muawiya shouted. 'A first class compartment has been reserved.'

'My ticket is second class!' Perry called back.

When they arrived at the first class section of the train Muawiya drew a whistle from his pocket and blew on it shrilly. Two porters in cast-off army uniforms immediately appeared, lifted Perry off the ground and thrust him through the open window of a compartment from which two other khaki-clad porters were ejecting the last of the fellaheen who had, it seemed, wrongfully taken possession of it. Shouting with laughter Muawiya sailed in through the window, propelled from behind. He drew a fat wallet from his pocket and gave the grinning porters fifty piastres each.

'The station-master is my brother-in-law,' he explained. 'He is sorry he cannot be here to present his compliments but he has to be in court this morning to give evidence against an eggs-and-bread man. Will you smoke one of these cigarettes, sir?'

The train was already moving out of the station. Blue irrigation canals flashed in the sun. The noise of Zagazig station subsided, and the fellaheen in the corridor began to clap hands and chant as the level delta landscape slid past.

'Muawiya!' said Perry incredulously, beginning to laugh.

For the first time that morning his hangover gave signs of lifting.

Muawiya spoke seriously. 'It is an honour for me to have your company in this way. I hope you do not think it impertinent of me to make these arrangements. Now we have two hours uninterrupted together. We can talk of poetry, anything.'

Perry simply could not make it out. Soothed and cheered by the motion of the train, he gazed at Muawiya and drew deeply on his cigarette. Was Zagazig really his home town? And even if it were, what possible motive could he have for making such a nuisance of himself at the lecture? Exhibitionism? Exasperation? Hashish? Muawiya looked perfectly normal this morning; but perhaps hashish did not give you the hangover that, say, whisky did? And what of Lieutenant Rashid? Why had the mention of Muawiya's name caused him to rush out of Colt's house with an indifference to etiquette that was rare in Egypt?

'If you wish to sleep I will tell these men in the corridor to stop their noise.' Muawiya's solicitude was becoming embarrassing.

'Is your full name Muawiya Khaslat?'

'Yes. Your name is Edgar, sir. Edgar Perry. There was a king of England called Edgar.'

At the first halt Muawiya called a vendor to the window and bought a sugar-cane six feet long. He would have bought one for Perry, but Perry said he had tasted it once and been sick. Muawiya casually lifted up the tail of his smart jacket and produced a knife he could have cut the throat of a camel with; he sliced off a convenient eighteen inches or so of cane and bit at it savagely with his large teeth; after some moments of vigorous chewing he spat the pith between his knees on to the floor and took another bite. Flies appeared. In a matter of minutes a mound of pith had formed. Muawiya stood up and pushed it beneath the seat with the side of his foot. The air reeked of the sickly stuff and still he had not satisfied himself.

He wiped his lips with a handkerchief. 'Why did I save your life, sir, may I ask?' He paused with a piece of cane half way to his mouth; he watched Perry shrewdly.

Perry was so nauseated by the syrupy smell that he stood up and opened the window. The compartment was swept by a sandy wind which seemed to lift Muawiya into the air. In reality he had jumped to his feet. He shouted, 'Flies! Flies!' and shut the window up again with a snap. 'It is impossible to eat sugar-cane, sir, unless the window is closed,' he explained. 'All the flies come in.'

'But the compartment is full of flies.'

'Sir, you let them in.'

'Not at all! They were here already!'

A quarrel about the number of flies in the compartment was so absurd that Perry made efforts to keep a grip on himself; after all, the fellow had probably put himself to a great deal of trouble to reserve this compartment — and what was more, he would almost certainly insist on paying for it. But the hot, sugary, fly-infested atmosphere was beginning to make him ill to the point where all he cared about was fresh air.

'Do you think I am pro-English?' Muawiya asked.

Short of climbing out of the window and hurling himself into a sandbank, Perry could see no way of escape; the corridor was so full of fellaheen they would cascade into the compartment once the door were opened. His resentment had now reached such a pitch that he began to believe Muawiya had intentionally cornered him in this way to have a tête-à-tête. And sure enough, when Perry ignored his question, Muawiya began to speak of his unhappy life, how his father always talked to him about money, never about his studies or about books; and that, said

Muawiya, was scandalous; because, after all, his father was a schoolmaster.

'I must have this window open.'

'But the flies!'

'Damn the flies!' If then they did have to quarrel let it be about flies and not about matters of any greater consequence! Perry took a breath and opened the window. Immediately a sheikh's tomb came in sight, a small whitewashed cupola in a grove of palm trees. Forgetting his sugar-cane and the flies Muawiya pointed excitedly and said, 'There is the tomb of some holy man. I am ashamed to say I do not even know his name. I am ignorant of my country and my religion. But that doesn't mean I am not a good Egyptian. Sir, —' and he put his face so close Perry had to turn his head away — 'Sir, I love you as a man but I hate England. I did not save your life because I am pro-English. I want you to understand me.'

The sheikh's tomb glided from view and Muawiya closed the window once more. The train was approaching Benha. A biscuit-coloured desert rose and fell in front of some low hills. The fellaheen in the corridor began standing up and sitting down, raising baskets and lowering them, arguing·and laughing in obvious preparation for leaving the train. In a matter of minutes, then, Perry would be able to escape from Muawiya by the simple expedient of walking into the corridor. He could afford to be patient.

'I don't want to talk politics,' he remarked.

Muawiya sliced off another section of cane. 'You and I have become dear friends, sir. Please, this sugar-cane is excellent. Are you sure you will not accept a piece? It is good for the liver.'

'Is it true that Zagazig is your native town?'

Muawiya shook his head and laughed. 'It is not true. I lied to you. But what else could I say? Zagazig is a town I know, but I do not come from there. My home is Damanhour. When I appeared at the Institute I knew you would think it strange if I could say nothing to explain why I was there.'

Perry was sitting as far away from Muawiya as he could contrive. His nausea had subsided a little. No doubt he had become accustomed to the sickly atmosphere; but his interest in Muawiya's remarks had quickened so perhaps this was a factor too. 'Then what were you doing in Zagazig if your home is not there?'

'Did I not tell you? I learned that you were to give a lecture and resolved to be present. You are my professor. What could be more natural?'

Perry thought there was a possibility that the fellow was speaking the truth. The dressing up in his best clothes, the long journey from Cairo specially taken, might well be the calculated flattery the occasional student was capable of. Nevertheless, Perry was not satisfied. He framed questions only to reject them before they were uttered; he saw himself groping in the dark towards an understanding — rather as he had groped in the Institute when the lights had gone out. Muawiya continued to bite at the sugar-cane and spit the pith on to the floor. He understood Perry's bewilderment perfectly and Perry formed the impression he would have carried solicitude so far as to help with the framing of these difficult questions; no matter how skilfully he would then have parried them.

'You *were* responsible for the lights going out, weren't you?'

'I thought it was an excellent joke, sir. Now I see I was foolish and I hope you will forgive me. It was most wrong. I am ashamed of myself.' Muawiya laughed out loud.

'Have you ever been in trouble with the police?'

'No. No more than anyone else. Sometimes an enemy will pay the police to make trouble.' Muawiya answered smoothly. The question had not come unexpectedly.

Thinking that he was now, probably, acting foolishly, Perry mentioned Lieutenant Rashid's strange behaviour.

Muawiya stopped chewing, emptied his mouth carefully, and said, 'What time was this?'

'About half past eight, I suppose.'

Muawiya smiled self-consciously and paused with his knife on the cane. 'He must have missed me. I did not see him.'

'Why do you think he should want to see you?'

A shrug and a smile. 'It is very easy. I am agent for a firm of educational publishers. I sell on commission. Clients pay by instalments. Rashid has bought some books on law and he is behind in his payments. No doubt he wanted to see me and explain.' Muawiya wiped his knife and slipped it under his jacket. 'But I shall not worry him. I shall wait for my money. After all he is a policeman.'

He saw the expression on Perry's face and began to laugh. 'You don't believe me. Sir, there is not enough sweetness in life. Have some sugar-cane and put some sweetness in your thoughts.'

After this Perry felt he could not decently inquire where Muawiya had disappeared to after the lecture. Encouraged by his silence Muawiya reverted to the incident in the Botanical Gardens of a few days before. He spoke with a noticeable complacency.

'They would have killed you, sir. I saved your life.'

'There's no need to keep rubbing it in.'

Muawiya's face lit up with amazement. 'Rubbing it in? But I don't understand. You think I shall ask you for some tit for tat because I have saved your life. I don't like tit for tat. You think I want some favour? You think I want some backsheesh? Once you called me a liar and I forgave you. Now you think I want tit for tat. All right I forgive you again. It is of no importance. But I did save your life! You must admit that!'

Muawiya threw the sugar-cane to the floor and brandished his ugly knife. His neck thickened with rage.

'For heaven's sake, man, calm down. I only asked you not to keep on boasting about saving my life. It makes me feel such a fool.'

Muawiya threw himself on to the seat at Perry's side and then twisted his body round so that he could look up into Perry's face. The attitude was a curious mixture of threat and cajolery. 'That is not the point. Did I not save your life? Did I not?'

Perry hesitated. He was startled by Muawiya's vehemence. He was also a little scared because Muawiya was holding the knife, point upwards, in his right fist: the approved grip, Perry understood, for a stab to the heart. Absurd to think of being murdered by a student under the curious eyes of half a dozen fellaheen — they were watching from the corridor window — and quite ludicrous that his assassin should be a man who had taken offence over a seeming lack of gratitude for having saved his victim's life!

In spite of his alarm, or possibly because of it, Perry began to laugh. What a preposterous situation to find oneself in! Muawiya jumped to his feet and took up a theatrical pose, legs apart, head thrown back, eyes fixed on an electric light bulb in the ceiling. The knife was still clutched in his right hand. 'You must not laugh at me.'

The dilapidated pink and brown tenements of Benha appeared and the train slackened speed to enter the station. Muawiya opened the window with a flourish and began to climb through, calling out as he went, 'I cannot travel to Cairo in your company. Be so good as to make yourself comfortable.' He still held the knife.

Perry told him not to be a fool and attempted to drag him back into the compartment. 'Of course you saved my life, you idiot. I am very grateful to you.'

'There are men who say I am not a good Egyptian because I save your life.' The words came out in a wail. Holding his tarboosh on with his left hand and clutching the knife with his right Muawiya looked into the wind. Perry supposed it was the wind that had brought tears to the fellow's eyes; but when he set one foot against the side of the carriage and dragged him back on to a seat Muawiya pulled a handkerchief out of his pocket and blew his nose noisily. Perry looked at him wonderingly.

'Sir, you must have no wrong ideas about me. I am a patriot. You must not trust me.'

It suddenly came to Perry that Muawiya's expedition to Zagazig and his extravagant behaviour there had no other purpose than the delivery of this simple warning: 'Do not trust me.'

As soon as Muawiya saw that Perry had taken the warning without offence he became gay once more. For the rest of the journey he chattered about matters of no consequence.

The summer sun was too fierce for an open-air siesta but by the time November came round Perry could usually be seen, naked to the waist, sprawled out on the balcony. He wore dark glasses. Through these, he gazed at the kite hawks which sailed effortlessly above the flat roofs and minarets of the city; once he was eating a sandwich on somebody's roof garden when one of these obscene birds had swooped down and taken it out of his hand; he saw the pale amber, curved beak, snatching sideways, he saw the sulphurous eye, and felt the momentary grip of the talons on his wrist. Worst of all his other hand came in contact with the breast bones of the bird as, instinctively, he had made a grab. The sandwich went and he was left with a bleeding wrist. Ever since then he had loathed and feared the birds. The dark glasses were worn not only to protect his eyes against the sun but also to protect them against the kites. But this he would have admitted to no one.

'Edgar!'

He pretended to be asleep. Mary was not deceived and he knew she was not deceived. Nevertheless he kept his eyes closed. When he heard her settle into the other basket chair he was annoyed she should have accepted his little act so easily, sat up and said, 'Hallo! So there you are!'

'I've been to lunch with the Princess.'

'Hassan told me.'

It struck Perry that her dress, her elbow-length gloves, and her winged hat were very nearly the same colour as the dome he could see behind her in the distance — a delicate biscuit brown. It pleased him that he could be sufficiently detached to make observations like this, and he said with a touch of savagery in his voice, 'How did you wangle that?'

She appeared to be radiant with triumph. In reality she was trembling with a suppressed merriment. 'The Princess telephoned for her story because she wanted to alter the end. When she discovered you had a wife I was invited to lunch. I took the story. After lunch she dictated a new ending and then handed the whole thing over again. Here it is!'

Her Highness had concluded the story not only with a description of the tombs of the Pharaoh and his favourite concubine but had also added detailed instructions on the best way of reaching them: time of departure from Cairo station, time of arrival at Luxor, which hotel to stay at, precautions necessary for the preservation of health, and so on. Perry could not see that this information added anything to the feminist message the Princess intended the story to convey.

'What did she give you to eat?' said Perry in an attempt at coarseness.

'She's the most insatiably curious woman I've ever met. She

felt my dress and asked me how much it cost. She said she'd never forgive you for not telling her you have a wife.'

'Well, have I?'

'That's perfectly true, Edgar. She said you were a domestic tyrant. She became so cross about it — you see, it's all part of this anti-man campaign of hers — that I had to defend you. Of course, I told her. I mean, I said you couldn't be expected to reveal the existence of a wife who wasn't *really* a wife. It would be embarrassing for you.'

Perry stood up and looked at her in astonishment. 'You said what?'

'You've no idea how delighted she was! It's quite absurd, of course, but what could I say? She dragged it all out of me. She asked question after question. She was insatiable. She said why didn't I send for James to join me out here, winter in Egypt was such a pleasant season. She said she'd pay his fare out because she was thinking of starting a ballet group here in Egypt and if James was a business man that was just the kind of help she needed. It's unbelievable!'

'The bitch!' said Perry. 'And you're a bitch too!'

Mary laughed and said, 'Oh, I can't sit still!' She and the Princess had had champagne with the cold chicken and she could still feel it tingling in her veins. Not for years had she enjoyed an experience so exhilarating. The old lady made such a fuss of her that Mary thought at first she had an ulterior motive. Perhaps she detected material for one of her stories. Perhaps she had been struck by the idea of discovering the point of view of an Englishwoman on her favourite subject, the equality of the sexes. Yet, on reflection, Mary had to admit that the true explanation for the Princess's interest was more probably a kindliness. Not a simple kindliness, a complicated kindliness.

The Princess had excused her presence in bed by saying she

rarely rose until after lunch. Her bed was a four-poster so large that, if walled in, it would have made quite a sizeable room. At night the Princess was shut off from the rest of the world by curtains of ivory-coloured lace; these curtains were now drawn back and elegantly looped up with green silk ropes. On the head-board was a plaque bearing a maze of Arabic lettering which Mary took to have some religious significance. The Princess sat up among her snowy pillows with a lace cap over her grey hair secured by a number of pearl-headed pins. Her earrings were pearls, too, and on a finger of her left hand — these were the details as Mary noticed them — was a huge emerald of the same shade of green as the ropes that held up the lace-curtains; and this, Mary realized, was the colour of the Egyptian flag. Mary knew she was in the presence of royalty because there was no sense of privacy. The two sets of double doors at either end of the room were folded back; during lunch an intermittent stream of visitors passed through: clearly, they were all members of the Princess's household — men in black jackets, gold watch-chains and tarbooshes, girls in voluminous blue gowns, Sudanese in white gowns and carrying poles. They were using the bedroom as a short cut and as they came to the end of the bed the men paused to make a profound obeisance. The womenfolk sank on one knee. Lunch was brought in by Swain, the English butler, who wore morning clothes as though they were fancy dress: as indeed they were in this setting.

Mary responded to this extravagance with an extravagance of her own. Even if she had wished she could not have remained discreet under the Princess's probing; as the minutes passed and the old lady's wonder grew Mary's excitement was fanned by her own incredulity: here she was, talking away to an elderly princess who looked as Queen Elizabeth the First must have looked in one of those many beds she was reputed to have slept in. Just anything was possible! The Princess had taken a fancy to her! This was to be only the first of many such intimate meetings! The most delicious confidences would be exchanged! Or, to put it differently, the Princess would listen to Mary's confidences with so much sympathy as practically to amount to the imparting of confidences of her own. 'Is the man married too?' she asked. 'Surely it would have been more convenient to send your husband a cable? Is he quite well, by the way? Last time he was here he behaved like a lunatic.'

The Princess said her circulation was bad and, to prove the point, popped both her feet out of bed and invited Mary to examine the dark veins. One of the blue-gowned girls placed slippers on the feet, another girl drew back the covers, and the Princess rose because, as she said, the time for composition had come. It was impossible to carry out any creative work while the circulation was sluggish. Her brain was at its best when she was taking exercise. Accordingly, she would walk up and down the room while she was dictating, and if Mrs. Perry wished to accompany her she was welcome to do so.

'But, of course!' the Princess exclaimed. 'That is *why* he behaved like a lunatic.' One of the maids had at last succeeded in placing a wrap over her; and now, while the secretary telephoned one of the Luxor hotels for information about the length of their season — this was necessary to round off her story — the Princess revealed that she had been thinking about Perry all the time. 'He tore his report up into little pieces and as good as threw them in my face. My husband was charmed because he likes original behaviour! But M. Perry was mad with love and jealousy! *Le pauvre!* How your husband must be suffering!'

'Your Highness, he is not suffering at all. He is completely lacking in imagination. Because I am here he appears to think the problem doesn't exist. Or perhaps he is saying to himself that it's a passing infatuation.'

'No, no, no, no! Believe me! I am old enough to be your

grandmother and I am a student of the human heart. Perhaps you are right. Perhaps he is a natural cuckold! Who knows?'

'How dare you talk to the Princess about our private affairs!' said Perry. He was getting ready to take Mary to the garden of the Anglo-Egyptian Union for tea. 'I could have forgiven you if it had been anyone else. But the Princess ought not to have to bother her head about things like that. She's too nice a person. Besides, it makes me look such a fool in her eyes. Ah! It's all very well for you to laugh, but you don't know the country. You don't know how important it is not to appear a fool. And that the Princess, of all people — '

'What's so special about the Princess, anyway?'

'Well — ' said Perry uncertainly.

❧ 3 ❧
❧

A PRISONER WITH PRINCIPLES

In the days that followed Mary thought a great deal about her meeting with the Princess and particularly about the words Her Highness had uttered so lightly: '*Le pauvre!* How your husband must be suffering!' The more Mary thought of them the more meaning the words seemed to acquire. Perhaps they were true! Perhaps Edgar was so much of a gentleman he was able to conceal his anguish. His very eagerness to press on with the report on the students' living conditions might be merely a symptom of his true feelings. Yes, she decided, there was little doubt that he was trying to forget his sorrow in work — for who, in his right state of mind would busy himself in a matter that was not only no concern of his but might, if Waldo was to be believed, land him in serious trouble?

Mary began thinking of herself as a woman of remorseless cruelty. Then why not confess and put an end to the farce? On thinking it over she decided that, having become accustomed to the false situation she had represented, Edgar would never believe the truth. Looking round for other ways to console him she at length decided to help with the report on the Gizeh tenements even if it did lead to a row of some kind. At least they would be in it together. Accordingly, they were to be found, one afternoon, in the second rack of a tram which bore them over the Nile bridges while they refused to buy bits of wire to clean primus stoves from a man who clung to the side of the tram and lectured them sonorously for most of the journey.

After the demonstrations and near-riots the situation had calmed down again. On the Cairo side of the bridges soldiers were posted to prevent any considerable body of students marching over from Gizeh; and discreetly tucked away down side-turnings were the riot squads, groups of sleeping soldiers who, at the blast of a whistle, could be expected to jump up, don steel helmets and small shields made specially for the work, climb into open army trucks and be driven off to the scene of disturbance sleepily waving their army-issue staves or cudgels in the air. At Gizeh, however, there was no sign of trouble. A brisk wind blew up the dust as though a thousand carpet beaters were at work and men walked about with tasselled scarves across their mouths. The sun stood over the Pyramids sending shafts of golden light through the clouded air.

Perry assisted his wife down from the tram but instead of making for the pavement he conducted her to another tram, a more luxurious type with glass in the windows, where he installed her in a first class compartment. At first she thought they were merely sheltering from the dust storm. Yet when other passengers came on board and the conductor came round for fares she looked for Edgar only to find that he was preparing to leave.

'This is a fast tram to the Pyramids,' he said. 'You'll be there in no time. If I were you I'd have some tea at Mena House.'

'But I'm coming with you.'

'What?' He appeared genuinely astonished. 'You can't do that!' He waved as the tram gathered speed. The acceleration was so rapid that already it was travelling too fast for her to jump off and they waved vigorously to one another, indignation on the one side and — well, what on the other?

He squinted into the flying dust until he saw the tram plunge down the steep incline that would take it under the railway and then turned, somewhat jauntily, to cross the road. The crumbling plaster, the exposed mud bricks, the gaunt stairwells and the brass bedsteads of the Gizeh tenements were before him. As a punishment for the demonstrations the government had closed the university for a month but Perry did not doubt that he would find the tenements occupied.

In preparing his earlier report — the one he had taken out of the Princess's hands and torn up — he merely examined a number of the students' rooms and made notes on the cooking facilities, the sanitary arrangements and whether or not there were chairs and tables. This time he was after statistics. He had no idea whether there were five hundred students in the quarter, or a thousand, or two thousand. There seemed to be no official list of rooms occupied and the existence of a street map showing university-approved houses seemed so absurdly too much to hope for that Perry had not even inquired for it. His plan was simple. By way of a beginning, he proposed choosing one street and asking the porter at each house or tenement whether the building contained students. Then he would count the number of rooms and the students in them. If he was fortunate he might even find a student willing to act as a guide.

But even this simple plan misfired. The first house he came to was a modest two-storey building of mud bricks which at some time in the past had been whitewashed. The walls now looked not unlike nougat and when Perry climbed the two stone steps to the passage he considered the possibility of the building stickily, cloyingly, caving in on him. A room to the right contained a bed so large that it touched three of the walls and left no more than sufficient space on the fourth side for the door to open. On the bed lay one of the largest students Perry had ever seen. He wore heavy, army-type boots, blue and white pyjamas, a tarboosh, and he lay with head comfortably cupped in his hands. From his English briar pipe rose delicate circles of blue smoke. At the sight of Perry he sat up and recognizing him for an Englishman said, in a friendly way, 'Sir, you are welcome to hide under my bed.'

'What for?' said Perry. He thought this might be an oriental greeting he had not heard of.

The student sat on the edge of the bed. 'Are you not pursued? Are not the students pursuing you? Is not your life in danger? But you are my guest. My name is Ahmed Mansour. I am an expert in agriculture.'

'As a matter of fact,' said Perry, 'I'm collecting statistics about the way you fellows live. By the way, I don't think we've met before, Mr. Mansour. I'm Professor Perry of the English Department.'

The student shook hands without standing up. When Perry produced a notebook and pencil his eyes widened with interest. 'Statistics? I will tell you everything because I believe in the scientific attitude. The years of superstition are past. I am an agricultural scientist. This is of importance to my country because it is an agricultural country. What sort of statistics do you want? Tell me and I shall give them to you.'

Hearing the voices other students had come down from the floor above to group round Perry in the passage just outside Mansour's door. 'What statistics?' one of them began to demand harshly. 'Here is an English professor who wants statistics.'

From his bed Mansour shouted in strident Arabic and the harsh-voiced student shouted back. So far as Perry could understand the situation Mansour was claiming him as a guest; even if he was a spy — and that had to be proved — he was first and foremost a guest, and as though to prove his point Mansour called over the heads of the crowd to the frightened porter for coffee to be brought. For by this time so many students had gathered they could fairly be called a crowd. They were packed into the passage so tightly it was impossible to move and the reek caused Perry to breathe cautiously. Other students were gathering outside the house — or so he judged by the cries coming from that direction — and Mansour, quite delighted to be at the centre of so much excitement, rocked backwards and forwards on his bed, puffing away at his pipe. When the coffee arrived the tray was passed carefully over the heads of the crowd, assisted by the very youths, it seemed to Perry, who were raging against him most violently. The courtesy charmed him. Nevertheless he could not help thinking he had made a mistake in coming to Gizeh before political passions had really had a chance to cool. Mansour delicately poured the coffee from its brass container into the little cups and then invited Perry to be seated. They sat side by side on the bed, sipping coffee in silence. The students, too, fell silent. The moment his cup was empty the trouble would begin again, Perry thought, so he began a careful explanation to Mansour why he was collecting information about the student population of Gizeh.

'A hostel?' said one furious-faced student. 'That would not be good. There is a hostel at Al Azhar and they go to bed at half past eight.' There were other reasons why he preferred liberty and he gave them in colloquial Arabic which brought a roar of delighted laughter. The orator was as strongly opposed to the hostel as ever but he was seduced by the laughter he had aroused. They were all seduced! What was this talk about a hostel? Was it true that specially large beds were to be constructed so that fifty students could sleep together? No work would be done in this hostel! Everyone would be exhausted, kept awake at nights by the snores! Hands reached out and patted Perry in delight. Their mood had violently changed. Instead of being suspicious they were noisily grateful for the laughter he had brought them.

'Outside, everyone,' Mansour shouted, standing on the bed. 'There are so many gentlemen the building will fall down. The floor is not strong, I warn you!'

When Perry emerged from the building with Mansour at his elbow he saw that the press of students in the street held up the normal traffic of old motor cars, asses and camels. Some of the students were clapping hands rhythmically. Most of the windows framed watching faces. After the initial excitement of the demonstrations a few days before a pall of boredom had settled on the quarter. The students had now apparently decided that the moment for dissipation had come, and the noise was so great that the tall, dirty-looking palm trees whipped silently in the gritty wind.

Still insisting that Perry was his guest Mansour gave instructions that he was to be supported out of this press of people to a safer place. As a result Perry, still holding his pencil and notebook, found himself supported on the shoulders of a couple of students moving unsteadily out into the throng who clapped. cheered, shook fists in mockery of a political demonstration and began to flow in the direction of the main street. Perry scarcely had time to wonder whether he was the only English professor who had ever been chaired by a mob of students before he heard the wail of a siren and an Egyptian army lorry came round the corner loaded with steel helmets, sticks and faces. It was a riot squad.

Soldiers dropped to the ground and began hitting out with their staves. Perry was released so unexpectedly that his legs gave way, seating him in the middle of the street while stones, thrown by the students, whirred overhead to be taken by the soldiers on their shields. An officer in the driving seat of the truck stood up, blew a whistle and pointed at Perry. When the students suddenly turned and ran, still shouting merrily, Perry was firmly seized by two soldiers, lifted to his feet and brought to the officer who, without hesitation, slapped him open-handed across the face and gave instructions for him to be taken into custody.

'Rarely does England show her dirty hand so openly,' he said stiffly to Perry who, now that he had begun to understand what was happening, could only believe that in some obscure way he deserved this rough treatment. If he did not deserve it a gross injustice was being done — so gross as to be incredible. He was lifted into the truck, the rest of the soldiers clambered up after him, and they moved off towards the river with the siren wailing once more.

Soldiers held Perry gently but firmly by the wrists to prevent him from escaping; they were obviously pleased to have made so easy a capture and patted him affectionately on the shoulder, saying in the kind of kitchen Arabic they thought English people understood, 'English no good. English finish. Strong Egyptian drive Englishman into the sea.' Or did the word 'bahr' mean not sea, but river? They were driving up the main street of Gizeh towards the Nile at about fifty miles an hour and it occurred to Perry that once they reached the bridge they might take it into their heads to throw him into the water. He had heard it was customary treatment for rioters and agitators— the sort of person they appeared to think he was. 'I am a British subject!' he called out. 'I demand to be put in touch with the British Consul!'

A soldier adjusted Perry's spectacles for him — they had slid down his nose — and followed up this act of solicitude by grasp-ing him round the waist, lifting him into the air, and tossing him over the side of the truck. Perry yelled and grasped his nose between thumb and finger. So certain was he of a long drop to the river that the pavement, when he landed, shook him like a bomb. The truck had stopped before he left it. Hoisted to his feet once more, Perry caught a brief glimpse of the

Nile darkening under the sunset and the lamps of distant bridges before he was pushed into a closed car, which immediately shot off towards the city centre.

'I demand to be released!' It was already too dark inside the car for Perry to make out who these men were, but he suspected that the officer in the steel hat who sat next to the driver was the one who had struck him. Their silence added to his anger. 'Don't you understand, you idiots? I'm a professor at the university. You're making a mistake.' He became more and more pompous, mentioning his friendship with Tureiya Pasha and the Princess. He explained that this scandal would probably reach the ears of the King himself. But they were coldly indifferent. The car sped down Kasr el-Aini and across the Midan Ismailia. Night had come with a rush here in the town and the interior of the car was splashed by the headlights of cars travelling in the other direction. Perry could not remember whether the city was under martial law. One month it was, one month it was not. You never knew where you were. If it turned out that martial law was in force these fellows could do just what they liked with him. Perhaps they were taking him out to the Egyptian army barracks at Abbassia.

Somewhere near the Abdin Palace, however, the car turned down a side street and braked noisily. There was no sense in resisting. By God, they'd be made to pay for this later on! But for the moment he must think of his dignity!

'What are you smiling for?' demanded the officer, flashing a torch in his face.

Now it was Perry's turn to keep silence. If he had been smiling (which he doubted) it could have been due only to that passing thought for his dignity! The officer came so close with his lamp that Perry could see, by the light reflected from his own face, the small green crescent and star on his lapels. One of the guards made a comment in Arabic. The officer laughed briefly and led the way, up steps and beneath a gloomy portico into an ill-lit stable of a place where groups of forlorn-looking people sat about on benches. It was, Perry realized with some relief, the very police station where he attended whenever he had trouble with his ration cards. He could even see, away to the right, the office where he normally did business: the door was open and the familiar sergeant wearing his enormous chevrons — large enough to be seen by low-flying aircraft the sergeant had once proudly told him — sat at his desk under a naked electric bulb.

'Forward!' said the officer. He removed his steel helmet and donned the tarboosh one of his men was carrying. 'Come on! What are you waiting for?'

These cries were intended not so much for Perry as to impress the men gathered in the large room or hall into which the party now moved. Perry had not been in here before and he thought it was like the zoo. There was the same animal reek. Two walls of the room were, in fact, taken up by huge cages, one containing men prisoners and the other containing women. One woman in a black veil shouted hysterically at the sight of the newcomers but the remainder of the prisoners appeared to be asleep or indifferent. In the centre of the hall a double row of policemen were drawn up for inspection in absurdly ill-fitting khaki uniforms. A police officer in blue tunic and breeches straightened a tarboosh here and looked down the barrel of one of their inoffensive rifles there. Without interrupting his inspection or so much as glancing towards the men who had marched on to his parade ground he began drawling nasal remarks to Perry's officer. Perry could see that he was angry to have his evening ceremonial interrupted in this way. Indeed, he was so angry that he kept them waiting by ostentatiously scraping a grease patch on one of the men's tunics.

Finally, he gave it up as a bad job, shrugged, and told a sergeant to march them out.

He yawned and turned slowly, stiffly, until he caught sight of Perry. 'Ah!' The grunt was so vigorous he might have been punched in the stomach. Already his black eyebrows had disappeared under the peak of his cap. 'What is this trouble?' he said in English. He ignored the officer and walked over to Perry. 'You are an Englishman! Is it that you are drunk?' He was badly in need of a shave and some sleep; there was weariness in every fold of his fleshy face. 'If you are drunk I will take you home. What do these men want?' The police captain was about fifty and, for reasons Perry could only guess at, he seemed to hate the army; and he particularly hated the representatives of the army he saw before him at that moment. National solidarity did not enter into the situation. He was on Perry's side against the officer — it was as obvious as if he had said so.

'I've been wrongfully arrested — '

Naturally the officer broke in here. He stood on his toes, he walked up and down, and the light falling from above gave prominence to the upper part of his face; the chin was narrow. As he turned this way and that to explain the circumstances of Perry's arrest he might have had a fox's mask on his shoulders, not a human face. Perry ascribed the fancy to the zoo-like atmosphere and in order to preserve a grip on himself began speaking in a loud, solemn voice. 'I am Professor Perry of the Faculty of Arts at Gizeh. I have been wrongfully arrested. In any case I am not subject to Egyptian law. The Capitulations take effect and I demand that the British Consul be informed immediately.'

'I'm very sorry,' said the police captain courteously, 'It seems more serious than I had imagined. There is no longer any imperialism. This soldier makes me lock you up. I must do it, you understand?'

Perry broke off. There was such genuine concern on the man's face — and, quite clearly, the poor chap was almost asleep on his feet, too — that Perry felt compelled to say something consoling. He remembered his disapproval of the Capitulations. If one chose to live in a foreign country one should live according to that country's laws. They shook hands.

'If you want to make a full confession,' said the police captain, with eyes firmly closed, 'including the names of all your accomplices and full details of your plot I can easily provide you with pen and ink and paper.'

'But damn it all — !' said Perry, taking fire again.

'I thought perhaps you wouldn't.' His eyes were opened abruptly to permit him the fitting of a key into the lock of the men's cage. 'Professor, sir,' he said as he ushered Perry into prison, 'this is, of course, merely a formality.'

Mary did not discover his whereabouts until past midnight and by that time she considered herself a new woman. Arriving at the Pyramids tram terminus she had planned as quick a return to Gizeh as possible; she would pursue Edgar through the tenements and insist on helping him with notes and observations — nothing, she thought, could upset him more! But the dust storm had subsided and the Pyramids printed themselves with such golden elegance on the evening sky it seemed a shame, having travelled so far, to return so quickly. She would punish Edgar by enjoying herself thoroughly! By the time she had walked to the Sphinx and back a round, red sun was disappearing behind a sand dune. The air had a nautical freshness. Her appetite was such that tea in Mena House cost fifty piastres and so much time that it was night before she reached Cairo once more. And she *had* enjoyed herself! She had enjoyed herself so much that Edgar was quite forgiven.

Mrs. Curtis, their resident landlady, was sitting in the dining-room with the door open; immediately Mary walked into the flat she was under observation by Mrs. Curtis who called out cheerfully, 'I've just succeeded in perfecting some liqueur apricot brandy. You look tired, my dear. Do get yourself a glass.' Mrs. Curtis was an elderly Englishwoman who ran a hairdressing establishment in Kasr el-Nil and sub-let a couple of rooms, with use of dining-room and kitchen, to the Perrys. Her liqueur apricot brandy (like her cherry brandy and her peach brandy) was prepared by dropping two or three of the stoned fruit into a decanter of ordinary Cyprus brandy — to give it character, as Mrs. Curtis said; more important it conferred a kind of respectability. Sometimes she added honey. She pretended to have a scientific interest in drink. Every sip was experimental. This evening she had extra reason for the pursuit of knowledge in that one of her chief competitors had just imported a de-frizzing machine from America. 'Well, dear,' she said with a note of calculated steadiness in her voice, 'a de-frizzing machine, how shall I explain it to you? It's a work of the devil! These Egyptian women, they don't like having frizzy hair, you see, lots of little frothy curls, so with a de-frizzing machine you can make it straight as a rat's tail! They cost two hundred pounds. I shall have to get one. It's that or ruin! Where's your husband, my dear?'

At eight o'clock Mary telephoned the Anglo-Egyptian Union in case Edgar had gone there to write up his notes and not remarked how late it was. Hassan trotted in from the balcony to say there was a man just like Mr. Perry coming along the street and was it time to serve dinner?

'No,' said Mrs. Curtis, 'we're not dining tonight until Mr. Perry comes in, even if we wait till two in the morning! Back to your kitchen, Hassan, and keep everything warm. I don't like the sound of this, my dear! Not at the Anglo-Egyptian Union!

Well, we'll keep our courage up! We'll not let a morsel pass our lips until he walks in.' She charged the glasses. 'If this liqueur brandy has a failing, my dear, I'd say it was over-sweet!'

'Let's have our dinner now,' said Mary who had allowed Mrs. Curtis to press three of her glasses upon her and was feeling a little drunk as a result. 'Then Hassan can go home.'

'Just as you like, my dear. Though I don't doubt that he is far more comfortable here than he is in his own home, aren't you Hassan? Whatever you do,' she whispered to Mary, 'you being strange to this country, don't ever give any of 'em so much as a lick of drink. It's a Moslem country, of course, and they're against alcohol on principle. But if you give 'em so much as that — ' and she showed how little remained in her glass — 'they lose all respect for women.'

Later that evening, after Mary had telephoned the Anglo-Egyptian Union once more, she and Mrs. Curtis stood on the balcony — they were six floors up — looking down at the lights of Bab el-Louk Square. Mrs. Curtis said that she hated to suggest it but, having been a nurse herself the thought came to her naturally, wouldn't it be a good idea to telephone round the hospitals? Or the police? she said. Or the morgue? Of course, in order to speak to all those places you had to know Arabic. After twenty years in the country she was glad to say that not one word of Arabic had ever left her tongue.

'Then what am I to do? I can't even telephone any of the men he works with. I don't know their numbers. Waldo isn't on the telephone.'

Mrs. Curtis took her back into the flat. 'Telephone the Palace.'

'But he wouldn't be there at this — oh, but of course!' What could be more natural, after looking round the Gizeh tenements, than a visit to the Palace for some sort of preliminary report? And once there, they would naturally ask him to stay to dinner. But in that case why had he not telephoned home? Was he angry with her? Perhaps he was beginning to punish her for James. Ought she not, then, to treat the move with disdain and go to bed?

The secretarial voice at the other end of the line saying, No, Professor Perry was not there; he had not been received that evening, touched her with chill. No mistake about it, she was cold to the tips of her toes. She said that it was the Professor's wife speaking; she'd be grateful if she could speak to Her Highness in spite of the lateness of the hour. That is, if she had not yet retired. Mary was so cold that she asked Mrs. Curtis if she would bring a coat — any one would do — while she stayed at the telephone trusting that the secretary would not put his receiver down.

'If you will speak,' said the secretarial voice, 'Her Highness is listening.'

'Your Highness, oh thank goodness!' Simply to put her anxiety into words constituted a relief. 'I think he has deserted me! The last I saw of him was three o'clock this afternoon when he put me on a fast tram to the Pyramids. But it was a trick, I can see it now! It's eleven o'clock and he hasn't come home.'

'This is Tureiya Pasha!' a strange voice announced. 'Good evening! Pardon me that I listen, but Her Highness wishes me to speak. Do you mean that your husband has divorced you? No? Well in that case he is missing and that is not good. Her Highness wishes you to come here, now, at once. You agree? Good, my dear. I give orders that you are to be admitted without delay.'

There was a gentle click as the Pasha replaced his receiver, the invitation was repeated in correcter English by the secretarial voice. The voice hesitated. 'Do you play bridge, Mrs. Perry? No? Ah, that is a pity. There would have been four of us.' And he, too, put his receiver down.

As soon as Mrs. Curtis understood the situation she insisted on seeing Mary safely to the Palace because at this time of night, she said, the streets of Cairo were alive with bandits. She came out of her bedroom wearing a brown cloche hat dating from the 'twenties, a tweed overcoat, and swinging a black wooden truncheon; it was about eighteen inches long and painted with the British Royal Coat of Arms. 'This,' she said, 'I don't want to alarm you, my dear, but this was my father's. He used to be a Special Constable in Buckinghamshire, dead these many years, poor soul. I don't want to alarm you but a woman's got to look after herself in this city after dark. Why, whatever are you doing here, Hassan? I thought you'd gone home long ago.'

The boy — he was no more than eighteen — came grinning out of his kitchen. 'I stay till Mister Perry come. If you go out I come too.'

'Good for you, Hassan,' said Mrs. Curtis and she gave him the truncheon to carry. 'A jab in the stomach is as good as a crack on the head. Remember that now. Well, are we ready? Right. Off we go, me first, you in the middle, my dear. Hassan last! Whatever you do, don't worry. We shall get through all right, never fear!'

For a whole minute the Princess sat in silence, looking at the playing cards she had impatiently thrown down on the table, and digested the news that Mrs. Perry had just given her. Mrs. Perry had made an impression on the Princess — though whether for good or bad Her Highness was not certain. At long last she had met, or so it seemed, a woman capable of outdoing her in the expression of contempt for the other sex. During her long life the Princess had enjoyed many turbulent scenes — in 1905 she had shot her first husband in the fleshy part of the calf, in 1922 she had dissuaded her second husband and her lover from fighting a duel; she would belong, she said, to whichever of them could drink a gallon of English beer first. Naturally, they were most unpleasantly sick! These scenes, and many like them, the Princess could look back upon with satisfaction but — and she would be honest with herself! — they lacked the artistry of Mrs. Perry's splendid gesture! To end a separation of many years by travelling the three thousand miles to Egypt for no other purpose than to tell one's expectant husband that one intended to leave him was as subtle as it was original. The Princess could think of no *coup* in her own career that an impartial critic would think more telling! She did not know whether to be admiring or jealous.

Her husband picked up the playing cards, saying, 'I can see this is a great shock to you, dear. It is not nice when a man we know disappears suddenly and then his wife telephones. So late at night it plays on one's nerves. Be generous with yourself for once! There are more important matters to occupy your mind. There are affairs of state! Be generous to yourself and forget about poor Professor Perry, just for tonight.'

Her Highness rang for the secretary on duty and he appeared with an apologetic look on his face, saying that he had failed in his attempt to find a fourth for bridge. 'There is only Swain and Her Highness would naturally not wish to play bridge with the butler.'

'I would if he were a better player. Swain is not a man of parts. But that is not why I rang. You have heard about Professor Perry. Find him at once!'

An expression of hopelessness spread over the secretary's face. 'It is not fair, Your Highness. When Afifi is on duty you never give him such difficult tasks. This is your revenge because I didn't find a fourth for bridge.'

'Do at once as Her Highness orders!' said the Pasha angrily. After the secretary had walked from the room with an exaggerated weariness, the Pasha kissed his wife's wrist. 'It is your royal character. This princely generosity would be unbelievable except in you. You receive and comfort an unhappy wife, you search for her missing husband, and yet you are a descendant of Mohamed Ali the Great. This will be remembered! All the world will read. It will be a chapter in the memoirs I am dictating to Afifi.'

The Princess yawned. 'How can you be so stupid! Mrs. Perry will be here, at my invitation, in five minutes and you ask me to forget about her poor husband. Perhaps it is not I you have in mind! Perhaps it is you yourself who wish to forget about Professor Perry. You think, in your heart, the old girl will go off to bed and then I can receive Mrs. Perry alone!'

The Pasha stood up, his mouth hanging open foolishly. 'What are you saying, my beloved?'

She laughed. 'I can see that you have a plan to seduce Mrs. Perry.'

In his torment he swayed slightly.

The Princess laughed boisterously. She shuffled the cards and her diamond rings flashed. 'Calm yourself, I was only teasing! Really, what a baby you are! But then, perhaps that is what I like.'

The Pasha was so shaken with relief that he went and stood at the window, gazing down into a courtyard where a fountain played under a coloured spotlight, until the secretary hurriedly entered the room some moments later and announced, 'Professor Perry is in prison. He is arrested and he is in the Abdin prison. He was leading a riot.' The secretary's face was huge with triumph. He had located Perry by good luck — the Palace switchboard operator had put him through to the police department as soon as the secretary had explained the problem — but he was not going to allow the Princess to think his discovery had been made without difficulty, danger, and the expenditure of considerable intelligence. 'He is a political prisoner.'

'Impossible! He is a baby new-born!' The Pasha spoke quietly because even now he had not quite recovered from the shock his wife had given him. 'What sort of a riot would Professor Perry be leading. Tell me that? What point of view was this riot expressing? Who was paying for it? No, it is absurd. There must be some misunderstanding.'

'Excellency, there may have been a misunderstanding, but there has been no mistake. Professor Perry is there. I spoke to the officer in charge myself.'

'Then why did you not order his release? Speaking in the name of Her Highness you could have done that. I must do it at once. I must see the poor man immediately. How he must be suffering! He is mentally unbalanced. He took a document out of Her Highness's own hands and tore it up. Clearly, he is not responsible for his own actions. Where was he arrested?'

'Gizeh.'

'Gizeh!' For the first time since the news of Perry's fate had been received the Princess moved and spoke. 'Gizeh! Where, no doubt, he was collecting absurd information for his absurd report. Darling!' she said to her husband, 'they've arrested that little man because it's a good way of striking at me, and through me at the Palace. Everyone knows that Professor Perry is under my protection! I don't care! They can hang him if they like! All they want is for me to go on my knees to them! It is a government of cannibals and bolsheviks! They will never compromise me! I defy them!' She walked up and down clicking her high heels angrily on the marble floor. The Pasha, who attempted to take her by the hand, was gestured away. 'Let them hang him for all I care! But they'll not dare to. He's English. The English Ambassador will make them release him. And then where do I stand? Professor Perry is under my protection. This is admitted. Do we not admit this? Then is a man to be released by a foreign ambassador when he is under my protection? No, you are right, my darling.' She kissed the Pasha on his cheek. 'You are always right. I must telephone the Prime Minister and insist on Professor Perry's release myself. Now I know who that will be! That is Mrs. Perry. She doesn't care tuppence for her husband either. If they delivered his head in a mail bag she'd take it all very quietly, I can promise you.'

A red light over the door had glowed and a buzzer sounded. When the door opened and Swain announced Mrs. Perry the Princess advanced impressively towards her with arms outstretched, saying, 'My poor child, how you must be suffering! You have had no news? Tell the Pasha and myself the whole story. But there is no story. He is not there. That is enough. How I admire your English self-control! All the time you are thinking, where is my husband? Is he alive or is he dead? Yet you look calm and beautiful. Perhaps you are glad. Perhaps you think only of marrying your friend.' Between themselves the Princess and the Pasha spoke French. From now on everyone spoke English. 'You must drink some wine. Let us drink some wine together and talk. Or would you prefer whisky?'

Mary shook her head without speaking. Even the thought of more alcohol brought an added wave of tiredness. The apricot brandy had made her sleepy and aggressive at the same time. She would have liked to remain in the guard room for a drink of the black coffee the Sudanese guards had immediately begun serving to Mrs. Curtis and to Hassan. But she had been hurried on to the drawing-room. 'As a matter of fact,' she said, 'there's nothing I'd like so much as a cup of tea, strong, without milk or sugar.' She sat down without being asked, emboldened by apricot brandy. 'You sent for me, Your Highness.'

'I thought we could sit and talk until news of your husband came in. Unfortunately you don't play bridge, I'm told.'

Mary saw that her request for tea was being ignored. No doubt she had offended against etiquette in asking for something she had not been offered. But instead of being embarrassed she felt spiteful. 'Then you've no news of my husband?'

The Princess allowed her eyelids to droop as though in grief or pain. 'No news. Naturally, I have the means to get information but there is no news yet.' She lifted her chin in the direction of her husband, and said, 'You haven't met Mrs. Perry before. I told you she was beautiful, didn't I? Come over here and look. See that lip? Who does that remind you of? Really, what a monster Professor Perry was, not to tell us at once that he had such a wife!' The Princess looked at him and added with a touch of complacency, 'Mrs. Perry has a lover too.'

The Pasha bowed slightly in Mary's direction and smiled without sincerity. He scarcely knew how to speak or act. By looking into his wife's face with a slight curling of the lip he thought to convey that Mrs. Perry could not be compared with the Princess for beauty. But he knew he was not succeeding. He was so bewildered by his wife's pretence not to know where Perry was to be found that he broke one of his strictest rules: he spoke in Turkish, assuming that Mrs. Perry could not understand him.

'If you don't behave I shall send you out of the room,' said the Princess, also speaking in Turkish. 'Have you thought,' she said to Mary in English, 'that Professor Perry might have killed himself in a fit of chagrin.'

'Chagrin?'

'As a discarded husband he would naturally experience chagrin.'

'He isn't that sort of person.' Mary felt the tears flooding to her eyes. 'Oh, I don't know! I don't understand people any more.' The lethargy brought about by the apricot brandy was beginning to clear, leaving her flushed and excited. 'It's your fault, sending him to Gizeh to make that report.'

'The Pasha's idea, not mine,' said the Princess, smiling.

Tureiya raised bunched fingers to his lips in a gesture that implored reason.

Mary turned on him angrily. 'You sent him to his death. Why don't you do your own dirty work? Oh! How I hate this country! Waldo was right! He said it was some palace intrigue.'

'Quite right!' remarked the Princess. 'It is all Tureiya's fault. I was against it from the beginning.'

The Pasha took several steps backward to express his astonishment. He was under fire from both women.

'The very idea,' said the Princess, 'of encouraging a foreigner to walk about in the poor quarters of the city. And somebody cuts his throat! Well, what else do you expect? It's your fault! The British Government will hold you responsible. How can you possibly defend yourself, that is what it would interest me to know. We shall have the British navy sailing up the Nile and bombarding the Mohamed Ali Club!'

'But Professor Perry is *not* dead!' The Pasha's voice was shrill with bewilderment. 'He is safe in prison.'

'In prison?' Mary ignored the Pasha and confronted the Princess who was coughing with laughter and dabbing at her lips with a lace handkerchief; the old lady was plainly delighted at the discomfiture of everyone.

'Is this true? Is he really in prison?'

The Princess rose and caught Mary's arm for support. She shook so violently with laughter that the Pasha rushed up in alarm. But the Princess waved him away. Her eyes were brilliant. Enormous tears of laughter coursed down her powdered cheeks. 'The Professor will be released at once my dear! I will make amends! But he's a strange man, you know. He tore up the report and scattered the pieces like confetti. Tureiya! Behave like a grown up man for once and telephone somebody. Tell them Perry must be set free!'

She kissed Mary firmly, first on one cheek and then on the other, before walking out of the room. She walked with great dignity, severely erect and unhurried, but giving occasional sighs and gasps of pleasure as she went. At the door, which had miraculously opened at her approach, she turned and looked back at her husband. 'Now that you are alone with Mrs. Perry I want you to remember one thing. No scandal!'

'Scandal!' said the Pasha in a low, trembling voice as soon as the door had closed behind her; and he went walking about the room muttering to himself, opening and closing his eyes abruptly, and occasionally tugging so fiercely at his hair that Mary would not have been surprised to see him bring away part of his scalp. 'Mrs. Perry! Her Highness talks of scandal. Do you know what scandal she means? She accuses me of planning to seduce you.' He hissed like a goose. 'My life is fire and ashes. No, no! It is all ashes! She humiliates me and then she asks me to telephone somebody. Who? It is useless. Your husband is in the hands of our enemies.'

'But what is he in prison *for*?'

'In Egypt,' said the Pasha in more normal tones, 'it does not matter what you are in prison for. What matters is that you are in prison.'

'I must get in touch with the British Consul.'

'The Consul? It is useless. Everything is useless. The city has martial law. The Capitulations are finished, except in theory. They are history. You know that? The Prime Minister is the Military Governor of Cairo. Everything is in his hands. Foreigners or Egyptians, it is all the same. He is our enemy. Her Highness tells me to telephone somebody. She is old. She forgets that Egypt is not like it used to be. True, I could advise His Majesty to intervene. But the matter is not important enough. I could not telephone and say, "Your Majesty, my friend is in prison. Will you kindly ask for him to be let out?" It is late at night. The King might be asleep. Though you know, Mrs. Perry,' said the Pasha with a solemnity that impressed Mary, 'I have telephoned His Majesty in the night. Many of the affairs of Egypt are directed from my desk.' He saw the effect he was producing and became almost jolly. 'Come, you and me, we will go in a car immediately to the prison, yes? I shall take some money and you will see!' He was ringing for the secretary on duty even as he spoke. 'This is Egypt. In moments of crisis money is always needed.'

'We're going to my husband now?'

'Of course. Her Highness has said Professor Perry must be released. There is only one way to release him and we shall take it. Let us meet in the hall in five minutes time.' And the Pasha, now smiling and apparently quite at ease once more, handed her over to the secretary on duty who, in turn, entrusted her to one of the blue-swathed girls.

Oh Edgar! she thought as she descended the marble staircase and passed the enormous tapestry of Louis XVI on horseback, you are in prison and I am on my way to release you!

During his stay in prison Perry acquired one useful art. A fellow-prisoner taught him how to remove a gold ring from a man's finger while pretending to shake hands with him. The instructor was an elderly man in a peasant's skull cap who had a curiously lumpy face from which tufts of hair sprouted at the angles of the jaw.

'And look!' said the man in a dialect Perry found it difficult to understand. 'Here is your wallet!' The old fellow squatted on his haunches looking earnestly, even reproachfully, into

Perry's face. 'I give it back to you, because you are my friend.' He tossed the wallet into Perry's lap. 'You are easy to rob, easier than an old woman. Are you a German?'

'English.'

The pickpocket was politely incredulous. 'Perhaps you are Russian. It doesn't matter. You are my friend. Look! I also give back your fountain pen! If you want to escape out of this prison I can arrange it for ten pounds.'

Perry did not wish to escape now. At first he had been angry in a dignified kind of way. He had stood rattling the loose-socketed bars of the cage shouting: 'Help!' and 'I am a British subject' but no one took any notice except an exhausted-looking man who was sweeping the area in front of the cage. He waited for Perry to stop shouting and came up to the bars, whispering, with downcast eyes, 'I also have children at home, O Pasha! Even five piastres would be very acceptable.' Perry felt the man's weariness descending upon him like a pall and he went and sat in a part of the cage as far removed from the other prisoners as possible. His situation was so incredible it did not allow him to be angry for long; instead, it brought him a melancholy satisfaction.

'As you are my friend,' said the pickpocket, 'I could get you out for eight pounds.'

'I don't wish to escape,' said Perry in his Linguaphone Arabic. He did not doubt for a moment that the pickpocket had it in his power to arrange an escape from this prison or any other prison in Egypt; for the moment, Perry was not even interested. Nothing would now satisfy him but the most abject apology from the army officer who had arrested him, another apology from the Military Governor of Cairo, and a third apology from the Chief of the Cairo City Police. There was no question of bringing in the British Consul or the Ambassador to extort these apologies; they must be given freely and sincerely to him as a man — as an individual, not as some political or legal concept like 'British subject' or 'state employee' — because it was as an individual that he had been outraged. Unless these apologies were forthcoming he would stay where he was!

When, therefore, some hours later he lifted his head and saw Mary, Tureiya Pasha, the Pasha's secretary and the Pasha's chauffeur lined up in front of the cage, Perry's first impulse was to ignore them. Seated as he was, in the far corner of the prison, he caught only the briefest glimpse of them — the four of them, standing side by side with rounded eyes — before the view was obscured by the rush of prisoners. Even in their sleep some instinct had warned them they were in the presence of great wealth. Arms were thrust between the bars, voices were raised in supplication, a shrill babble broke out from the women's cage; and then, as suddenly, the prisoners fell silent. They turned from the bars and slunk back to their own particular spot on the floor and there stretched out in sleep. The four newcomers on the other side of the bars had been joined by a fifth: the weary police captain in charge of the station.

'Edgar, are you all right?' said Mary.

Perry raised a languid right arm in salutation but remained where he was in his corner. The harsh single light swinging overhead in the draughty airs of the barn-like building put ugly shadows into her face. She looked many years older, almost middle-aged; Perry was so struck by this transformation that for the first time in his life he experienced pity for her. When she turned to the Pasha and said, 'They've been torturing him! He's too weak to stand up! He doesn't know where he is! Oh! What have they been doing to him?' — when she said this, Perry struggled to his feet, walked to the bars and succeeded in catching one of her gesticulating hands. He patted it consolingly and said, 'I'm perfectly all right. You must have been worried about me. Oh! Stand back, Your Excellency,' he called to the Pasha, 'or my friend here will have your wallet.'

Perry had become aware that the pickpocket was standing at his side.

'Release this English gentleman at once!' said the Pasha to the police captain, not even looking at him. The Pasha's secretary had been whispering into the captain's ear for some time.

Perry dropped his wife's hand. 'I positively decline to be set free.'

The Pasha bent forward to obtain a closer view of Perry's face. 'Mad! Mad! Mad!' the full moist lips were murmuring under the neat moustache. 'Il est fou! Vous voyez?' The Pasha straightened up triumphantly and told the police captain in French, Turkish and Arabic that the poor professor was undoubtedly mad. The Pasha had made this diagnosis many days ago and now, alas! it was confirmed! There was no room for doubt! Only a shrewd man would have been able to detect the earlier signs but M. Perry's present state was plain for anyone to see! Not want to be released, indeed? Of course he must be set free, at once, and taken to hospital!

Perry was reminded of the jungle silences he had read about in books. No one made a sound in the prison. All were listening to the police captain scratch the side of his chin.

'Do you know who I am?' said the Pasha in Arabic.

'Yes, Your Excellency,' said the officer but the Pasha had already made off. He stood in front of the open door with legs planted well apart, gazing in the direction of the street. The police officer made no attempt to follow. Instead, he stood in front of Perry rolling his head from side to side so that occasionally the light fell directly into his left eye and Perry could see that it was angrily red, as though a blood vessel had burst.

'Professor, sir,' said the man, in scarcely more than a whisper,

'You are an Englishman and you will understand this. His Excellency's man has offered me a hundred pounds to let you go. If I argued he would make it two hundred pounds. Would this happen in Scotland Yard?'

'I've no intention of leaving until I've had an apology from everyone concerned.'

'Sir,' said the police officer, raising his voice. 'Would this happen in Scotland Yard? No! And it does not happen in Egypt either!' He spat dogmatically on the ground and crushed the place under the toe of his boot.

'A good man,' said the pickpocket. 'A true patriot.'

'Edgar, darling, don't be pig-headed!' said Mary. 'I know you've had a terrible time but if you refuse to come out I shall stay here until you do come out.'

'No,' said the police captain heavily. 'You must go home.'

'I'm not going home without my husband!'

'No! No! No!' said the police captain, moved to such desperation that he now began to shout and tramp up and down addressing in a mixture of anger and self-pity anyone who cared to listen. 'I graduate from the Faculty of Law and enter the police force,' he shouted in Arabic, 'because I was told there were good prospects! And what happens? I work all day and all night! I have not shaved for eight days. All this happens to me. Now I no longer have any ambition! I want quiet and sleep. And what do I find?'

A heavily-moustached police sergeant looked in to see what was going on; at the sight of the captain he hastily withdrew.

'Lady,' said the captain in quiet, controlled tones, 'your husband the professor is in prison but it is only a formality. Please go home now and don't worry me. If you do not go with His Excellency — see, His Excellency is going — you will have to stay in my office for the rest of the night. You can't go home by yourself.'

'That's quite true, dear,' said Perry cheerfully, 'I'll be all right.'

'How I despise you, Edgar!' Mary drew away from him. 'You seem quite unable to face up to your responsibilities. Very well, stay in your dirty, filthy prison for all I care!'

'His Excellency says you're not to lose heart,' whispered the secretary between the bars. 'Be patient for tonight and in the morning His Excellency will intervene with the responsible authorities. It is a mistake,' said the secretary, stealing a glance at the captain, who was listening intently, 'to deal with subordinates but the hour was so late His Excellency had no alternative.'

'I'm not coming out,' said Perry stubbornly.

Before Mary left she weakened to the extent of pushing some cigarettes and matches through the bars. Perry took the opportunity to seize her hand once more and, this time, kiss it gently.

'Do try and get some sleep, darling,' she murmured. 'Oh dear, I've been deceiving you so terribly. Never mind, I'll come and tell you all about it in the morning. If only we spoke Welsh, or something, then we could talk and nobody else would understand.'

Perry stood watching her walk through the doorway on the Pasha's arm, chauffeur and secretary bringing up the rear, and would then have returned to his corner but the police captain called to him and produced a bunch of keys. 'You will come with me to the office, sir. There is a gentleman there to see you.'

In the unshaded glare of a powerful electric light Muawiya sat with his eyes closed. At Perry's entry they opened and fixed uncomprehendingly on the bare white wall before him. Then he took the cigarette from between his lips and breathed smoke out of his nostrils. An open hand hissed over his unshaven chin. Picking up a tarboosh from the table he placed it squarely on his head and turned for the first time to look in Perry's direction.

His voice trembled with emotion. 'Sir, you were wrong to begin this work without my assistance. Why did you not ask *me* for the statistics of Gizeh? I could have given you all the statistics any man could want. You need not have put yourself to any trouble. Why should I have to learn of your plans from other students? Ordinary students! Quite ordinary!'

A sergeant — the one with the heavy moustache who had been frightened by the captain's anger — brought coffee and Perry could see no reason for not drinking like the others. All three buried their noses in the cups.

Muawiya shivered. 'The evenings get cold. Sir, you have met my friend, Police Captain Asfur?'

Asfur rose laboriously to his feet as though he had never seen Perry in his life before and shook his hand with some formality. 'It is an honour to have you in my custody, sir!'

'Dr. Perry is a professor of literature. He gives me my course on Shakespeare.'

'Shakespeare,' said Asfur, rubbing his angry right eye and yawning, 'is a universal genius. Perhaps I made a mistake in choosing a legal career. But it is all destiny.'

Perry felt no surprise at finding Muawiya in the police station; indeed, the fellow seemed inescapable. Take a picnic in the desert and Muawiya would almost certainly emerge from a rock tomb with a ready flow of conversation. There was conversation on the present occasion. The reason for Perry's presence was ignored. Out of deference to his literary interests Muawiya tried to engage Asfur in a discussion of the film of 'Jane Eyre' which was at that time being shown in one of the Cairo cinemas.

But Perry was ill at ease because, quite obviously, the conversation had overtones. He could detect the overtones without understanding them. The two men spoke in English — Perry himself took but a grudging share of the conversation — and their surface remarks were platitudinous but clear. Discussion was handicapped because, as it turned out, neither of them had actually seen the film. Yet events were moving in some unspecified direction — and Perry was helping them on by the inconsistency of his own behaviour. Half an hour before he had said he would not leave prison until he had received satisfactory apologies from the men responsible for putting him there. Yet here he was in the police captain's office drinking coffee!

At half past one by the cheap alarm clock on Asfur's desk there was a long silence. The three men sat and listened to a late tram grinding its way through the quarter; finally, Muawiya put his hand palm downward on the table, made a soft aside to Asfur in Arabic, and looked at Perry.

'Police Captain Asfur tells me that it is all a mistake for you to be here and he would be very glad if I took you home now.'

Perry looked at Asfur and the man turned away, shrugging and drawling out in his nasal, sleepy English, 'I told you, sir, it was a formality.'

Unexpectedly, Asfur removed his tarboosh, threw it to the floor and took a wild kick at it. The first time he missed. The second time he drove it through the open door and they could hear it rolling about in the corridor outside. Asfur's head was covered with small grey curls, like the head of an old negro.

'The Pasha said you were mad. Is that true?' Asfur waited for the answer with his head on one side. 'No? It is too much to believe, a sane man in Egypt. Sir, we are all mad here. But I must be philosophical. I must put it out of my mind.'

Asfur followed his tarboosh out into the corridor and closed the door behind him.

'I can't very well go now after I've taken a stand,' said Perry. 'It would be inconsistent of me.'

There was a touch of insolence in Muawiya's voice. 'You must be a philosopher like Asfur, sir, and put it out of your mind. Come, quickly please or you will get me into great trouble. I will walk with you. It is too late for a tram.'

Muawiya opened a small door which Perry had not previously noticed. The urgency in Muawiya's voice was difficult to resist. Subsequently Perry was able to recollect that he did Muawiya's bidding to avoid getting him into the trouble he had mentioned — although if Perry had stopped to think he would have seen he was being bamboozled. As he accompanied Muawiya down a dark passage Perry was so taken up with thoughts of how he could explain his escape to Mary and to the Pasha he would have taken a wrong turning if Muawiya had not restrained him. To be seen at liberty so shortly after his refusal to be set free would certainly cause the Princess, for example, to think him quite unprincipled.

Muawiya opened another door and they stepped into the moonlight. Perry now found himself trembling in the cold and he stamped his feet in an attempt to generate a little heat. Down the street intense flashes of light went up from a gang at work on the tram lines with welding equipment. Except for these workmen there was no one in sight.

'I think I'd better go back,' Perry mumbled.

Muawiya gasped and gave him a push that was almost a blow.

'Do you want to get me in trouble?'

The two men walked in the moonlight, avoiding the shadows, until they came to the centre of Abdin Square. Here they could talk quietly with no danger of being overheard.

'Why don't you say something?' demanded Muawiya.

'What do you want me to say?'

'For example, you might say how surprised you are that I succeeded with Asfur when an important man like Toureiya Pasha failed.'

'You were there when the Pasha came?'

'I heard everything.'

From Perry's point of view this made the situation even more irregular. What a fine show of defiance he had put on when there appeared no real chance of freedom! And at the first opportunity for escape he had at once forgotten all self-respect! That Muawiya had heard his defiance and subsequently become the instrument for his moral defeat Perry found particularly irksome, and he seriously considered walking back to the police station. Asfur could scarcely refuse to lock him up again.

Muawiya laughed. 'Why don't you ask me how I could arrange for you to be set free? I will tell you the answer. It is because I have no hundred pounds like the Pasha.'

-'I am really rather cross with you,' said Perry stiffly. He abandoned the idea of returning to jail for fear it might involve him in even greater indignities and set off rapidly, still shivering, towards the palm trees of Bab el-Louk Square.

Muawiya trotted at his side, incoherent with astonishment. Perry repeatedly cut short his questions and protestations, but when they arrived at Sharia Sidky Pasha where the flat was located, he began to wonder whether he had been too harsh. He invited Muawiya to come up and have some hot coffee.

'What for are you angry?' Muawiya demanded hysterically. 'I am your saviour. What for don't you understand?'

Even at that hour men could be heard playing trick-track in a shuttered café across the street. Muawiya gave out womanish sighs of distress and began clicking his finger joints. 'Why? Why?' he asked. 'I would get you all the statistics of Gizeh. All! There is no need for you to trouble yourself.'

'You've put me in a false position. But I'm much more cross

with myself than with you, Muawiya. Look here, old chap, you thought you were doing the right thing.'

'Why do you hate me like this?' Muawiya demanded.

Perry groaned. 'I do not hate you. I have very complicated feelings, it's true. But I don't hate you. Indeed, in a way I'm grateful to you. Do you know what I thought when I found myself in prison — me, a completely innocent man?'

Perry could see that his apparent lack of gratitude had caused Muawiya a great shock and, in spite of the lateness of the hour, in spite of the biting cold, he was anxious to set out the full complexity of the situation.

'When I, an innocent man, was shut up in prison I did not feel innocent. I felt I *must* have deserved it. Otherwise the whole situation would have been too fantastic.'

Muawiya pulled himself together sufficiently to light a cigarette. He did not offer one to Perry.

'I really felt my sins had found me out,' said Perry in a whisper.

Muawiya drew so hard on his cigarette that his face could be seen in the glow. He spat into the gutter. 'That is because you believe in justice. I have not seen justice. I do not know whether there is justice anywhere. When anyone hurts me I do not think I deserve it. I think of revenge.'

He turned abruptly and walked off, the metal studs on his shoes striking fire from the pavement.

⊛ 4 ⊛

⊛

HOSTILITIES ARE DECLARED

FOR TWO DAYS NOTHING HAPPENED. Perry was uneasy. On the third day he left the flat when Mary was not looking, crossed the tram lines of Bab el-Louk Square and made his way to the Midan Ismailia and so to the Nile. There it was, churning muddily under the arches in the usual way. To the south were the white sails of pleasure craft. Here, close at hand, with the sails furled and an old man at the tiller, a grain barge was being dragged against the current by two harnessed men. Perry was still so shaken by his extraordinary arrest and still more extraordinary liberation that he looked at the familiar scene with a mild disappointment. Because he had been through so much it seemed inexcusable that everything else should be unaltered. The Nile had not changed its course. The Pyramids (he could see them in the remote distance) stood in the same place. And no doubt the stars, when they appeared that night, would form their usual pattern in the sky.

Mary took the tiresome point of view that his release was due to the intervention of Tureiya Pasha. The police captain had naturally wished to put up a show of incorruptibility, but no more than a show! To believe that a mere student like this Muawiya he spoke of should succeed where the Pasha had failed was absurd. Only someone of the Pasha's consequence could have hushed the matter up so completely. Why had the newspapers no mention of the affair? If he had been arrested by the military and handed over to the police for safe keeping why had the military not made inquiries about him? (Mary had made Perry tell his adventures in great detail.) No, his present freedom could only be explained by the action of some really influential person!

'But you know very well the government wouldn't do anything to please the Palace.'

Mary smiled, a little contemptuously, and said he obviously knew very little about Egyptian politics if he believed issues were as clear cut as that! True, she herself had been in the country only five minutes but she had acquired the feel of the place. The Palace and the government were continually bargaining with one another. His release was the kind of favour one combatant grants to another. A *quid pro quo*. But he was too English to understand this kind of horse trading!

A little of the Princess's condescension, Perry thought, had gone to Mary's head; to be just, though, he had to admit that the Egyptian sense of intrigue was highly contagious. Even he, in telephoning the Pasha to inform him of his freedom, had enough common sense to *pretend* he knew it was due to the Pasha's intervention; and the Pasha had enough vanity to make not the smallest murmur of denial.

Perry had soon abandoned his plan of getting locked up once more and so regaining the only advantage over the authorities he could possibly enjoy: refusing to leave jail until he had received an adequate apology. The lock-up had become more disgusting in restrospect than it appeared at the time. And even if he did succeed in becoming a prisoner once more there was no guarantee that the army officer who had arrested him in Gizeh could be shamed into grovelling. Perry's change of heart underlay, in all probability, much of the uneasiness he felt as he gazed at the Nile. How weak he was! How irresolute! No wonder Mary revealed her contempt by reading aloud at the breakfast table long, boring letters from women who had been at school with her.

Mary herself was both problem and rebuke. How gladly he would have welcomed advice about her from some wise and imaginative friend: but the two people of whom he immediately thought, the Pasha and Waldo, were not really capable of taking Mary's measure. The Princess then? She would laugh at him. She had no delicacy in these matters. In her hands problems broke into pieces and were, so to speak, swept up by the servants. How could he possibly explain to one so irreverent his sense of failure over Mary?

For some time he had done his best to believe her story about having a lover but now he was beginning to confess defeat. With all the good will in the world Perry just could not believe in the fellow. Mac-something-or-other — what was his name supposed to be? He did not exist. But how could Perry reveal to Mary this dreadful suspicion?

A less perceptive man would have thought Mary was falling in love with him all over again. She had certainly changed. When he came home from jail she had heard him enter the flat in the small hours and peeped round the door of his room in an alarmed, wholly touching way, dressed (he was quick to notice) in a pair of silky, clinging pyjamas. Once satisfied that it really was Edgar she had not stopped to put the kind of questions one might have anticipated. She did not want to know how he came to be free; at least, not for the moment. Her astonishment lasted only long enough for him to see her face transformed — rounded, made childlike, almost glowing with emotion. He was struck by the size and beauty of her eyes. They made him step towards her. But a short while ago she had appeared middle-aged in the harsh police station light and he had felt sorry for her. Now, he could only be elated. The room was warm after the cold night. Her body was warm. Momentarily he held her under the arms with his two hands, feeling the warmth and softness of her body and marvelling at the respectability of the situation. After all, she was his wife!

She had kissed him on the lips, and still he held her. Magically, the arrest, imprisonment, Muawiya's intervention and his subsequent release had come to mean only this: the warmth and softness of his wife's body. She said nothing. He too kept silence. Their breathing sounded strangely loud. After everything that had happened, in spite of her boast of possessing this supposed Scots lover, a moment had come when, between them, all that mattered was sexuality. To Perry it seemed that they had dazed each other. Neither moved. Because of the curious way he was holding her she had to reach out her head in order to kiss him. Their bodies did not touch. He might have gathered her in his arms but he did not. She might have put her arms around his shoulders but she did not. They stood, six inches apart, glowing in each other's presence, yet not looking at each other. Perry looked fixedly at the open door for a while; when he suddenly glanced at Mary's face he saw that her eyes were closed.

'Can I make you some coffee?' she had said.

Remembering this scene, a man might have thought she was falling in love with him all over again, even if he would also remember that he had declined the coffee on the plea that it would keep him awake and she had immediately withdrawn to her own room for the rest of the night. The highly charged atmosphere might have argued less the existence of the Scots lover than Perry's defeat of him; but the highly charged atmosphere was not the only factor that required interpretation. More suggestive was the business-like questioning of the following morning and her insistence that Tureiya Pasha was ultimately responsible for his release. She told him that the university did not properly appreciate him, otherwise they would have given him more salary. She said it was incredible

Waldo had not heard of the arrest and stirred himself on behalf of a colleague and fellow-countryman. In other words, Mary talked and behaved like a faithful wife. Besides, she received no letters except from her mother and these schoolfriends. Perry knew because it was his job to bring up the mail every morning from the box in the hall. What lover failed to write letters, even if he was a Scotsman?

Two days — two and a half to be precise — had now passed since Muawiya brought about his freedom; a time of chafing and stern self-criticism. At the very moment of distress over his weak handling of Muawiya, Perry had discovered an embarrassment in the false situation which Mary appeared to have contrived for herself. Why she had done so he could not imagine, but then he did not profess to understand women. He looked over the brown Nile to the palm groves of Gizeh and felt the sunny warmth of the morning settling over him, so very gently, its mantle of inertia. Why not, he caught himself thinking, sit here quietly in the sun for a while and then stroll as far as Groppi's for a coffee? But this was treachery! He rubbed his eyes and gave his cheeks small, invigorating taps as he did in the bathroom every morning: inertia was the enemy! Perry swung off vigorously in the direction of the flat, determined to compensate for his weakness over the false arrest by taking a strong line with Mary. For a change he would act like a man of principle. He would charge her with having no lover at all and, once he had forced this confession from her, demand to know what she meant by it.

'Good morning, sir!' said an unmistakable student-voice from the obscurity of the hall the moment Perry entered it. 'We have been waiting for you. We have come to invite you to take a picnic with us.'

After the brilliance of the street the small hall where the porter lived and the lift was housed was so dark that Perry could not see who had spoken. He groped forward until his fingers came in contact with the handle to the lift door, opened it and so automatically caused a small bulb to glow in the lift's roof.

'I beg your pardon!' said Perry, not because he had failed to hear.

'A picnic at Sakkara.' The speaker's great bulk looked familiar, though he certainly was not one of Perry's students. 'We shall have an excellent picnic there, among the tombs.'

From his boots to the crest of his tarboosh was a good six feet — an unusual height for an Egyptian — and he weighed at least fourteen stone. Broad nostrils spoke a certain amount of negro blood. At the realization Perry did not recognize him bushy eyebrows rose and the head was thrust forward on its thick neck. 'Ahmed Mansour of the Faculty of Agriculture, sir. You left my room to be arrested in the good cause of better living conditions. We come to pay you homage. This is my friend Boghos.'

Boghos, a dignified youth with a few turns of white cloth round his tarboosh, seized Perry's hand, kissed it on the back and applied the spot to his forehead. He said nothing but, by the burning intensity of his small brown eyes, conveyed profound respect.

Perry thought he was a fanatic. 'Come on up to the flat. But it's quite out of the question that I should come on a picnic. Very nice of you to suggest it, though. You see,' he added, at a loss for a convincing excuse, 'I've got my wife to think of.'

'Madam can come too,' said Mansour.

These two young men, Perry reflected, had learned from the porter that he was out and waited patiently in the hall, not presuming to make their presence known upstairs. It had the effect of making him feel discourteous before he started; inevitably they would be disappointed and, if he knew Egyptian students, go off with a flea in the ear; an attempt must at least be made to placate them with coffee.

'Good news,' said Mansour as the lift creaked them up to the fourth floor, trembling as it went. 'University is open tomorrow and we go back to our studies, all happy.'

They had, all three of them, actually entered the flat and Perry had told Hassan to bring coffee before this remark took effect. Perry was pre-occupied with other problems; if he did not immediately charge Mary with her deception it might be days before he could again work up sufficient momentum. And yet the absurdity of launching the topic in the presence of two students was obvious.

'University opening, did you say?' he exclaimed. 'But that is quite impossible.' Mary entered the room and he found himself appealing to her. 'Did you hear that, Mary? These fellows say the university is opening. I've never heard of anything so absolutely — Oh, you don't know each other! Mr. Mansour — my wife. Mr. Boghos — my wife.'

The students stood side by side, bowing gravely and putting a hand to lips and forehead.

'So absolutely what, Edgar?' Mary was dressed for going out, shopping probably, and gave the impression of not having much time to waste.

'Well, so absolutely — '

By re-opening the university the authorities had declared their opinion that all danger of student demonstrations was past. This opinion was normally arrived at after a period of calm and to a man who, little more than two days previously had been arrested for fomenting trouble in Gizeh, it could only appear slighting. There were at least two hundred students cheering him when the riot squad arrived. Was that nothing?

'How do you know the university is opening?' he asked Boghos and Mansour.

'It is in the Arabic newspapers. It is quite certain, sir.'

Not until Hassan brought him the *Egyptian Mail* and Perry could see the brief announcement for himself did he really believe. 'Well, it's absolutely outrageous!' He threw the paper on the floor. 'They can't pretend they don't know about my arrest. D'you know, Mary, these fellows were actually chairing me. Weren't you, eh? I wonder when that happened last to an Englishman in Egypt. Now they want me to go on a picnic to Sakkara. Can't go, of course!'

'Madam,' said Mansour heavily, 'Professor Perry is a good man who wants to do good for the students. He was arrested because he wants better living conditions for us. All the students say he is a saint. We offer this picnic as a mark of respect. And you are invited, madam. You will be most welcome.'

'How very, very kind of you,' Mary was touched by Mansour's solemnity. It opened up a prospect of heroic sacrifice in the service of the unfortunate students. 'Why ever can't we go?'

But for the presence of the two students Perry would have explained that the acceptance of their invitation might give the appearance of assuming the leadership of a faction. He did not wish to make himself conspicuous in this way. 'You wouldn't like Sakkara,' he said. 'It's very nice of these fellows to ask us but they're always having dust storms over there. You with your sinus trouble would — '

'Sinus trouble?' Mary looked at him in surprise.

Mrs. Curtis always referred to the room in which they were seated as the saloon. It was circular and dark because the only light came through the frosted glass panels of eight doors which led into the other rooms of the appartment. Eight straight-backed chairs sheeted in white were ranged round the circumference as though held there by centrifugal force.

Boghos rose from one of the white chairs and took up his

position at the centre of the room in a way that seemed to promise a political speech of some length. He was, however, handicapped by the English language. 'It is good to see you at liberty, sir.' As he weightily delivered these words — the first since his arrival — he gestured with his right hand in Perry's direction. 'I do not speak of justice. I do not speak of injustice. I speak of Sakkara! Come!' He clasped hands over his heart. 'You will make us happy and honoured. No dust storm. I promise you no dust storm.'

'Sakkara!' Mary spoke in a way Perry recognized as an attempt at provocation. 'That's where the Step Pyramid is, isn't it?'

'Also the Sepulchre of Ti and the Serapeum. Madam Perry, you must come, really you must.'

Perry did not know whether to be exasperated or charmed. Having drunk his coffee he fetched a bottle of sherry and some glasses from the dining-room. Mary was the first to decline and Mansour followed her example on religious grounds. Boghos, on the other hand, was a Christian and free to accept a glass. He sat swilling the sherry round and round, occasionally taking a sip and revealing his distaste by the way he wrinkled up his lip over his white teeth. Perry sat with the bottle on the floor between his feet.

'Mrs. Perry and I can't come on this picnic. It's really very kind of you to ask us. I'm very grateful. But a picnic at Sakkara is not possible. To tell you the truth, I haven't quite made up my mind what to do about my arrest. It may be important to prove I wasn't on friendly terms with any of you fellows. You saw the way that army officer struck me? He took me by surprise, of course.'

'What is an Egyptian picnic like?' asked Mary.

'Cold chicken,' said Mansour in a loud voice, 'tomatoes, cheese, boiled eggs, bananas, dates, oranges, bottles of beer for the Christians, and coffee. We can sit on the sand or go to the house of Mariette Pasha. It is empty. No one lives there. We smoke cigarettes and play cards.'

'Many Moslems drink beer on a picnic too,' said Boghos. 'I have seen them.'

'It would be different if you were students in my own department,' said Perry. 'You're not even in my Faculty. I'm sorry, but there it is.'

Mary wanted to know how one reached Sakkara and Mansour was beginning to explain when Perry picked up the sherry bottle and his glass and walked through the dining-room to the balcony. A scavenging kite shivered its feathers, opened its hostile, dun-coloured beak and slipped sideways off the stone parapet; the creature circled and rose while Perry shouted at it. Really, the brutes would be foraging in the kitchen next! Perry shouted once more and listened for any comment that might come from the saloon. But there was no comment. No one had heard him. The voice of Mansour boomed on, describing, no doubt, every step of the way to Sakkara. Perry drank another glass of his South African sherry and looked out over the roofs of Cairo with a feeling of melancholy helplessness. Judging by the animation of the conversation in the saloon they had not even noticed his absence.

'My dear Mary,' he said, returning suddenly, 'you know it really is extraordinarily kind of Mr. Mansour and Mr. Boghos to invite us like this and it's mean of us to say no. Well, we have to say no! But let's all go round to Groppi's and have lunch! Now, what do you say?'

Perry had no sooner made this proposal than he experienced the undeniable warm emotion of generosity welling up inside him. Why was he making this gesture? At some point between the balcony and the saloon the impulse had come to him. Take them all out to lunch! But just where it came to him, just when, and why he could not say! One moment he was drinking sherry and squinting in the morning sun. The next moment he was in the dark saloon, with the initiative in his hands once more. For the past two and a half days he had waited on circumstances with the one result, it seemed, of causing himself to drop out of public and official notice. The authorities thought his riot such a poor affair that they had not hesitated to reopen the university before the dust of his arrest had settled in the Gizeh streets! It seemed that he could even walk out of a discussion, like this one on the Sakkara picnic, without causing comment. Events threatened to pass him by. Perhaps it was only natural, after all, that he should take the initiative and meet the admittedly well-intentioned Mansour-Boghos invitation with an invitation of his own.

'But Waldo is coming here to lunch,' said Mary.

'In that case he can join us at Groppi's. We'll leave a message with Hassan.'

'But we can't do that!'

'Oh yes we can, my dear!' Disregarding the presence of the two students Perry kissed her lightly on the brow, the cordial effect of his lunch invitation now tempered by melancholy; suddenly remembering her supposed lover he was touched by compassion and held her hand tightly all the way to the lift.

Only in the seclusion of Shubra did Waldo wear the full regalia: at the university and here, in town, he dressed unobtrusively. Ostentation was quite foreign to him. It was foreign, also, to the spirit of Islam. When he crossed the crowded floor of Groppi's open-air restaurant and climbed to the tudor lounge where the Perry party awaited him he was therefore wearing a European style suit in a bright blue then fashionable among the Cairenes. As a recognition of the circumstance that he was a professor at the national university and therefore a civil servant he wore a tarboosh. And as a concession to his desire never to appear quite consistent he wore a pair of yellow hide slippers with pointed, upturned toes.

He was in a good humour. Although Mary had not mentioned Edgar's adventures in the note sent to invite him to lunch — indeed, the lunch had been organized for the very purpose of telling him — Waldo appeared to know all about the arrest, the imprisonment, and the means by which Edgar had been set free. Waldo was delighted. He stood over the table, his shoulders forced back and his body apparently leaning away from the party so that he appeared a little out of normal perspective and impossibly tall. The tarboosh was a remote red pinnacle. 'By the way, Perry,' he said after remarking how glad he was to see him looking none the worse for his exploit, 'You've still got my reading glasses. I'd be very glad of them back. It's damned inconvenient. Who are these chaps?'

He had touched the back of Mary's hand with his moustache.

Perry introduced the two students and Waldo gave them a military nod before sitting down. He appeared to have formed the view of Perry's arrest that it was one of those colourful escapades people put into their memoirs for light relief. To be more exact it was the kind of happening Waldo would put in *his* memoirs for light relief; his mouth twitched and it seemed not too impossible to make out the words that were passing through his mind: 'A man on my staff called Perry was arrested in the winter of that year. He was, in reality, an inoffensive creature with steel-rimmed glasses which he was always losing or smashing. However, etc.'

Waldo did not ask for Perry's version of his arrest. He appeared quite uninterested in details of any kind. By the time he had settled himself in a chair it was clear that he had already heard quite enough for his purposes — enough to provide an excuse for talking about himself. He was lost in a vein of reminiscence. On the death of King Fouad Waldo had, he said, made one in the funeral procession which stretched for oh, he knew not what distance. Everyone was on foot, naturally. He himself was in full academic dress. On his right hand and on his left hand were colleagues, also in full academic dress and, d'you know, there were fellows there he had not seen before and was never to see again!

'I must say,' he interrupted himself, 'that Groppi's is a rum place to come for lunch. Matter of fact, I don't think I've been here this time of day before.' He looked round curiously at the other patrons of the restaurant, corpulent young men with incipient beards, in the main, who sat quietly lunching off millefeuille and eclair. Perry had quite forgotten that Groppi's was not the place to provide a grave repast but the arrival of Waldo had so discouraged him he lacked the energy to insist on going elsewhere. Suffragis brought omelettes, cheese sandwiches, fresh dates and beer in such quantities that they had to use a second table to support it all.

'Mary and I like a light meal in the middle of the day,' Perry remarked brazenly. He did not think that Waldo's experience at King Fouad's funeral was in any way worthy of comparison with his own unfortunate adventure. By mentioning it Waldo was, surely, implying nothing less than a comparison? Waldo had not, however, finished.

'After some time I found myself next to a Swiss who taught economics in the Faculty of Commerce, or so he told me. And d'you know, as we went along we fell to talking about Social Credit. I'd never heard of it before. This Swiss explained it so interestingly that I quite forgot where we were. From time to time I would look up and see the schoolchildren and the soldiers and so on who were lining the streets, all with tears running down their faces, and, of course, I naturally wondered what was the matter with them. I'd quite forgotten I was taking part in a funeral. We walked four miles. It was very hot. If it hadn't been for Social Credit I think I should have died. And then, when we got to the big mosque, there were soldiers sacrificing buffaloes in the sun, cutting their throats. All the road was running with blood. And the flies! Well, we weren't going to paddle through all that so we went home in taxis. I never saw that Swiss again.'

Mary had not been eating for some time. With elbows resting on the wooden arms of her chair she leaned slightly forward, the better to observe the expression on Waldo's face. 'Don't you understand that Edgar was beaten up and thrown in a filthy wog jail!' She spoke so loudly that the cake-eaters at neighbouring tables turned and stared. 'As head of his department the very least you can do is to see that he gets an official apology, yes, and compensation! His suit was quite ruined!'

'Professor Perry is a hero,' said Ahmed Mansour. 'His campaign for improved living conditions for students makes us all love him.'

'Oh come! It can't be as bad as all that!' Waldo was annoyed by the failure of his story about King Fouad's funeral and more than ever disinclined to take Perry's misadventure with any solemnity. 'Anyway, I can't understand what he was doing in Gizeh to get mixed up with a rumpus like that.'

Perry had drunk three beers and now felt his body exuding a relaxing sweat. For the first time since coming out of prison he was reasonably composed in his mind. He smiled at Waldo. 'I was, of course, raising a riot. Unsuccessfully, it seems. They tell me the university is opening tomorrow, so my little effort can't have made much of an impression.'

'Don't talk like a fool, Edgar.' Mary continued to stare at Waldo.

Boghos Effendi had been drinking beer too. Before speaking for the first time he raised an admonishing hand in Waldo's direction. 'We students invite you all to a picnic. We thank Professor Perry for his work. Our living conditions are terrible. Truly we live like animals!'

Waldo's angular face lengthened abruptly. The glass half-way towards his mouth was replaced on the table; yet so stiffened by suspicion had he now become that his lips remained parted to receive it for some seconds after the new thought had, so obviously, struck him. 'Perry you don't mean to say you actually went on preparing that report?'

'Certainly.'

'After I had expressly forbidden you to do anything of the sort?'

Perry nodded and took a bite out of a chicken sandwich.

'Am I to understand that you were actually in Gizeh working on this — '

'I was gathering statistics. Mr. Mansour here was being most helpful. I don't recollect Mr. Boghos, though I don't doubt he was there all right.' Perry licked the butter off his fingers. 'They chaired me, Waldo. Now, as a matter of interest, has there ever been anything like it in your experience of the country?'

Whatever version of the events in Gizeh Waldo had heard, and from whatever source he had heard it, quite plainly it had not been as detailed as Perry would have wished. Perhaps Waldo had thought he had been picked up by mistake out of a crowd of onlookers.

'Well, I'm sorry, but the Dean will have to know of this. The sooner the better. Can't you see what a difficult position you've put me in? Now, I ask you, if you were in my place what would you do? You see, the question is unanswerable!'

'See the Dean? What on earth for?'

Waldo's face darkened with anger. 'I intend to make it quite clear to him that no member of my staff is dabbling in Egyptian politics. I can't believe the Senate knew you'd been stirring up trouble in Gizeh when they decided to reopen the university. It is sheer madness. I tell you — and I speak with twenty years experience — it is sheer madness. We shall have the town in flames. I might be called upon to resign. How could you be such a fool! Disobedience. You disobeyed my orders! That is what hurts most. We must go at once.'

While speaking he had not neglected to eat or drink. The last fragment of egg and the last drain of beer disappeared with his closing words. Waldo stood up and placed his tarboosh on his head. He was made to feel particularly foolish by the memory of his so-recent high spirits. He hated the kind of inconsistency this seemed to reveal. 'Why has there been nothing about this in the papers? The whole thing has been grossly misrepresented to me. Muawiya Khaslat never said a word about your actually leading this demonstration. Well, really!' Waldo flung his arms about in a frenzy of anger and bewilderment. He remembered, too, what a failure his story about King Fouad's funeral had been and this memory introduced a note of hopelessness into his voice. 'All I've ever asked is a loyal staff and a quiet life.'

Waldo continued his speech in a strong whisper because he realized that by this time he had aroused the interest of everyone in the tudor lounge. Even at the distant bar men in white suits were turning on their stools. 'We must go to the Dean at once. In this country it's important to get your account of events in first. Perhaps we're too late already. We haven't a minute to lose.'

'Really, Waldo, I come here to celebrate — '

'At once!' In a provocative attempt to be confidential Waldo gave Perry a sharp nudge with the knuckles of his right hand. 'And alone!'

In spite of the bullying tone (to which Perry attached little importance anyway) an appeal was being made to his sense of responsibility which Perry found it difficult to resist. As a teacher at the state university he was a member of the civil service; and, in Egypt, the civil service was politics. When governments changed, deans in the various university faculties tended to change too; and, as Perry sat under the shadow of Waldo Grimbley in Groppi's tudor lounge, he found himself admitting a certain responsibility to report his quasi-political activities to the man best qualified to value them at their true worth (Perry did not trust Waldo's judgment) and who was, moreover, the man most likely to suffer a change of political fortune if a member of his staff put a political foot wrong. That man was, of course, the Dean. Perry did not think he *had* put a political foot wrong. If the Dean only told Waldo as much it would serve to pacify him. Presumably he would then give up his feeble attempts at bullying. But that was not the main point. Perry was most swayed by the urge, which had come quite suddenly, to follow a professional course of conduct for a change. Let us take the Dean into our confidence by all means!

'I couldn't possibly go and see the Dean and leave my wife and my guests in this way. If you insist on leaving now then I must insist that Mary, Ahmed Mansour Effendi and Boghos Effendi come with us.'

Waldo's obviously new yellow slippers squeaked at the implied rebuke. 'I don't want to seem discourteous, Mrs. Perry, but this really is important, and it's a matter only involving your husband and me, so perhaps we could drop you at your flat. Unless we get to the Dean's by half past two he'll be taking his siesta.'

'This is not a matter for the Dean,' said Mary. She was as angry as Waldo but in firmer control. 'It needs taking up on the highest level. The way they've insulted Edgar ought to be taken up by the Embassy. Of course I shall come with Edgar to see the Dean if you're so determined to make him go. I can't understand you! I hope Edgar goes on to make a report on the students' hovels that will shame the lot of you at the university, and the government too! Why are you so busy keeping him quiet? Anybody would think you didn't believe in Progress.'

Not daring to interrupt, Waldo had been opening and closing his mouth. When the end came the unmistakable capital letter at the beginning of Mary's last word so disconcerted Waldo that he turned to Perry and said, 'Very well! It's agreed that your wife comes. But I'm not having those students!'

With a courtesy that Perry found touching Mansour and Boghos had already withdrawn at the first sign their presence might prove embarrassing. Unaccustomed to Groppi elegance they stood uneasily at the head of the stairs leading to the *patio* talking quietly to one another. Mansour appeared the more uncomfortable of the two. His large bulk contrived the impression it was not receiving enough air, rather as though Mansour feared to fill his lungs properly lest he should break all the glass and porcelain in range of his breathing.

'They are my guests,' said Perry. 'I won't go without them.'

'What does it matter, dammit?' Waldo shouted in a tone of surrender.

As Waldo, followed by Perry, Mary, Mansour and Boghos, made his way to the street rage gave such dignity to his bearing that he received glances of admiration from mustachioed men in heavy overcoats who sat with fingans of coffee under their noses. Quick to sense the impression he was making, Waldo produced a string of heavy, amber beads from a pocket and walked past the glass counters into the sunshine of Sharia Adly Pasha, sliding the beads between his fingers in a hastily assumed religious gravity which lasted until the whole party was sitting in a taxi, on their way to the house in Dokki where the Dean lived in term time. In order to persuade the two students to come on the expedition Perry had warned them he would decline their invitation to Sakkara if they failed him now; they sat on a single turned-down seat, shouting jokes in the Cairo *argot* to one another and to the driver. They had quite recovered their self-possession.

'P-please, Waldo! P-please, Edgar,' said the Dean once more. 'Do b-believe me. It is the greatest of honours and pleasures to see you all. Above all, I have the inestimable privilege of meeting Mrs. Perry for the first time. It does not at all matter that I was going to the races. You will have saved me just that little bit of money.'

Abbas el-Hakim had the slightest of stammers. He was a modest little man of about fifty with a round, much-lined, humorous face; since taking his doctorate at Cambridge in the 'twenties — he was a historian — it was widely rumoured that he had never opened a book. Undoubtedly he must have had considerable political shrewdness to rise to the eminence of his present position, but much of his energy and enthusiasm went into horse racing. He was popularly supposed to be 'Bahram', the racing correspondent of one of the Arabic dailies. He could never be brought to admit as much. Indeed, he was ashamed of his enthusiasm, saying that racing would be impossible without gambling and gambling was against the laws of religion. When Waldo and his party had arrived, then, to find the Dean in brown and white shoes, a black and white check suit, and carrying a pair of field glasses, in the act of driving off to the Gezireh Racecourse, he could scarcely be expected to show genuine delight.

Waldo professed great concern lest the Dean should miss his afternoon's sport and Perry thought it prudent to follow his example; but Abbas maintained his customary smiling quiet, and led the way to the salon. An old man in a felt skull cap came in from the garden rubbing earth off his hands; he threw back the shutters and the ostentatious furniture, gilt and red velvet, was exposed to the afternoon sun. Banana fronds outside the window threw shadows across the faded carpet. The considerable size of the room and the bareness of its unpapered walls made on Perry the usual impression: that no Egyptian lived in a house; he camped out in one.

'It's about this demonstration and so on the other day,' said Waldo, 'when Mr. Perry was arrested!'

Abbas did not want to hear serious conversation until they had taken refreshment. He offered Mary a cigarette and stood in front of her chuckling and making small talk until the gardener, who had hastily tied a blue sash round his waist, brought in the tiny cups of black, sweet coffee. Mansour and Boghos sat unobtrusively in a corner in spite of the Dean's repeated invitation to draw nearer so that they could take part in the general conversation. He looked gently into the face of each of his visitors in turn, tapped a cigarette on a gold case the size of a playing card, and raised hands and eyebrows as though to say, 'Who will light this for me?'

Waldo reached him first. 'Did you know Mr. Perry was arrested?'

'No.' He appeared indifferent to the news. Finally expelling the smoke from his lungs, the Dean smiled into the sunlight. 'Do b-believe me, it is such a pleasant s-surprise to be called on in this way, at half-past-two in the afternoon, by five people — and three of them strangers to me! Three new people to know! This is very kind. I do not even wish to know why you are here. It is enough that you have arrived. P-pray do not think of the race meeting. I shall not! Mr. Perry, how is your distinguished pupil? Does the Pasha make progress? Alas, I fear not! Yes?'

His slightly formal and old-fashioned English gave the impression of a deeper irony than, in all probability, was intended.

Perhaps the Dean intended a little teasing; but nothing more.

'When you are eventually given the Order of the Nile, Third Class, I hope you will remember, my dear Edgar, that I was the instrument bringing you and the Pasha together. Your services to the Egyptian State will surely be recognized. Remember me in the hour of your glory! In the meantime, you have been arrested? What is this I hear?'

It was perfectly true, although Perry had forgotten the fact, that when the Palace had first felt the need for an English tutor they had approached Abbas who sent for Perry and asked permission to nominate him. If anyone in authority did seek to make political capital out of Perry's arrest there was a possibility the Dean might be more intimately involved than the normal healthy mind would suspect.

Waldo looked at the students Mansour and Boghos in a way intended to make them climb out of the window. 'You'd better tell the Dean what you've been up to, Perry.'

'How dare you speak like that!' said Mary. 'You talk about Edgar as though he's done something wrong. You act as though you're jealous of him! Why are you so unfair? I cannot understand why you don't show some spark of indignation over the way Edgar's been treated. Anybody would think you were jealous of him.'

'That is but justice!' Mansour rose to his feet and came forward with his coffee cup in his hand. 'Mr. Grimbley is not my professor and you are not my dean so I can speak freely. Mr. Perry is noble and a martyr.' He placed the cup in the gardener's outstretched hand and retired to the corner once more where he and Boghos sat whispering loudly to one another and glancing up at Waldo.

'You see?' said Waldo to Perry. 'I wanted to come alone. You insisted that everybody else should come too. Now look what's happened!'

'Frankly, I don't see why any of us need have come. You're such an extremist, Waldo.'

'Mr. Dean — '

Abbas raised a hand. 'Come, Edgar, I am getting bewildered! What is happening? What is all this about? Tell me, now, with your own lips. Then we shall go into the garden and drink some tea. Or perhaps you will all come to the races with me. It would be a great honour. There is still time. But now, tell me! Why are you a martyr? Why are you noble?'

'You see,' said Waldo when Perry had finished a sketchy account of his adventures, 'however foolish Mr. Perry has been, he has not been doing anything political. That's why I insisted on his coming along to give you his own version. As for being arrested and locked up, well of course that's just a joke. It could happen to anyone.' And Waldo began laughing, obviously delighted by the composed way Abbas had listened to Perry's story.

Now and again Abbas had put in a question. Would Perry recognize the officer who had arrested him if he saw him again? Had the Pasha given a time limit for the preparation of the report? Was Muawiya good at his studies?

Waldo sat up. 'I say! That's the fellow who came and told me about this hoo-ha! He didn't tell me he'd got you out of jug. What's his game, eh?'

'Do you gentlemen know Muawiya Khaslat?' The Dean turned in his chair and looked at Mansour and Boghos.

'Yes,' said Mansour.

'Moslem Brotherhood?'

'I don't know,' said Mansour promptly. 'Neither does Boghos.'

'What is the Moslem Brotherhood?' Mary showed by the gentle note in her voice that she had taken a liking to Abbas.

'It is a group of religious nationalists. Some would say

fanatics; but I? No. There are some good men. It is wrong to say they are a secret society. They are strong, of course. Very religious, and that makes for strength. Muawiya is undoubtedly a member. He would never have got your husband out of custody otherwise.' He turned to Perry. 'Really, Edgar, how shamefully you have been treated.'

Mary looked at Waldo with her chin up. 'I'm glad to hear someone else thinks so too.'

Waldo was so interested to discover that one of his own students was a member of the Moslem Brotherhood (a gang of fanatics, to be sure) that he returned Mary's gaze unseeingly. When he awoke to the hostility of that gaze he was momentarily confused and said, unguardedly, 'Really, Mrs. Perry, I don't know why you should be upset.' Your husband is perfectly safe; all's well that ends well — this was the note he undoubtedly meant to strike. But by placing the emphasis on 'you' instead of 'upset' he had clumsily made a remark of quite a different order.

'I don't know why *you* should be upset,' he remarked.

The words sounded like an obvious reminder of Mary's declared intention to leave Perry and return to England; and it was a measure of the distance events had carried them since the discussion in Waldo's flat that the three people principally involved, Perry, Mary and Waldo, now revealed embarrassment.

'I mean,' said Waldo, 'some people would look on the funny side.'

Mary opened her mouth as though to speak.

Abbas clapped his hands gently to show approval. 'Let us say no more of this matter. Edgar, let us not protest to anyone. Let us not ask for retribution. It would only lead to a lot of publicity. You know what a sense of humour we Egyptians have. You would cover yourself with ridicule. I should be covered with ridicule. And, to be truthful, it *is* a little ridiculous!'

The Dean chuckled. 'How I should have liked to see you in prison, Edgar.'

'It wasn't my idea to come here, you know,' said Edgar. 'Waldo insisted.'

'Quite right, quite right. Waldo is wise in these matters. Let us agree, shall we, to laugh about it? Shall we laugh about it, Mrs. Perry? I see you are somewhat severe. If we do not laugh there will be such a lot of trouble for us. Please, Mrs. Perry, let us agree to laugh. Then all Edgar has to do is promise to give up his idea for making a report.'

'I don't see why I should have to do that.' Perry felt his anger stirring.

'Neither do I,' said Mary.

'Professor Perry must not give up his noble mission,' said Mansour. Boghos stood up and took a step in Perry's direction as though to sustain him, at this moment of crisis, along the martyr's path.

Waldo allowed his creaking yellow slippers to take him up and down the room. He was so agitated he could not bear to look at anyone. 'I knew this would happen! This means disaster!'

Even Abbas had stood up. 'Edgar, I don't want to have to forbid you to carry on your investigations.'

'Damn it all, Mr. Dean, why shouldn't I carry on?' The energy Perry had discovered in scaring off the kite that morning began now to course even more vigorously in his veins. After two days of hopelessness he had taken the initiative by carrying his little party to Groppi's for lunch. Now he would go a stage further. He would show an iron will for a change and see what came of it.

'Why shouldn't you carry on? The reason is very simple.'

The Dean took Perry's hand and held it — a childish gesture which Perry found innocently pleasing and certainly more persuasive than any argument the Dean was capable of putting forward. 'The Palace — and it is for the Palace you are working, no matter what you think — the Palace is not particularly interested in students and their welfare. But the Princess *is* interested in political advantage.'

'Let's go and ask her!' said Perry.

'I beg your pardon.'

'I said, Let's go and ask her. If I understand you properly you're implying my report is a political stunt to discredit the government. As a matter of fact the Princess is against my making any sort of report. Very well, it's the Pasha. Let's go to the Palace now and ask him.'

Abbas allowed Perry's hand to fall and turned sadly away. 'Edgar, dear, you are being impossible. This is out of the question.'

'Why?' said Mary.

'It is not impossible,' said Boghos.

'Mr. Dean, Waldo,' said Perry, working himself into a fury, 'do you think I'd allow myself to be a political pawn? I insist that we all go to the Palace immediately and reach an understanding. Or aren't you interested? Don't you care what kind of squalor your students live in?'

The Dean turned and looked at the gilt woodwork and red velvet of the chair on which he had been sitting; he put out one hand and fingered the ornate convolutions of the back, as though to assure himself of its objective existence. Waldo, who had been stiff and silent with astonishment, thawed into a grimace of horror but the Dean shook a hand in his direction as though to silence him. 'Let me think,' the Dean appeared to be saying.

The gardener went round collecting the empty coffee cups, sniffing and sighing like an old hound. The Dean called his attention to a cup he had overlooked and everyone listened to jingle of crockery and the slip-slop of his footgear as the old man retired towards the kitchen. The Dean made a complete circuit of his chair, obviously still thinking hard, and took up his position in front of Mary.

'Can't you make him see reason?'

For some moments Mary had been studying herself in a mirror which happened to hang conveniently, thinking that the biscuit-coloured suit required gayer accessories than the spray of jet flowers, but she was prompt to say that in her opinion Edgar was being quite reasonable. She smiled across at her husband to show her approval. Approval? No, it was stronger than that. She offered her admiration. Here he was, standing up for his beliefs, in a manner little short of the heroic! Almost gaily she went over and took her plucky stand at Edgar's side, showing that if he was to suffer for his convictions at least he would not suffer alone.

'Edgar is quite right! We ought to go to the Palace at once and have the whole thing gone into.'

'To the Palace!' said Mansour and Boghos, not quite together.

'Look here! Those two aren't coming!' Waldo spoke hurriedly and then corrected himself. 'But of course nobody is going to the Palace. It is out of the question!'

'I'll go by myself,' Perry was saying. 'If nobody else wants to come I'll go to the Palace alone, and I shall tell them you've forbidden me to make any more investigations at Gizeh for political reasons.'

Mary held his arm. 'I will come with you, Edgar.'

'To the Palace!' said Mansour and Boghos raggedly.

'Gentlemen!' said the Dean, who had already donned his tarboosh and picked up his binocular case as though even now he had not given up hope of appearing at the races. 'How do we know that Their Excellencies will be at the Palace to receive us?'

He stood back for Mary to pass through the door and then hurried on into the dusty sunshine to see her safely seated in his big American automobile. He became formal and spoke of Professor Grimbley and Professor Perry. The fact that he had asked Perry a question and given him no opportunity to answer revealed how troubled he was.

'I always give the Pasha a lesson at three this afternoon and he hasn't telephoned to cancel,' said Perry. 'He's bound to be there.'

Waldo appeared, blinking in the sunlight at the top of the steps. 'Mr. Dean! Why put up with this blackmail? This is a matter for Faculty discipline. Perry! You must be mad. Get out of that car at once and apologize to everyone.'

With the exception of Waldo everyone had, by this time, taken their seats in the car, Abbas at the wheel, Mary, Perry and Boghos in the back and Mansour on the floor at their feet. The atmosphere was made up of such an explosive mixture of anger, elation, self-conscious heroics and outraged pride that time for further argument or hesitation was out of the question. If Waldo had not jumped for the running board when the car had described a circle on the Dean's golden sand he would have been left behind; and, even so, the car was a quarter of a mile down the road to the English Bridge before he managed to jerk the door open and take his rightful place on the seat at the Dean's side.

'I draw the line at these two students,' he shouted. 'They're not even in the Faculty of Arts.'

'Professor Perry has invited us to accompany him to the Palace,' said Abbas. 'He has invited all of us. We shall accept his invitation in full. To the letter.' He pretended not to notice the movement of cars and people northwards, in the direction of the racecourse. 'We shall all ask an audience. Then justice will be dealt out. I am not a fool. I understand my own country.'

'Nobody's going to make a fool out of me!' Perry looked aggressively at the back of Waldo's head. 'The trouble with you people is — '

'Now, now, Edgar!' said Mary in a wifely voice. 'It won't do any good to lose your temper.'

Perry would have liked his party to be even larger. Muawiya should have been there. The police captain, Asfur, would have been welcome too. Perry would gladly have led a crowd into the Palace. The time had come, he felt, when he must justify himself in public opinion, not in any vulgar, demagogic kind of way but by having thirty or forty interested people there when he interviewed Their Highnesses in the presence of university authority and made it clear that he was no one's political pawn, that his intentions had never been anything but philanthropic and that if anyone tried to thwart him now it would only be due to the most unworthy and cowardly motives. The Dean could not possibly have driven fast enough to please him.

As the car drew up to the main gate of the Palace two Nubian guards came out of the sentry boxes and spread their arms wide. The wooden gate was firmly closed and the high brick wall, surmounted by steel hedgehogs, would have deterred a sterner onslaught than any Perry might have intended; nevertheless, the two guards, in their snowy turbans and ankle-length gowns of blue and gold thought it necessary to strengthen the defences by standing with arms extended. At the sight of Perry they went to the sentry boxes and returned with a heavy wooden staff each.

Perry was the first out of the car. The brilliance of the afternoon sun caused him to step into the shadow of the Palace wall where he looked into the scarred, puffy face of the smaller guard and said, 'You know who I am. We've come to see the Pasha.'

The guard swung his staff over Perry's head, causing it to give out a curiously loud, angry buzz. The second guard struck the pavement in front of Perry's feet, laughing and shaking his head. In the past Perry had always got on very well with these guards. They always seemed merry. They had once tried to sell him a gold ring for ten piastres. But this afternoon, although they laughed, they said not a word. They were gradually forcing Perry back towards the car.

The Dean spoke to the men in Arabic and even then they said nothing. Perry was standing in the roadway with the two staves whirring in front of his face. Over the Palace wall he could see the Italianate entablature of the building itself, a smoky red against the sky. The hedgehogs caught the sun, a palm tree in the grounds lifted its fronds silently, a small white cloud appeared. He shut his eyes and heard the Dean start up his engine once more.

'Doesn't the Pasha want his lesson?' Perry said foolishly. 'If I'm kept waiting much longer I shall report you.'

But, of course, the guards could only have been acting on orders. He was shut out! The Pasha, or the Princess, or both, had given orders not to admit him!

'Edgar!' Perry opened his eyes and looked round to see the Dean leaning out of the driving seat with a sad smile on his face. He spoke mildly. 'It is no good, Edgar! Jump in now! Be a good boy! There is still time to go to the races.'

Perry stood in the road explaining to Mary, with a note of incredulity in his voice, just how he had been humiliated. The shock made him look here, there and everywhere with a hen-like rapidity. The guards leaned on their staves, watching quietly and ignoring the jeers of Mansour and Boghos. Waldo threw his arms about in quiet conversation with the Dean.

'I don't believe the Princess knows anything about this.'

Mary turned and would have made for the Palace gate if Perry had not caught her by the arm.

'There is still time to win a fortune at the races,' said the Dean enticingly. Waldo made the mistake of laughing noisily.

Holding Mary with some firmness Perry set off in the direction of Kasr el-Aini. He heard nothing she said. As a matter of fact she was unable to get more than grunts or monosyllables from him for the rest of the day.

'Sir,' said Muawiya, 'students tell me that you and Mrs. Perry are to take a picnic at Sakkara.'

Perry nodded but said nothing. They were walking back to Cairo after the first morning of lectures since the university had been closed. Perry forebore to ask Muawiya why he should be going to Cairo when he lived at Gizeh, in the other direction.

'I do not wish you to go on this picnic, sir.'

They passed the Dean's house, crossed the tram lines and approached the English Bridge. Muawiya was puzzled by Perry's silence.

'It is shameful that students in the Faculty of Agriculture should have a picnic for a professor in the Faculty of Arts. All my friends in the English Department are ashamed. They say that only the English students can help you with the statistics. The Faculty of Agriculture students do not even want a hostel. They are not advanced enough, sir. The English students would like you to give up the other picnic and have a picnic of our own at the Barrage. It will be much nicer for Mrs. Perry at the Barrage.'

Muawiya seemed to bear no ill-will for Perry's lack of gratitude over the escape from custody. Yet his presence distressed Perry. His mention of 'statistics' and 'hostel' was quite enough to make that particular scheme appear perfectly absurd. For

Perry to look ahead and see his shadow accompanied by the bulkier shadow of Muawiya was to feel he was following, through the clear sunlight, a symbolical representation of his own haunted life. Now there was a gap between the two shadows. Now Muawiya was trying to look into Perry's face and the gap closed up. The student wore a tarboosh, so his shadow was blunt-headed, even shark-like, as it came into the attack. Occasionally the attack came from the right when the student had dodged round to that side in avoiding pedestrians coming from the other direction. Perry saw his own shadow as a mild-mannered, elderly fish making its way through the ocean while a voracious monster bit succulent lumps out of its side as it went. Perry became so depressed that he walked under the trees, right up against the railings. Here he could cast no shadow.

The student's voice trembled. 'If you do not accept our invitation we shall say you do not like us.'

Perry walked faster. In future his relationship with Muawiya would be correct to the point of coldness. It was intolerable the fellow should think he had rendered a service of importance. On the contrary, it was entirely discreditable. Whenever Perry thought of the way he had walked out of prison, without exacting the smallest murmur of official apology, he was sick with shame. Muawiya was involved in this shame. It was absurd that he could not see it. He ought to realize that merely to be in his company was enough to cause a *malaise*.

Yet before he could insist on Muawiya's keeping his distance there was one question to which Perry must have the answer. His sufferings had made him too cynical to think that Muawiya would answer truthfully. But he was compelled to put the question as a small boy is compelled to touch wet paint.

'For the last time, sir,' said Muawiya, his voice quavering with self-pity and jealousy, 'why do you go on this picnic?'

They halted at a bus stop. 'If I answer that question will you answer one for me, Muawiya?'

'Of course. Why not?' His eyes widened with pleasure.

'Are you a member of the Moslem Brotherhood?'

'Yes, of course. Why not?' Still the wide, happy eyes.

'The police captain. Is he a member too?'

'Oh yes. A good man. Patriotic and religious.'

'And the police officer at Zagazig? You know, the one you sold books to?'

'All, all Moslem Brothers.' Muawiya laughed. He had so far recovered his good spirits as to sound mocking.

Perry was astounded. In spite of his supposed cynicism he did not doubt these answers. He thought of the Moslem Brotherhood as people at one time had thought of the Mafia. Muawiya spoke as though it were the Boy Scouts. His manner was convincing.

'Sir, if you come with me I will introduce you to one of the chief men in the Brotherhood. He is a sheikh from Al Azhar. We are all good men. We are good to *you*. Now, sir! My question. Why do you go on this picnic?'

Too late Perry realized his indiscretion. He had been so eager to question Muawiya about the Brotherhood that he had not counted the cost. How could he confess that he and Mary had finally decided on the picnic because the Dean and Waldo had forbidden them to go? The Princess and the Pasha might desert him, the Faculty might bar his path, but once having begun his report on the Gizeh tenements Perry was determined to finish it. If necessary he would publish the shocking details at his own expense! He would rouse the country! The picnic was a declaration of hostilities! But how could intimate confessions such as these be entrusted to Muawiya?

Perry knew that he was blushing. He tried to walk faster. 'No, no. Some other time, Muawiya.'

'But, sir! We made a bargain!' Muawiya was becoming emotional again.

'It's not a bit of good, losing your temper!'

Mutually outraged, the pair crossed Kasr el-Nil Bridge at a trot. Perry was given strength by the memory of Waldo's laugh outside the Palace. He could still hear it, like the creak of a tree in winter.

A PROSPECT OF TOMBS

W<small>HO WOULD RIDE AND WHO WOULD WALK?</small> At Badrashein
station a man waited with a string of pearly asses, sleek as mice,
ready and willing to trot through the groves of Memphis to the
pyramids and tombs, five miles away, on the desert escarpment.
Fifty piastres, there and back! It was for nothing! The man
affected to turn away in disgust at the offer of forty piastres.
The train, which had brought the party from Cairo, pulled
laboriously out of the station, children and beggars swarmed
across the line from the village, and the hard brilliance of early
morning was mellowed by the rising dust.

'No,' said Mary. She would not feel safe on a donkey. She
would much rather walk.

'We shall have one donkey between us,' said the spokes-
woman of the five women students. 'We can take it in turns.'

'Sir!' Mansour was distressed. 'Mrs. Perry would be perfectly
safe. All the time I should hold the donkey's head.'

'We'd much prefer to walk, Mansour. Really! It's such a
wonderful morning.'

Boghos hired one animal to carry the panniers of food. The
men students stood clapping hands rhythmically in a circle that
enclosed a wild-eyed, half-naked, village youth who danced
with a long staff in his right hand. They began singing. Even
the donkey man joined in, grinning broadly and shuffling his
feet in a little dance. Everyone was imbued with a gaiety so
much under control that it was almost solemn.

For one of the students Badrashein was home. He was a slim youth with fluttering fingers and, when it became clear that the English martyr and his wife intended to accept the hospitality he shyly offered, his agitation became painful to see. Mary and Edgar descended two steps to the dark reception chamber of the student's house and drank milky tea from ornate Japanese cups. The student — what *could* his name have been? Perry was never to remember! — served the tea himself. His hands shook, the cups jingled in the saucers, a clock ticked tinnily in the gloom, whispers could be heard behind a screen, and the rest of the students called gaily from the street, 'Oh sir, oh lady, we must go.'

'How wonderful it all is!' said Perry as they stepped into the sunshine.

Mary began hurrying. 'Edgar, I know I shall be sick in a minute. The smell! Can't we get out of this village?'

'The hospitality, the friendliness, the gaiety! Don't you see? Listen to them singing! Listen to them laughing!'

The main street, no more than eight feet wide, appeared to be conducting them to the pink walls of a mosque. At the last moment a gap between the mud brick houses was seen to the right. Mansour called out the places of interest as they made their way westwards. The house of the *mudir*! The shop of the Greek grocer! The new police station!

'All the time,' said Mansour, 'we tread the sacred dust of our ancestors. This was Memphis, the greatest city in the world.'

A buffalo with the metallic sheen of a blue-bottle luxuriated in a muddy pond where the countryside began. The women students had already taken charge of Mary. She sat side-saddle on a trotting ass. No doubt she had decided this was the quickest means of escaping from the reek of Badrashein; and now that she was breathing pure air from the west she did not dismount. The girls ran at her side, clapping the ass's flank. Perry saw that she was laughing, and pointing up at the ripening dates.

Ahead there were pale trunks and wave upon wave of fronded green. The dates hung among the greenery like so many swarms of bees. As the party made its way westward the palm grove closed in behind them yet always, here and there through the trunks, Perry could pick out the dull glitter of desert. As yet, there was no horizon. Instead of following the main track, some of the students made winding, adventurous trails of their own. They disappeared, on right and left, behind the trees; then appeared again, further off or surprisingly nearer. Perry could scarcely understand the excitement that was possessing him. The only other time he had been to Sakkara he had made the journey on horseback across the desert from Gizeh. This palm grove gave him a new experience. Walking between Boghos and Mansour he felt wildly happy.

'All Memphis!' Mansour stopped and made a dramatic sweep with his hand.

A bare-footed Beduin girl in a black veil drove a couple of goats past, staring boldly. An older woman followed, leaning on a stick and jangling with brass head ornaments.

'In England, this time of year, the rain! And the cold!' Perry spoke the first nonsense that came into his head. 'Sometimes you get a mild winter, of course.' He wanted to call attention to the radiance of the Egyptian morning. The others did not seem to be as aware as he was of its purity. Every step forward was in response to a scenic invitation. It would have been impossible to sit down and rest even if he had wanted to. There, for example, straight ahead, was a monstrous pearly Sphinx, squatting across their path. It flashed in the sun. Shadows played along its body like the ripple of muscles.

For Perry this was the final emotional touch. Although he had not seen the alabaster sphinx before he knew perfectly well what it was, one of the two most celebrated remnants of

Memphis. In his present mood of exaltation he could not face it. Mary had dismounted from the ass and in company with the rest of the students was patting the monster and making admiring remarks. Perry turned aside and made for the other celebrated remnant: a huge statue of Rameses the Great which lay on its back under a corrugated iron roof and protected by four stone walls. There was no mistaking the building; all the street vendors of Cairo had picture postcards of it. In the photograph it looked more like a boat house than it did in reality; but Perry knew where he was going. He entered the building, climbed the steps to the catwalk which had been built for viewing purposes, and looked down at the stranded monarch with an impossible yearning. Yearning for what? He pulled out a handkerchief and blew his nose. He was elated and embarrassed at the same time.

Hearing a scuffle on the steps he turned and saw Boghos regarding him with his fanatic's stare. They looked at each other for some moments. Just when Perry was about to make a remark Boghos turned, scuttled down the steps, and burst into the open, calling, 'Mrs. Perry, the Professor is up there. He is looking at Rameses and crying.'

Perry called out from where he was, 'I'm all right, Mary. There's nothing the matter.'

A silence followed which reminded him of the silence when the light went out at Zagazig. He had the same momentary fear. Perhaps they had all stealthily left, abandoning him to Rameses and the Sphinx. The women students began talking together and he heard Mary's firm tread on the steps. A moment later her broad, sensible brow appeared. Once more he found himself admiring her widely spaced, grey eyes.

'Come on up!' He took her hand gaily and assisted her up the last few steps. 'There is nothing the matter. See?'

Students were crowding up the stairs behind her. To his

dismay Perry saw that he was not going to be able to give Mary a convincing explanation for his display of emotion. Yet now that everyone knew about it he was no longer embarrassed. Mary looked at him with a touch of apprehension.

'My dear girl,' he said, 'I've never been so happy in my life before! This is going to be a completely happy day!'

'All this strain — ' she began.

'A day of happiness!' He began to shoo the students back down the stairs. 'On to Sakkara! We're going to enjoy ourselves.'

Mansour took the view that the martyr had walked far enough. The time had come for him to ride. In spite of Perry's protests the panniers were removed from the ass carrying them and handed over to four volunteers. Encouraged and advised by all present Perry now mounted the beast. He obediently sat well to the rear — this 'seat' was unanimously recommended — and found that his dangling feet barely cleared the ground. Saddle and stirrups were, of course, missing.

'Y'Allah!' shouted the students.

Mary's ass was already trotting into open country with a neat cloud of dust round its hooves.

'Let me know when anybody else wants to ride.' The bridle was put into Perry's hands and the ass trotted off between the palm trees with one ear pointed forward and one pointed (accusingly, it seemed to Perry) at the rider. Neck and neck the two asses crossed a bridge over an irrigation canal, everyone laughing, their crisp shadows pointing the way they had to go. Perry would have liked to shout, 'It is perfectly true, what Boghos Effendi said. I was crying!' But the mob was already demonstrating, by their high spirits, that they would have thought it a matter of no consequence. All right! He was crying! Now he is not crying! Indeed, he is laughing! What does it matter? See, there is Sakkara on the hills!

'All Memphis!' said Mansour as he puffed along at Perry's side.

Tethered oxen, as pink as porcelain, grazed the berseem pastures on either hand. A stately line of dark casuarina trees struck north for Gizeh between a metalled road and a blue canal. Crossing this road the asses' hooves set up a surprising splutter which was smothered the moment they reached the dust track on the far side. The party was already climbing out of the valley. Seeming to tremble in the sun, the Step Pyramid showed pale against the sky; broken, a heap rather than a form, and very near. Elsewhere, north, east and south, the horizons were remote. The lines of casuarina, the palm groves here and there, the single road, the occasional white wing on the river, were set about the spacious scene as though to play tricks with perspective. The sun flashed on a Citadel window, fifteen miles away.

Before setting themselves to the final climb everyone stopped for a rest. Mary dismounted and walked over to say something and Perry was struck by her colour. She looked radiant. He patted her hand.

'Listen!' he said to everyone.

They all fell silent and listened.

'Not a sound,' he breathed. They sat listening to the desert silence until the four young men with the food panniers caught them up. Then Perry insisted the time had come for the asses to have a rest. He and three others would carry the food.

'We are almost there,' said one of the girl students. She was the first of them to speak to Perry, although they had already struck up a gay intimacy with Mary. They climbed ahead over the sand and shards showing thick ankles under their belted overcoats.

At the custodian's office Mansour presented his free pass from the Department of Antiquities (they were supposedly making an educational visit) and a bent, one-eyed man counted the party through a gate. The necropolis was heaped in mounds of broken stone before them. Ten minutes later they had crossed the ridge, looked westwards over the dunes of the Libyan desert, north to the distant minarets of Mohamed Ali's mosque, and descended a gradual slope to a single-storey building of recent date. This was the now empty house of the archaeologist Mariette and the very place where Mansour and Boghos had planned to hold their feast.

Muawiya Khaslat emerged from the front door as the party approached.

'Welcome, Professor Perry. Welcome, Mrs. Perry. Students of the English Department are already here.' He waved both hands joyously. 'All, all are welcome. Come and eat!'

Perry could not conscientiously pretend surprise. He had expected some such *coup*.

By catching an early Fayoum bus from Gizeh Muawiya and his friends had alighted at a point not two miles from Sakkara and established themselves in Mariette's house a good hour before Perry and his party arrived. And whom had Muawiya enrolled for such a stunt? Perry looked round. There was Hilmy, the respectable-looking boy with glasses. There was Jabbur, a thick-necked youth who had once been shot in the face during a demonstration and had a withered cheek. And there was a round-faced Saudi Arabian whose name Perry could not remember. He was relieved to find the contingent from the English Department so small. If it came to a fight the four of them could scarcely be expected to inflict serious damage on Mansour's party.

Ignoring everyone else Muawiya stood shaking Perry's hand and smiling into his face. 'In spite of everything you are my favourite professor. In spite of your cruelty and your persecution of me I had to see you at Sakkara.' He was wearing a shabby brown overcoat and a voluminous camel hair scarf. Obviously he was overjoyed with the situation he had created. Not having shaved for at least three days he was as blue as a burglar round the chin; the very roughness of his appearance gave to his joy a kind of drunkenness. 'I expect that lady is Mrs. Perry.'

The discovery that Mary and Muawiya had never met was, for Perry, the most surprising feature of this encounter. Two people so well known to him and unknown to each other? It seemed a flaw of nature. As Perry said the appropriate words Muawiya touched Mary's outstretched hand with the tips of his fingers and bowed abruptly.

'You're the Moslem Brother.' Mary looked down on him from the slight advantage given her by the slope they were standing on. 'I don't care what they say about you. I am very grateful to you for getting my husband out of prison — '

'Now, Mary — '

She turned on Perry. 'Of course I shall thank him.'

'He has no right to gate-crash. The very idea, getting here first with a lot of food!' He looked round. 'Anyway, it's much too early to think of food yet. We ought to look at some tombs.'

'Yes, that is right, sir!' shouted Mansour. He and Boghos were unloading the food panniers and carrying the contents into the house. 'You and Mrs. Perry and the girls and everyone, you go and look at the tombs. Be careful not to fall in the mummy pits! When you come back in one hour your lunch will be served.'

Having gone into the house to make sure that no interference with his own lunch arrangements was in progress Muawiya stood by Perry's side. 'It is honourable that Professor Perry and his wife eat lunch with English Department students.'

A cold wind, appropriately enough, blew sand in their faces. The women students rushed to the lee of the house, twittering like birds. But the wind dropped as suddenly as it had sprung up, leaving Mary, Perry, Muawiya and such other students who were listening to the argument all facing east. The happiness of the Memphis palm grove seemed far away indeed! Here they were, high up among the tombs, arguing who should eat with whom! Muawiya was all the more provocative because his presence could only be due to a genuine regard. One did not buy a lot of expensive food and catch an early bus from Gizeh merely to annoy an English teacher. There were other, simpler routines. His action sprang from such a depth of feeling, such jealousy for that matter, that nothing would satisfy him but the outrageous. To make matters worse Mary appeared impressed.

Muawiya was so excited that, as he spoke, a bead of spittle appeared on his lower lip. Excitement gave elegance to his movements. He threw out one hand like an actor and turned on one foot so that the skirt of his coat flew out. Calling aloud in Arabic he stood in front of the open door summoning whoever was the leader of the Faculty of Agriculture party to come out. The last of the food had been checked on to a trestle table by Mansour and he appeared in the porch swinging an empty pannier and frowning down at Muawiya. (He was six inches taller.) Muawiya seized him by the hand and drew him towards the Perrys. Mansour did not resist. He bit his lower lip and showed the white tips of his teeth. For some reason the women students were exclaiming loudly; perhaps they thought Mansour was to be subjected to some indignity.

Muawiya raised Mansour's arm in the air. 'Sir, we shall wrestle together! Whoever wins, he will be the victor and you and Mrs. Perry will picnic with the victor.'

'For the last time, I will *not* eat with you.' As an afterthought, and because he sensed Mary might seek some compromise, Perry added: 'Neither will my wife.'

'I should kill him.' Mansour laughed. He was so much bigger than Muawiya that his boast did not sound idle.

'To die in this way would make me happy.' Muawiya addressed his remarks to Mary. 'What an excellent cause! But when I am dead you would have no appetite. The picnic would be spoiled. It is much better and more gentlemanly, it is more civilized and cultured, to have a donkey race.'

'A donkey race!' All the students, without exception, were delighted. Even Mansour threw his head back and chuckled. Perry walked about with his hands thrust into his coat pocket insisting that whoever won the race he and his wife were the guests of Mansour; they would eat with no one else. But the asses were brought from behind the house, and a joyful argument about the course took place. Mansour and Muawiya wished to go as far as the Serapeum and back. The rest of the students preferred a rougher track in the direction of the Sepulchre of Ti, presumably because there was a better chance of the riders falling off. Everyone — even Mary — was determined that, whoever ate with whom as a result, there could be no finer way of starting a picnic than this race among the mummy-pits. Students climbed hillocks of debris to spy out and suggest routes of greater complexity and danger. The girls had persuaded Mary to the flat roof of the house where they would have a good view whichever way the donkeys ran. Jabbur, the youth with the withered cheek, offered to bet Perry fifty piastres that Muawiya would win.

'Listen everybody!' To Perry's surprise everyone stopped chattering and looked in his direction. 'Listen!' He drew a white handkerchief from his pocket and allowed it to flutter in the light wind. 'Mansour! Muawiya! The course will be one complete circuit of the house. Now come here! Bring your donkeys here. When I drop this handkerchief, you understand, that's the starting flag. You'll go once round the house and make for me. I'm the winning post. Is that quite clear?'

Perry's change of heart brought cheers and, from the girls on the roof, a round of polite clapping. Even Boghos threw off some of his normal severity and showed pleasure. He grinned and patted Perry on the shoulder. 'The Egyptian asses are very strong. Have no fear.'

This confidence was not shared by everyone. When Perry put the field under starter's orders, shouted, 'One! Two! Three! Off!' and dropped his handkerchief there was a rush to help the asses with their burdens. Hilmy and Jabbur ran on either side of their candidate, Muawiya, supporting him awkwardly under the buttocks; two other young men performed a similar service for Mansour and the asses trotted forward with surprising speed. At the first corner Muawiya was in the lead and Mansour shouted for more supporters; his present team seemed incapable of the lift his rival was getting. Muawiya was a smaller man, anyway. It was plain enough already who was going to win. Muawiya gave an ululation of triumph as he sailed round the corner with daylight clearly visible between him and his mount — to that extent had Hilmy and Jabbur succeeded in taking a grip on him. Indeed, as the party disappeared from view it looked as though the ass were having to scamper to keep up.

As if it mattered who won! Everyone was in such high spirits it no longer seemed important who played host, Muawiya or Mansour. Food and drink were in abundance. When the time came they would feast — and feast together! The race! What was the race? It was a preliminary blood-quickener, an appetite-sharpener! Dust hung in the air. The excited yells and cheers were muted by the echoless desert into a reedy mingling of cries with a touch of remoteness in them.

'Don't forget,' Perry was shouting. 'I am the winning post! They must actually pass me before the race is over.'

The caretaker of the house, an elderly man in a dirty white gown and slippers, scuffled through the sand in Perry's direction with a tray bearing two cups of coffee. Perry waved at him, saying, 'Not now! Later!' The man was either deaf or stupid because he came on, smiling like a child — and with the appeal of a child — over the pleasure he was about to give.

Beyond the caretaker Perry could see the corner around which the asses must come. Behind was a sweep of desert, so level under the reddish Libyan hills, that it might have been a lake. Nothing moved against the lake but the smiling old man with his winking coffee.

'Out of the way. You'll be knocked down.' Perry waved his handkerchief in excitement as what appeared to be a crowd of struggling human beings and animals were displayed, as though hanging between sky and ground, against the backcloth of wilderness. Presumably they were touching ground but the dust made it difficult to be certain. A violent silhouette of gesticulating hands, tarboosh tassels, crouching forms and ass's ears had burst into view from behind the house. Was it possible they were actually carrying the asses as well? One of the beasts set up a horrifying bray and the silhouette expanded menacingly in Perry's direction. He could now see the asses had gained extra helpers on the far side of the house. They were not, it was true, being carried by these helpers but the young men had rallied in such numbers the beasts were scarcely bearing any weight and could not have fallen; they were so closely supported it would have been impossible even to drop dead. Perry waited until he made out that Muawiya and his cohort were in the lead and began to clamber over a hillock of debris, calling out as he went, 'The race is not over until you pass me! I'm the winning post!'

The caretaker with his tray of coffee broke into a run. Unless the coffee were drunk within a matter of minutes it would be cold; and everyone knew that once cold it was good for nothing. No man boiled up cold coffee. The caretaker managed to gasp this out as he made his way up towards the cave where Perry had planned to take refuge. He seemed unaware that he was being pursued in his turn.

'Oh, come down, Edgar! That's a dirty trick!' Mary's voice carried up to him by some acoustic effect in spite of the louder brays, cries and groans, in his immediate rear.

Perry replied by waving his handkerchief. The cave, when he reached it, was no bigger than a fox hole. Perspective had played him false. But the dying down of the sounds of pursuit told him that the race was over anyway, and when he turned he saw that the asses, as silvery as the shadows, were standing riderless. Mansour and Muawiya were making the ascent on foot. They came, their faces shining with sweat and grinning, hand in hand like children.

'Bring the coffee with you!'

Muawiya turned back and relieved the caretaker of his tray. Perry sat and waited. A tiny avalanche of splinters broke away from beneath one of his feet, making (the morning was so still) a wholly disproportionate thunder. The upturned faces of the watchers below were motionless. Clearly, they expected some gesture of him.

'Now,' said Perry when the two students were standing in front of him. 'Drink this coffee. You've both deserved it.'

He took the tray and, in spite of their protests — the coffee was intended for him! — insisted on their drinking.

'For the victors!' he called down.

'We have no time to lose,' said Muawiya, breaking in on Perry's rejoicing. 'Unless we see the Tombs of the Sacred Bulls and the Sepulchre of Ti before lunch there will be time for nothing this afternoon.'

A PROSPECT OF TOMBS

'Let us go, sir!' said Mansour, courteously knocking the sand from the seat of Perry's trousers.

'Let us go by all means.' Perry was charmed by the way matters had turned out. If the race had served to bring the gate-crashers and Mansour's party into harmony who was he to object? — even if Muawiya had, apparently, planned the rest of the day in some detail.

In the course of time Perry was to develop a theory about the grave crisis which occurred during the picnic at Sakkara. He would claim that it was a perfect illustration of the twentieth-century dilemma. Man was a political animal. He was also a human being. When, in one individual, these two characters came into conflict — as happened at Sakkara — the outcome was inevitably muddled. At the time Perry was too frightened and, a little later, too concerned not to make a fool of himself to think up a theoretical explanation for Muawiya's conduct. Not to appear absurd! It was becoming a guiding principle in Perry's life at the very time he found it easiest to get into absurd situations. He could think of only one person with greater talent in this respect, and that was Mary.

Fear and folly! Perhaps Sakkara, with its claustrophobic tombs and bull sarcophagi, had made its own contribution to the muddle!

By three o'clock in the afternoon there were few who still had an appetite for tombs. Lunch had been a great success. They had sat down, more or less indiscriminately, on benches at the trestle tables and any question about who was the guest of whom did not arise. The gaiety was noisy and infectious. Even a descent into the Persian Shaft was less horrifying on a full stomach. But the heated depths did their stupefying work and when the party climbed into the open once more most of them looked for sheltered spots where they could sleep in the sun or tell fortunes with playing cards. Mary claimed to tell fortunes by palmistry and was hidden from sight by the excited girls.

Muawiya lay on his belly watching Perry closely. 'It would be a shame if we missed the new tomb.'

Perry was reluctant to move. He reclined in the angle made by two huge blocks of masonry, beautifully protected from the wind which had sprung up again. The masonry served as a sun-trap and he was using his overcoat as a pillow. He did not care if he never set eyes on another Egyptian tomb. But the fact that Muawiya was giving the invitation made a certain difference.

'What d'you mean, a new tomb?'

'Not two minutes' walk. It is not open to the public. The mummy is still there.'

Perry stood up and looked round. However oddly the fellow might choose to show his regard, arranging illegal jail breaks and gate-crashing other people's picnics, he had been on his best behaviour for the last few hours; it might be an agreeable conciliatory gesture to visit a tomb in his company. Perry put his overcoat on. Mary was busy telling fortunes and the only male student in sight was asleep.

'Well, if you're sure it's not far.'

The ground hereabouts had been vigorously worked over by the archaeologists. At the bottom of deep trenches were the dark openings of burial chambers and shafts leading off, presumably, to still remoter workings. Ravines were bridged by weathered planks. The student stood in the middle of one of these planks, his red tarboosh the only strong colour among the tawny devastation, looking about and frowning. When he returned Perry said, politely, it must be difficult to find one's way among the workings. Muawiya studied the detail of their surroundings and made no answer.

'You're lost, aren't you?' said Perry bluntly.

Muawiya grunted and made off down a narrow passage which gave access to workings some twenty feet or so below ground level. A number of modern doors, secured by wooden bars, were set in the walls of the excavation as though leading to subterranean rooms. Perry knew nothing about archaeology but it seemed an unlikely spot for a newly-discovered tomb and when he complainingly joined Muawiya the student grinned, apparently to acknowledge his mistake. The wind could be heard brushing the sand over the lip of the excavation.

'You were surprised to see me today.' It was an inconsequential remark and Muawiya coughed out a laugh to see the expression on Perry's face. 'This happy day! Now we are alone for the first time! We can talk for the first time. Sir, why do you hate me?'

Perry turned and would have walked back up the passage to ground level but Muawiya caught him by the shoulder and swung him against a door.

'Sir, I am sorry to say it but I am going to kill you now with this gun.'

The door had given out a cavernous boom when Perry struck it. He listened to the sound intently with one hand gripping the wooden bar for support. Even now he could hear the reverberation pulsing away through the rock chambers. The moment of silence arrived and Perry cleared his throat, stood up and remarked uncertainly, 'I beg your pardon! What was that you said?'

The remark sounded so feeble that Perry, even at such a moment, felt shame. He was convinced that Muawiya had uttered a simple truth. Any moment now his finger would whiten over the trigger of the neat automatic pistol and Perry would die. For the first time in the history of their acquaintance he did not doubt one of Muawiya's promises. It seemed a reasonable promise. In spite of his fear (and Perry was too frightened to draw breath) he found himself acknowledging that Muawiya had some justification. On the train from Zagazig he had even given a warning which Perry had chosen to ignore. No one was to blame but Perry himself. Very well! Stand up and die!

'What was that you said?' Perry repeated the question foolishly and looked up from the blue circle of metal to Muawiya's face. The fellow had pursed his lips together; his eyes had gone dead, expressionless. Why did he not fire? The wind whispered round the excavation, a fine shower of sand fell on Perry's head.

When Waldo and the university authorities heard of his murder what would they say? At first they would be shocked. Mary would have a free first-class passage back to England (all these points occurred to Perry as he stood waiting for Muawiya to fire) but after a while they would say it served him right. Waldo would even have the pleasure of pointing out that he had vetoed the Sakkara picnic. Now look what had happened! Poor, misguided Perry! He thought he was making common cause with the students by going off on picnics and agitating over their living conditions. With what result? One of the students shot him in cold blood! The moral was clear. Always carry out the instructions of the Head of your Department!

Perry was so annoyed that he began breathing once more. Time, which had apparently stood still, now set itself in motion. Muawiya lifted the weapon to shoot him through the head. At this moment Perry's fear was not of death; he feared the way his death would make him appear ridiculous. With the creak of Waldo's laugh in his ears, Perry ducked out of the line of fire and, springing forward, seized Muawiya's right wrist. To his surprise Muawiya made no resistance until he tried to take the pistol from him, when he turned away, raising the weapon in the air. In the struggle Perry knew he was fighting a man who simply was not exerting all his strength. When, finally, he was wresting the pistol out of Muawiya's grip the right side of his face was suddenly scorched and he knew a shot had been fired. A moment later he turned, with the gun in his hand, and saw the hole drilled through the very door Muawiya had thrown him against. There was no silencer on the weapon. Then why had he heard nothing?

'Did you hear it go off?' All Perry's curiosity was directed on this acoustic freak. He was still alive. Muawiya had not shot him through the head. But a shot *had* been fired and he had not heard it. The side of his face burned. Was he suddenly deaf?

Muawiya grabbed at the pistol at the very moment figures appeared on the edge of the excavation and Perry knew from their excited shouts that he was not deaf.

'I'm all right!' He saw Mary and waved. The shot must have sounded or Mary and the students would never have heard it and come running. He was still so confused by his experience that when Mansour and two other students appeared he tried to hand the pistol back to Muawiya who did not take it but gripped him by the wrist.

'Edgar, what are you doing with that gun?'

'I'm all right.'

'Come quickly,' Muawiya shouted unexpectedly, 'Professor Perry has tried to kill himself.' He wrenched the gun out of Perry's hand and ran across the floor of the excavation to a point immediately beneath Mary. 'Here! Catch it! I saw Mr. Perry steal away and followed him. He is not safe alone. See! He tried to shoot himself.' Muawiya threw the weapon out of the pit and the women students, who had now arrived, gave dramatic gasps of horror as they saw it sail through the air.

'I caught his hand.' Muawiya began a serious speech but

only the girls remained to listen. Mansour was already at Perry's side. One of the girls began screaming. Mary rushed down the passageway and had to force a way through the excited crowd. Mansour saw her coming and shouted for the students to make way but they were so worked up that they ignored him. He pushed them back, yelling angrily, 'Let Mrs. Perry come.'

'Oh, let me get to him.' Mary struck out with her fists.

When finally she broke into the space Mansour had succeeded in clearing Perry was leaning against the door and apparently sweating from one side of his face. The right hand side was scorched. He had lost his right eyebrow but his spectacles — which were undamaged — had protected his eyelashes and the eye itself. Across his cheek lay a brick-red stain. Everywhere but on the stain itself his face was bathed in sweat.

'Well, Edgar, I never expected anything quite so stupid, I must say.' Mary gently removed the spectacles and wiped his face with her handkerchief. 'I really had no idea I meant so much to you.'

Perry wished for silence and solitude. He would have liked to walk into the desert until he came to some remote, airy and well-constructed tomb where he could sit and arrange his thoughts. But silence and solitude were out of the question. He walked up the passage into the sunlight, supported on the one side by Mary and followed by students who shouted reassurances to the waiting girls. Muawiya himself came forward with a great show of solicitude and took his right arm. Perry made no resistance. He saw that the fellow had recovered the pistol and was flashing it in the sun.

The two asses were brought. Rumour had it that the Cairo train left Badreshein at five o'clock so the time had come, in any case, for them to start on their return journey. Perry found himself mounted on one ass with Muawiya trotting at his side and giving out, to the whole posse of students, vivid details of the way he had saved the professor's life. No doubt it was a form of mockery. But Perry was less provoked by Muawiya's imagination than by Mary's solicitude. Whenever he glanced in her direction he saw that she was regarding him with a brooding, maternal warmth which made him want to dig his heels into the ass's side and gallop madly ahead. How dare she think he would kill himself! And on her account!

As it was he urged his animal over the edge of the track and down a steepish incline which would cut their journey by a quarter of a mile. With a cry of alarm Mary followed suit. The two asses wisely slid part of the way on their haunches, raising billows of dust, and kicking out madly once they reached level ground. Mary had fallen off as soon as her mount sat down but Perry was still clasping the neck of his beast when it began kicking and braying. The girls ran to Mary's help but she waved them aside and slid through the dust calling, 'Edgar! Where are you? Are you hurt?'

Perry sat up and watched the two asses trot away in the direction of the Nile. Miraculously his glasses were unbroken and as he gazed through the fug, not really caring whether he was riding or sitting, it occurred to him that the longer he postponed telling the truth about Muawiya the more difficult it would be to convince anyone. Mary, for instance. Then why not tell the truth now?

Gripping him under the arms, someone hoisted him to his feet and began beating the dust out of his clothes with open-handed slaps that made him stagger. He made out the frowning, anxious face of Muawiya.

'Sir, you lay there and for one moment I thought you were hurt. Thank God you can stand up!'

'You murderous, sarcastic — ! Where's that gun? Give it to

me at once.' Perry would have made a serious attempt to
choke him but that Mary and the rest of the students were
coming down fast; if he attacked Muawiya they might wonder
why. They might ask questions. Mary, in particular, would be
insatiably curious. And before he could take a grip on himself
he would be confessing the truth. If it came to choosing between his evidence and Muawiya's the courts would inevitably
choose his. Besides, the gun could be traced and Muawiya,
or one of his friends, proved to be its rightful owner. He
would be jailed for fifteen years. This was a long time for so
incompetent an assassin! Thoughts rapidly clicked into
significant position.

Perry's jaw was rigid with anger. This enabled him to speak
fiercely and yet remain inaudible to anyone but Muawiya.
'How dare you say I was trying to shoot myself! I've never been
so insulted in my life!'

'I didn't mean to insult you! I meant to kill you!'

'Why? Damn it all, I've a right to know why.'

'The fact remains — I could have killed you easily. You are
not such a fool to think you stopped me by yourself. Here is
the gun if you want it.'

'No, don't give it back to him!' Mary was upon them.
Attended by Mansour and Boghos she loomed through the fog
of dust and tried to snatch the gun from Muawiya's hand. But
he put it back in his overcoat pocket. He bent a little, looked at
Mary sadly, opened his mouth as though to speak, changed his
mind and walked briskly away. Everyone watched him in
silence.

'He was crying too,' said Boghos. 'It is very funny. He is
crying just like Professor Perry when he was looking at the
statue of Rameses.'

'Muawiya!' Perry hastened in pursuit. The student looked
back and quickened his pace. He was walking due south, a

direction that would bring him to nowhere in particular. 'Muawiya, for heaven's sake stop!'

'What do you want?' He paused until Perry came up to him. 'The gun.'

Muawiya was crying, wrinkling up his face like a monkey. He produced the gun, handed it over, and with no further word continued on his way. Perry slipped it into his pocket and walked back to the rest of the party.

'I don't want you to talk about this. It's the end of the matter as far as you're concerned, d'you understand? I want you to forget this — this picnic at Sakkara. Now let's make for Badreshein.'

'But what about Muawiya?'

'What about the asses?'

The sun had lowered sufficiently to cast long shadows and make the landscape look solid once more. The western slopes of desert and heaped masonry were quite red. Distant cultivation, berseem and palm and the lines of casuarina settled into a smoky blue which became heavier as they walked forward. And it was clean and calm — calm to the point of sleep. To Perry's eye the countryside had been washed over. If rain were not quite out of the question he would have thought a shower had washed the dust out of the air, and from the distant trees and the cultivated acres.

The burn on his face tickled fiercely. The asses were caught and the girls took it in turns to ride. No one spoke. Mary took his arm and pressed it understandingly as they walked. At the first canal he was tempted to take the gun from his pocket and throw it into the water. But he reflected that one of the students would certainly come back later and recover it; and what was more his action would be misinterpreted. They would think he was making a gesture to show repentance.

'How do you feel now, darling?'

It was the first time she had called him darling since her arrival. If he was not a repentant suicide what was he? The difficulty of thinking up some other role defeated him. Between them, Mary and Muawiya had made truth almost out of the question.

❂ 6 ❂
❂

THE OFFICIAL RESPONSE

The Princess and the Pasha had been married for ten years. Now that she was seventy she doubted whether she would marry again. The present arrangement had worked much better than anyone could have foreseen at the time of the marriage — Tureiya a mere thirty-five, unusually handsome, with a private fortune that was overshadowed by hers but large enough to increase the difficulty of bringing him to heel if he showed independence. Yet discipline had never been necessary. After a while they had fallen in love. It was quite unexpected and it went on and on, this warm, autumnal flush of feeling that made them write to each other if they were separated only for a day. The Princess had her own explanation for their success: in the first place, she had grown old and unadventurous and, in the second, she and Tureiya had complementary characters. Whereas she was all fire and imagination her husband had the practical instincts of a Greek grocer.

With this theory in mind she frequently gave way to Tureiya on matters of small importance, such as encouraging Perry to prepare his Gizeh report, and cracked down on a scheme to switch one of their Delta estates from cotton to sugar. It was all a matter of scale. The larger a problem the more poetical were the considerations involved; the more, that is to say, she dealt with it herself. Perry was simply not in this class of problem. Perry and poetry were at opposite poles. So, when her husband decided that Perry was irresponsible to the point of real lunacy and would probably involve them in political embarrassment if encouraged, Her Highness agreed on his dismissal.

The Pasha had made an observation of compelling astuteness: 'Monsieur Perry is a fanatic. I can see that he is the sort of man who prepares a report and then thinks it ought to be carried out.'

'What is more,' said the Princess, 'he is a natural cuckold.'

They were in agreement, then, about Perry's dismissal but the Pasha had no wish to upset him with the bad news. He could have given him his *congé* over the telephone, when Perry was proffering thanks for his supposed intervention at the Abdin police station. For the decision had already been made. But this would have been too cruel! And a letter of dismissal? One had only to think of one's emotions on opening a letter containing bad news. Much better to give the guards instructions that the next time M. Perry presented himself at the Palace he was to be turned away. His rejection would appear, somehow, an act of nature. It would be like a storm. And who caused storms? If M. Perry were impious enough to challenge God himself then he would be unworthy of the delicate considerations which were now governing the Pasha's actions. But M. Perry was not an atheist. He would see that we were all instruments in the hands of Destiny. He would suffer no shock and he would bear no rancour. To be on the safe side the operator at the Palace switchboard was told to snub him if ever he rang up.

Quite a different situation was created by the news that Perry had tried to kill himself.

Tureiya was near Tel el-Kebir at the time, shooting duck in the marshes. With his help there would have been a similar result but because the Princess had to act alone the result was brought about more quickly. The Pasha would have seen immediately that he was, so to speak, in charge of the Perry situation. He would have given advice and this advice would have led them into tortuous courses. He would have wanted a full-dress debate. He would have consulted the secretaries. He would have appealed to friends for counsel. And finally, no doubt, he would have told a secretary to telephone Professor Perry's apartment. Lacking the benefit of her husband's guidance the Princess telephoned as soon as the crisis arose.

'Ask him,' she said to Afifi, 'what in God's name he has done with my story.'

Publication day for the first number of the feminist magazine was a month away and two young women, Vice-Presidents of 'The Daughters of the Nile' organization, had pasted proof copy into the spacious dummy all morning. Here was the editorial in French, Arabic and English. Here was the portrait of the Editor in her diamonds. Here were the photographs of the jewelled handbags from the Editor's collection. And here was the article on 'Cleopatra, Stateswoman and Patriot' which the Editor had been moved to write at the last moment. But where was the English translation of the most important item of all: the pathetic story of the Pharaoh Amenhotep and his little concubine? The pearl earrings of the Vice-Presidents swung in agitation over the scissors and paste.

'Who knows?' said the Princess. 'He may have destroyed it in his passion. He is always tearing things up.' She listened on an extension while Afifi spoke from another room.

Since the picnic at Sakkara, Mary had lived in a world where colours were brighter and music — the weird music from the radio in the barber's on the corner — more dramatic. Suddenly her life had been lifted on to another plane: the plane of art. Edgar's breakfast of cereal and fried eggs had possessed the heightening of tragedy — he had left one egg and read the morning paper in silence. When he set out for the English

Library she kissed him so passionately that she cut a lip on his teeth. He had an aura. Like a hero of classical antiquity he lived in a world of histrionic irony where other people knew more about his situation than he knew himself. For example, Mrs. Curtis knew what happened at Sakkara. And Mary knew that she had no lover. But of both these facts — and of an even more important third — Edgar was ignorant and his ignorance gave poignancy to the way he ate his breakfast eggs under the steady gaze of the two women. No, it was not ignorance! That was the wrong word. It was innocence, a noble innocence.

Mary had let Mrs. Curtis into the secret, in spite of Edgar's instructions, because she felt she had to confide in someone or doubt that the shooting incident had ever taken place. Was it money? When Mrs. Curtis learned there was no money trouble she was doubly shocked. Men had shot themselves before now because of money trouble and no one thought any the worse of them. But the poor man must be off his head if he took the Egyptians so seriously he allowed anything they did or said to upset him. Mary had smiled at this interpretation of Edgar's behaviour and explained there had been a lovers' tiff. But there was no cause for alarm. Mrs. Curtis need not worry that Edgar would make a second attempt. Mary had paid a visit to the gynaecologist at the Anglo-American Hospital and when she told Edgar she was pregnant a reconciliation would naturally follow. This was the third fact of which he was ignorant.

'Mr. Perry is not here,' she said into the telephone. 'Who is that speaking?'

Afifi explained he was speaking from the Palace of Her Highness who required the immediate delivery of a certain translation. If Mr. Perry was not there he must be found.

Mary put the receiver down with a bang. In her mind she

was once more outside the closed Palace gates with the silent guards whirring their staves round Edgar's head. How could she possibly express the indignation she felt? It was clearly of no avail to lose her temper with an underling. And, to be quite honest, so much had happened since the rebuff that Mary required time to work up the anger that loyalty to Edgar required. More time, anyway, than Afifi was prepared to give her.

'I do not intend worrying Mr. Perry just now,' she said when the telephone rang once more. 'He has more important matters to think about.'

Afifi breathed heavily. He was clearly at a loss to imagine a matter of greater importance to Professor Perry than the Princess's translation. When the voice of the Princess herself cut in on the breathing it showed a natural impatience with Afifi for not saying so.

'What matters, Mrs. Perry?' said the old voice, wiry with rage.

'Oh, Your Highness!' Mary was so startled by this illustrious intervention (she had forgotten the Princess's habit of listening on an extension) that she blurted out what she thought was the truth. 'He tried to shoot himself.'

'Get off the line, Afifi.' The Princess spoke in a more agreeable tone. There was a rattle as the secretary replaced his receiver and the Princess continued. '*Tried* to shoot himself? Was the weapon not in good working order?'

Mary felt herself relaxing with pleasure. The Princess was the one person capable of appreciating the confused splendour of her situation. The setting was irradiated by her interest. Shadows were deepened and beauties enhanced. Colour flooded in. Until the Princess spoke Mary had not realized how much her drama depended on the quality of the audience. The Princess asked when and where and was there any chance he had been bluffing. Until that moment Mary knew that she and Edgar had been playing to bare boards. The Princess did not inquire why Edgar should have wanted to shoot himself. Her voice brimmed with assumptions that stirred Mary like round after round of appreciative applause.

'Mrs. Perry, I am sending a car for you immediately. Poor child! Come as you are! This is a matter on which you will need to unburden yourself. You will find me alone. No one will disturb our tête-à-tête. Put on your prettiest dress. At times like this one needs to know one is looking one's best.'

'But he's only gone to the library. He'll be back for lunch.'

'Then we have an hour and a half. In any case I do not suppose he is at the library. He is probably drinking somewhere. They always do.'

The car arrived so promptly that Mary was still dressing. The Sudanese stood in Mrs. Curtis's 'saloon' twirling his flat cap and whistling through his teeth, much to Hassan's admiration. At the sight of the boy, goggling round the kitchen door, Mary hesitated and then said, 'If Mr. Perry is back before me say I've taken his translation to the Princess and I shall be home for lunch.' The translation, duly completed, had been discovered in the desk. Even with suicide in his heart Edgar was punctilious and as she sank into the cushions of the Rolls she imagined him patting the envelope with the bleak but noble thought that it would pay her passage home.

Poor dear! The Palace walls, the same blue-smocked guards at the gates, the single dead-looking palm, so lately the scene of Edgar's humiliation now served only to intensify her compassion. Perhaps he would be angry with her for coming to the Palace. At the mere lifting of the Princess's finger she had come running! Edgar would have every justification for being cross with her. A helplessness fell upon her. As the limousine entered the Palace gates she understood, for the first time, the extent of her treachery. And yet, even Edgar would surely wish the Princess to have her translation! This was no comfort. She could not deceive herself. The wifely course of action would have been to tell the secretary to fetch the translation himself. The chauffeur opened the car door and she walked up the marble steps into the vast hall of statues, monsters in bronze and porcelain, thinking that if she burst into tears the Princess would despise her. Let me not cry! Dear God, she thought, let me not cry now!

The Princess rose from her divan as soon as Mary was ushered into her presence. Her blue-tinted hair was piled high and she wore a curious, silky gown in old gold which began at her throat in a Russian-style collar and flowed copiously to the hem of green zodiacal figures and so swept the carpet. Her tiny red slippers peeped from beneath.

'This morning,' said the Princess, 'I am a mother to you, my dear.' She approached Mary lifting her arms, so that the full sleeves fell back and revealed the weight of bracelets on her wrist. 'Come and sit with me. I was working on my magazine, but this is more interesting. I dismissed my assistants. Oh, now please don't protest — ' Her thin face was flushed with merriment.

'Why did you have my husband insulted the other day?'

'Insulted?'

'When he arrived to give the Pasha a lesson the guards turned him away.'

'But he didn't try to kill himself because of that. Eh? No, I thought not. Did the guards beat him? No. Well, it is all of no consequence. For myself I do not know why he was turned away. It was a matter between the men. I will find out if you wish.' The Princess drew Mary down beside her on the divan. 'Do not stiffen yourself so! After all, just think, perhaps my husband was being rude. He has no manners. I apologize on his behalf. Now, you see, the matter is closed and I forbid you to mention it again.' She looked keenly into Mary's face. 'So, you have broken your husband's spirit!'

'Oh no. Don't say that. He loves me.'

'It is the same thing.'

Any danger that Mary might begin weeping had now passed.

'You are quite sure,' asked the Princess, 'that it was not a trick? Saved by a student, and in a mummy pit from what you tell me! Remarkable! How many women can say their husbands have shot themselves for love? Their husbands, mark you! Not lovers! In my own life even the lovers tried to shoot each other, not themselves! As for my husbands! Can you imagine Tureiya shooting himself in a mummy pit? Poor little man, he might! I think I should be too old, if he did, to be anything but sorry. But you! You! ' said the Princess, almost girlish in her excitement, 'You are young and you have your triumph! Do not weaken! Do not let him drag you back out of pity! You come from England! You dismiss your husband! He shoots himself! You go home and marry your lover! See in this mirror!' The Princess picked up a hand-mirror and held it, in a trembling grip, before Mary's eyes. 'Dear, you are like a rose! You glow! You are perfection!'

Mary took the mirror and studied herself. The Princess was right. This morning her eyes had a clearness and her complexion a radiance which spoke back at her from the glass. She looked in silence, as though at the features of a stranger, and returned the mirror to the Princess with a smile.

'I'm going to have a baby.'

The Princess stood up. 'Extraordinary! Does your husband know? But of course he does. That was why he tried to shoot himself. Cuckold's courage! But you have been audacious!'

Mary jumped to her feet and followed the Princess to the centre of the room where she was bending over a specimen case.

Mary was about to speak when her eyes fell on the contents of the case, the largest and most brilliant butterflies she had ever seen. For a moment she had the illusion that the jewelled wings were in motion but this was only a trick of the surprised eyes.

The Princess touched the glass with a finger. 'What do you think? This monster with the orange in his wings. Are they not beautiful? Why are you angry with me again?'

Mary looked from the butterflies to the green and brown fleck of the Princess's eyes. 'The father of my baby is naturally my husband.'

'But this is ruin! What are you saying? Your lover in England — '

'There *is* no lover in England. How dare you suggest anything so wicked? First you insult Edgar and then you insult me! How dare you, I say!' Mary smacked the specimen case so violently with the flat of her hand that the Princess stepped back out of flying splinter range.

'No lover, Mrs. Perry. Do you mean you lied to me?'

The glass of the specimen case was too thick to be broken even by the heavy blows that Mary was now delivering with clenched fist.

'You talk as if I were a prostitute.'

A blue-gowned woman attendant appeared in the doorway, obviously horrified, but the Princess dismissed her with a wave of the hand. 'Do you seriously mean to tell me, Mrs. Perry, that you have *never* had a lover? I'm sorry to upset you but what are you saying? *Never*? I am old. I no longer understand the world. Everything changes. Nothing is constant. See, now you have upset *me*! No lover! All invented! What can one say? Why should she say she had a lover if she hadn't a lover? But no, she must not answer! Who knows what other horrors she might reveal?'

The Princess caught hold of a chair and was about to lower

herself to the divan when Mary came to help her. The Princess looked at her as though she had forgotten her existence. 'Why play your joke on me, Mrs. Perry? Your husband — yes, I can understand. But me? Why should you lie to me?' She folded her legs beneath her and sat with a straight back. 'Perhaps it was not a lie. Perhaps you deceived yourself too?'

Mary was calm again. She stood, looking down into the Princess's brown eyes. 'Yes, I deceived myself too. You are right, Your Highness.'

For perhaps a minute the thin, pale face was stiff with speculation. 'Come,' she said at last, smiling to inspire courage. 'Sit down with me. We have met late in life. Let us talk no more about it. You are forgiven. If you had been presented to me in your youth! But we will not talk about it. Do not despair! I promise you there is hope. After the birth of your baby you will have more poise. You will be beautiful. A new start in life will be very possible. Courage! Sit quietly for a while and strength will come back to you.'

Tureiya was so discomposed by the news that he was still wearing his knickerbocker hunting suit at dinner time and was rebuked by the Princess in front of Swain the butler. He had shot fourteen brace of duck at dawn, sent the finest to His Majesty, eaten well, slept all the afternoon in a houseboat and been praised by the Princess for leading a manly, outdoor life. Oddly enough, he did not look on Perry's reported act as further evidence of his insanity. Judging by the way she told of Mary's visit Her Highness appeared quite satisfied with the way matters had turned out and, taking his cue from her, Tureiya was prepared to indulge his most generous feelings.

In Professor Perry he immediately saw the victim of frustrated idealism. He was not unlike Perry himself. They were both men of vision. But whereas he, Tureiya, had patience and saw through the immediate difficulties to the more glorious future the poor professor had quickly lost heart. Thrown into prison, abandoned by those who had encouraged him, even — so the Dean had written to say — forbidden to continue with his report on the students, Professor Perry had taken a gun from his pocket, put it to his temple, pulled the trigger and — ? Then what had happened?

In the act of slipping into the dress jacket which the valet held out for him the Pasha paused. Her Highness had not told him precisely why Perry's suicide had failed. Tureiya had always had a secret, horrified interest in suicide and he tried to imagine what could possibly have gone amiss. The weapon jammed? But no, quite obviously, someone must have stopped him; otherwise, how would the news have leaked out? One did not say, 'I tried to shoot myself but failed.' Tureiya felt cold at the very thought of putting a gun to one's head. No matter what happened to him he would never have the courage to do it. Never! He was a coward. Very well, he was a coward! Seeing that the valet was still waiting he pretended he had been considering his diamond cuff-links. He ordered them to be changed for jet; he said they would be more in keeping.

He determined to get in touch with Perry if only to ask, 'When you pulled the trigger, tell me: what did you think about?' Throughout dinner, where the guests were the previous Prime Minister but one and his wife, Tureiya tried to think of some way of arranging a meeting with Perry where he could surprise him. He wanted to confront Perry without the slightest warning, put his question and receive the unprepared answer. In this way Tureiya believed he would hear the truth. It was not a bit of good giving the man time to think of something poetical.

The telephone was probably as good a method as any. But Tureiya wanted to see the expression on Perry's face; he wanted to see the eyes. How could you know a man was not lying if you did not see his face? And even the telephone did not confer absolute surprise. It was impossible for Tureiya actually to dial Perry's number himself; a secretary would have to do this and make the necessary announcement to whoever answered at the other end. Even if that person were Perry he would, therefore, have a warning. And if it were someone else he might have minutes in which to prepare himself. There was also the possibility he would refuse to answer. Her Highness had hinted Perry was displeased by the manner of his dismissal.

The Princess! Tureiya looked down the table and saw that his wife was unusually lively. She was too far away for him to hear what she was saying but judging by the way the ex-Prime Minister was covering his face with his napkin it could not fail to be exceedingly witty. Tureiya saw the contrast he made with her. She was rational, like a man; she had intellect and wit. He, on the other hand, was in some ways more like a woman. He was ruled by his heart; and above all he had imagination! The Princess was probably telling Perry's story and making a joke out of it whereas he, Tureiya, could only too easily imagine himself in the poor man's place and tremble. He wanted dinner to be over as quickly as possible so that he could, in private, question the Princess more closely. Now he could hear what she said. The Pasha's immediate neighbours had fallen silent. But why was she speaking about Mme Perry? Why was Mme Perry of such interest? Even in telling Tureiya of the Perry adventure Her Highness had appeared to dwell with peculiar satisfaction on the situation of Mme Perry. She had said she proposed making a real friend of Mme Perry.

An idea struck Tureiya with such violence that he was scarcely able to check a cry and the Princess looked along the table with a quick smile, thinking he had laughed. To cover up he began describing his duck hunting adventures in a loud voice. No sooner had the ladies withdrawn than Tureiya made his apologies to the ex-Prime Minister and instructed the secretary-on-duty to get the Dean of the Faculty of Arts on the telephone. He would take the call in the library. Yet, delighted as he was with his scheme for surprising M. Perry, he thought it prudent to make no mention of the matter to the Princess. Possibly she would point out some powerful objection and in his present excitement he did not wish to know of an objection even if it existed. He saw himself rushing out on M. Perry, from behind a screen, say, and putting the vital question with such force that M. Perry would *have* to answer with complete candour. 'Tell me,' he imagined himself saying as he stared into Perry's eyes, '*exactly* what was in your mind when you pulled the trigger.'

Yet the actual encounter was very different. After some discussion the Dean agreed to telephone Perry and ask him to appear at his house in Dokki the following morning at eleven o'clock, no matter what his other commitments were. If Perry had to cut a lecture he, Abbas, would explain to Professor Grimbley when he saw him. The present matter was of an importance transcending ordinary Faculty routine. But what was the present matter? Here the Pasha laughed and became conspiratorial. If he was concealing it from the Princess what could be more natural than his desire to keep Abbas in the dark too. He said so. Secrecy was essential. The dish was seasoned by it.

His eagerness was such that when the Rolls drew up before Abbas's house the next morning at 10.45 he had raised his hand as though to open the door without waiting for the chauffeur. The hand rose but did not fall; it became a gesture of greeting for Abbas himself, who, backed by the gardener in a clean gown and crimson sash, came down the steps and seized the handle for Tureiya to emerge into the sunshine with his cane and his yellow gloves and his English-cut suit of sporty brown overcheck.

'Abbas Bey! I must be concealed! The car behind the house! All is arranged? He is coming?'

The Dean ushered the Pasha up the steps and into the sparsely furnished *salon* where he had received Grimbley, the Perrys and two students on a previous occasion which naturally came to his mind. 'It is a p-pleasure to see you in my house, Your Excellency. But there is no need for me to say that. Now, before Professor Perry arrives no doubt you will wish to tell me what lies behind this m-meeting.'

The Dean spoke in Arabic and the Pasha replied in French.

'Not now, Abbas Bey. My advantage will be lost if I explain. Imagine the scene. I shall come out of that door there. You will be holding M. Perry in conversation here. I shall confront him. Thus! Then, you will see. It is quite extraordinary, I promise you.'

They sat on the gilt and red velvet chairs sipping coffee.

'Excellency, forgive me. F-forgive me, I say. I c-cannot agree to this. I owe it to my position. I am Dean, you understand.'

The Pasha set down his cup and laughed excitedly. 'Abbas Bey, you will never forget this day. Suddenly I shall throw open that door and advance on him.'

'Excellency, no!' Abbas el-Hakim wrinkled up his face. 'Y-you will never forgive me but as Dean I must insist that I know everything in advance. You must tell me now what you are going to accuse Professor Perry of.'

Abbas spoke with dignity and a wholly unexpected force.

Tureiya was amazed. He could not believe that the Dean did not wish to take part in the wonderful game he was preparing. 'I? Accuse M. Perry! No! Very well, I tell you. This is your house. I am your guest. Listen! Professor Perry has tried to kill himself with a gun!'

'What are you saying?'

'With a gun! He put it to his head. He pulled the trigger. Click! Nothing happened. He put the gun down. A friend seized it. Now, tell me! What was in M. Perry's mind when he heard that click?'

Abbas pulled a handkerchief from his pocket and wiped his face. He did not know the Pasha well. Until that morning their dealings had been limited to a few chance encounters at the Mohamed Ali club and, of course, to the matter of Perry's appointment as the Pasha's English tutor. Abbas could not guess what political move he was now making. As yet, the matter was most obscure. But, depend upon it, a political move of sorts it would certainly turn out to be. Abbas was too wary to be caught easily.

'Are you certain of this, Excellency? How do you know?'

'The Princess has taken Mrs. Perry under her protection. But he will be here at any moment. Abbas Bey, I beg your permission to withdraw.'

He stood up but Abbas clung to his arm and insisted on knowing just why it was important to surprise Perry.

'But Excellency,' he said when Tureiya had explained the stratagem. 'This is bad psychology! If you wish to draw the truth from him you must not appear suddenly. He will suspect a plot. In any case he will be dumbfounded. Much better to win his confidence, draw him out, and then put your question in the scientific way. I mean coolly; without excitement.'

Abbas expressed his suspicion of Tureiya's motives by doing his best to frustrate the tableau Tureiya was working for. He could scarcely forbid it. He could at least pose as a rational man.

'Abbas Bey, you are right!' Tureiya was immediately convinced. 'That is just what the Princess would have said. Why do I receive good advice so late? No one advises me. My secretary is a fool. M. Perry is a nervous man. Of course, he would be dumb with surprise. As for winning his confidence, there is no need for that. M. Perry and I are men of the same stamp and between us there is a natural confidence quite different from — from — ' His eyes protruded somewhat and now they glistened with satisfaction. He could not think of a word to describe the kind of confidence possible between ordinary men (inferior to the confidence between Perry and himself) but at least he would know what to say to Perry when he arrived.

'Your Excellency is most kind,' said Abbas in a neutral tone. He was standing at the window and had been watching Perry pay off his taxi and walk up the gravel drive to the house in what he diagnosed as an incurious frame of mind. Perry was obviously not wondering why the Dean should summon him to his private house. He looked at the gravel and, when he came to them, the steps. But he did not raise his eyes. He walked slackly and was, Abbas surmised, in a mood to continue the suicide attempt at the point where he left off. Abbas was touched. He went into the hall to meet Perry, held his right hand and said in little more than a whisper, 'Tureiya Pasha is here. We know everything and you must not worry. We want you to know that you are among friends.'

At this revelation Perry swung his head awkwardly. For the first time Abbas saw the right side of his face where his cheek still bore a red smudge and he wore sticking plaster on his eyebrow.

' — the Pasha!' he said loudly. Remembering that this word had never been mentioned in their English lessons he said the only rude word in French he could think of. '*Merde!* I wish no disrespect to you, Mr. Dean.'

The Dean had heard the English word at Cambridge and was glad he had dissuaded the Pasha from making a surprise entry.

'M. Perry,' said the Pasha cordially. He had heard all and now came forward to take Perry's arm and conduct him to one of the red velvet and gilt chairs in the *salon*. He spoke in French. 'You and I understand one another. I understand your anger. That surprises you, but it is true. I will tell you something. We are men in the same mould!'

Perry asked Abbas what he had meant by saying that he knew everything.

'We know', said the Pasha, 'what happened at Sakkara.'

'How do you know?'

The Pasha frowned. The interview was not going to plan. 'Certainly it is not in the newspapers. But in Egypt there are no secrets. Everyone is outspoken.'

Perry refused the coffee the gardener was offering to him. 'And what did happen at Sakkara?'

'What happened at Sakkara? You had a gun and you tried to shoot yourself. Now I can see that you are wounded. So the gun was fired. It was knocked from your hand. That is what happened. Yes?'

During the silence the gardener blew his nose loudly.

'Yes,' said Perry.

The Pasha showed an open hand as a sign of frankness. 'I am your friend. Have confidence in me. As soon as I heard this news I was stirred to tears. M. Perry, there are few men in this world capable of understanding you but I am one of them. I resolved to give you a message of good cheer. Idealists, like you and me, must not be discouraged. The world progresses, even poor Egypt progresses, because idealists are not discouraged. We must press on.'

'What was the name of the person who took the gun from you?' said Abbas.

'Muawiya Khaslat.'

'This is of no importance,' said Tureiya, almost gaily. 'Now tell me, M. Perry — for it would give me the greatest pleasure to know, and I put the question in the interest of science — what was in your mind when you pulled the trigger?'

'I don't want to discuss it.'

'This is important knowledge about the human mind. Why do you not trust me?'

'It isn't a question of trust. I just don't wish to discuss the matter.'

'You see,' said Tureiya to the Dean, 'you advised me wrongly. He will not answer me. He is too bitter. I understand his bitterness; I share it; the world is a bad place. But he ought to answer me. Don't you see, I am so *curious* to know.'

The pitch of Perry's voice rose with his anger. 'You are not bitter and you don't understand. It matters damn all to you that I really believed there was some chance of building that hostel.'

Tureiya looked at the Dean. 'I do not understand. What is he saying?'

'Excellency, M. Perry is clearly very excited.' The Dean spoke in Arabic. 'I do not think it proper for you to stay. He is not in a fit condition to discuss his experience.'

'What did he think?' The Pasha clasped his hands. 'That is all I ask to know. Perhaps he thought of his wife. And that is another thing. You would think he would wait at least until his child is born.'

Perry looked squarely at Tureiya for the first time.

'What child?'

There were tears of mortification in the Pasha's eyes. Because of the Dean's stupidity he had failed to extract the information which had seemed so precious to him and there was no way of knowing when such an opportunity would present it again. Suicide was rare in Egypt. It was a European custom. Although Perry repeated the question and would have prevented the Pasha from leaving the room if Abbas had not pushed him to one side, communication between the two had broken down. Disappointment made Tureiya aware only of himself. He scarcely knew where he was or why he was there. Abbas piloted him through the door and down the steps while the gardener ran to warn the chauffeur.

'When the sun shines,' he said to Abbas in parting, 'one is warm and happy. One is like a child. In spite of everything, why should a man *want* to die?'

The gardener took it for granted that his house duties were over. He replaced his tarboosh with a felt skull cap and tucked his robe into his loosely-fitting drawers. Under the banana fronds there was, apparently, a tap; for at that point he bent down and a lawn sprinkler began revolving in the middle of the coarse-looking grass. A rainbow rose and fell. A dry tang was beaten out of the ground as though it were a threshing floor being damped down for sweeping.

Abbas stood at the open window, rebuking the gardener and saying that coffee must be brought for his remaining guest. The gardener had found another tap and an artificial rivulet was flowing through black earth. He squelched about, barefooted.

'Hamed!' Abbas called patiently. 'Hamed!'

At last the gardener heard him and ran off to the kitchen. Abbas swung one of the shutters over to exclude some of the sunlight.

'Mr. Perry!' He sat so near to Perry that their knees almost touched. 'I suggest that you did not attempt suicide. I suggest that Muawiya Khaslat tried to murder you and you fought him off.'

They sat in silence until a boy of about fifteen — not the gardener — brought in a tray with a glass of water and a cup of coffee which, this time, Perry did not refuse. He drank until he could feel the grounds between his teeth. He sipped water and thanked the boy quietly.

'Why should you think that?'

Abbas shrugged. 'Well, it is more reasonable.'

'Reasonable? What do you make of a fellow who saves me from being beaten up? Later on he helps me out of jail. Then he shoots me. As Dean of the Faculty of Arts what is your attitude to a man who behaves like that?'

Abbas produced a packet of English cigarettes and they both smoked. Abbas held his cigarette down, between his fingers, so that the blue smoke met round his wrist. 'As Dean of the Faculty of Arts I am an Egyptian and I say nothing about it. N-nothing at all! You understand me?' He flicked ash on to the carpet and drew deeply on the cigarette. 'He tried to kill you?'

'He didn't try very hard.'

'He likes you! Why should he try very hard?' Abbas walked to the window and breathed smoke into the sunshine. 'But you are not like me. You do not live in an occupied country. You are one of the occupiers. It is mysterious to me why you do not denounce Khaslat. He would be d-dealt with — most severely.'

'Have you thought,' he went on, when Perry did not reply, 'what it will be like to have a student under you who has tried to murder you? All the other students will know it too. After a while he will tell them. His pride will demand it.'

'He didn't pull it off. What's there to be proud of in that?'

Abbas shook his head impatiently. 'After some time pride will drive him to try again. And then he would not be at all sentimental about it.'

'You make me wonder,' said Perry ironically, 'what the teachers' trade union would have to say about this situation.'

Abbas chuckled. 'Or the British Council.'

'I mean about a Faculty dean who thought one of his students sentimental for not making a good job of shooting the English professor.'

'That is just what I had in mind, Mr. Perry.'

They listened to the buzz of flies and, outside in the garden, the sound of pulpy vegetation being cleared. Whenever their eyes met Abbas smiled. He appeared in no hurry to bring the meeting to an end. Winkling the truth out of Perry brought him as much satisfaction as backing a horse at long odds — mainly because it confirmed his belief that he was shrewder than most. He knew, too, that Perry liked his frankness.

Perry stood up. 'I've a lecture at twelve.'

'I'll drive you myself. I have to go to the university.'

Abbas called his farewells to the silent house — his wife was, no doubt, somewhere in the background — and led the way down the steps. The car had been standing in the sun and the leather seats were hot to the touch. Perry sat back and closed his eyes, hoping that Abbas would have nothing further to say. Tureiya Pasha's mention of an unborn child had shaken him far more than the Dean's penetration.

They took the road along the Nile. Abbas drove slowly, as though they were out for the air.

They passed the English Bridge before he spoke. 'I wonder whether I ought to advise you to resign and leave the country. In your own interest. For safety. Could you find a post in England?'

Perry, with eyes still closed, was savouring the river air. 'I beg you not to be alarmed on my account, Mr. Dean.'

He could feel the car accelerating and, as the sun had left his face, knew they had turned by the French Embassy and were travelling up one of the avenues that led, eventually, to the university. In his mind's eye he saw the silvery, rather impressive dome bearing down on them. To the left were the

Zoological Gardens with the pessimistic cranes and Muawiya walking away from him with a split coat. On the right, the Botanical Gardens with the hooligans from Al Azhar and the ever-present Muawiya dragging him under a bush and swearing he was a Frenchman. Was it imagination? Or did he really hear the cry of the mob even now?

'I'm not going to be frightened out of Egypt by anyone.' He sat up and opened his eyes. 'In any case, Muawiya's had his one and only. He makes a pretty poor assassin.'

They were not at the point he had imagined. The Botanical Gardens were on the left and the shouting came from the right, from the grounds of the university itself. As the car swept round to the gates Perry glimpsed a splutter of red tarbooshes through the railings and heard the Dean exclaim that they were undoubtedly Arts students; otherwise they would have been on the far side of the quadrangle, on the steps of the Faculty of Law. There was sufficient colouring in his voice to convey the pleasure he felt that for once his own students were taking the lead.

'And there goes the head of his department Professor Waldo Grimbley,' he said sonorously, 'being treated with no respect.'

'Waldo? Where?'

'Straight ahead. With a brief case. There! Didn't you see that strong young man give him a push?'

As yet fifty or so students were not a mob. No one was sitting on a comrade's shoulders to cry slogans. They were a loosely knit, but hostile little crowd, shouting, 'Professor Perree, Libertee!'

Waldo walked, with shoulders back, undeviatingly towards the Faculty steps, contriving the impression that he had not noticed his mockers. His outer garment was a loosely fitting cloak — an Egyptian *abayeh* — which added to the impression that he was some predatory but noble bird being mobbed by choughs. Suddenly he broke into a run and the students would have run with him had they not noticed the Dean's car with Perry inside it. They crowded round clapping and grinning. Some booed the Dean.

'Assassin!' they called after him as he walked up the steps with Perry in his wake. Perry was patted on the back, his hand was shaken by some and kissed by others but they were prevented from entering the building proper by a rush of janitors who gave loud cries of horror at the blows they themselves dealt out.

'What a dreadful occurrence,' the Dean was saying to Waldo. 'It would be a good thing if you came up to my office and had some coffee. And you, of course, Professor Perry.'

Waldo's neck had thickened with rage. 'I saw them! I know their names! I'll fail them, by God! I won't have them in my department!' He looked at Perry suspiciously. 'What have you been up to? They were kissing you. I saw them.'

'You must be calm, Professor,' Abbas remarked in a sugary voice. 'Because a dreadful thing has happened. You must be calm. You must gather your strength. When we have reached my room I shall — '

'Abbas, what the devil are you talking about?'

The Dean's solemnity was puzzling the anger out of Waldo and by the time they had reached the office he was mute with expectation. Perry examined the coloured photograph of His Majesty which was displayed over the Dean's desk and sank into a leather armchair, feeling that he could have little responsibility for what followed. A one-eyed servant opened the shutters and stepped on to the balcony where his appearance was greeted by derisive cheers from the students who had gathered below.

'I have to inform you, Professor Grimbley,' the Dean said as soon as the servant had left the room, 'of a happening that touches us closely. It was nearly tragic. But thank God he was saved by the prompt action of one of his students. Professor, during a picnic at Sakkara Mr. Perry tried to shoot himself. You did not know this? I thought not. Everyone knew it but you and me. The students, it seems, have a theory. You and I drove him to suicide. We forbade him to get interested in the welfare of the students. So he tried to shoot himself in despair. There is only one thing we can do to give the lie to this story. We must go out on to that balcony, the three of us, and show the students that we are in harmony. It is particularly important that Mr. Perry should look happy. Come now!'

'Perry, d'you mean to say you went on that blasted picnic after — '

The Dean clapped his hands. 'Another time! Please! My students are in a bad mood. They must be conciliated.'

Waldo continued to snarl but Abbas caught him by the hand and led him to the balcony. The three of them, with Abbas in the middle, emerged on to the balcony and were greeted with cheers.

'Look happy, Mr. Perry! Look happy, Professor Grimbley.' Abbas himself could scarcely speak for laughter.

Mary must have seen the Princess. It was the only explanation. She had told the Princess, the Princess had told Tureiya and he had blurted the news out in the presence of the Dean not suspecting that it was news to Perry too. Now that Perry came to think of it, Mary had eaten no lunch the day before. When he returned from the library he found her wearing one of her best suits and scolding Hassan more violently than was necessary for some mishap in the kitchen; and the grilled fish, when finally served, appeared to reduce her to nervous silence. He now thought he saw why. She was pregnant and could not bring herself to confess. Oh yes! It was easy enough to tell the

Princess. But how could she tell her husband with no sacrifice of dignity that she was to bear him a legitimate child when she was supposed to be having an affaire with a Scotsman? Perry's heart went out to her. Her position was cruel.

'Mary, darling,' he said on a telephone he had found in one of the Faculty offices, 'I want you to have lunch with me at the Union. I want to have a serious talk with you. No, we can't talk over lunch in the flat. What's that? Well, there's Mrs. Curtis. What? That doesn't matter. We'll have it warmed up for dinner.'

Giving Waldo and Abbas the slip had been easy, but making an escape from the university premises was a different matter. The crowd before the Faculty building was swelling rapidly and as it commanded the route to the main gates escape could only be made by unorthodox means. Eventually he had to climb the spiked railings opposite the English Department, dodge quickly across the road into the Botanical Gardens and make his furtive way down to the tram route. In the distance he could hear cheering of such rhythmical vigour he could only think the students were staging a full-blooded demonstration. As this would be a demonstration in his favour it would not surprise him to learn that, by this time, Muawiya had taken charge.

At the Anglo-Egyptian Union there was the customary pre-lunch stir. Cars performed half-circles on the gravel, the Sudanese waiters carried drinks into the garden and the usual party of Englishmen sat up at the bar on tall stools. Perry collected his mail and walked through the public rooms in case Mary had already arrived. He retired to the lawn to avoid getting involved in a conversation and marched up and down at a point from where he could keep the entrance in view. What was he to say to her?

In his anxiety he forgot where he was and began to trot; it was a youthful habit which recurred at moments of stress —

oh! to get *on* with life! he found himself thinking. To seize the nettle as quickly as possible! — and he ran quite quickly along the edge of the flower border under the quiet gaze of the drinkers on the tall stools. At least, they seemed quiet when he glanced through the open windows in their direction. Heavens! What was he doing? They would think he was crazy. He stopped, cleaned his glasses and made off soberly in the direction of the front gate where, as luck would have it, he saw Mary and knew he had no breath to speak.

'Edgar! Are you all right?' She paid off the taxi and hurried over the gravel. Her face was shaded by a wide-brimmed hat. Eyes, unnaturally large (and beautiful!) looked out at him. 'Are you ill?'

'All right — in minute — running — all right!' For a moment he could only gasp and lean against a tree, knowing that he was crimson-faced and sweating. 'Been limbering up! Exercise! Perfectly all right! What'll you drink! Let's sit down at this table.'

Their table was so remote it was almost in the garden of the Egyptian Army Officers' Club which lay next door, a white-painted building with a handsome portico and a bandstand. Perry looked at the Egyptian officers crossing and uncrossing their legs as they sat about drinking coffee and said, 'I suppose I ought to take more exercise. Perhaps we ought to join the Sporting Club.'

'Edgar, what has happened? You said you wanted a serious talk.'

He scarcely knew which matter to raise first, the baby or the supposed lover. If he chose the baby his tone would need to be loving and confidant, a calm affirmation of his joyful father-hood without — somehow — any touch of complacency to imply that the situation could have been no different. If, on the other hand, he chose to emphasize her virtue by first dissipating the myth of the Scots lover he would need to be particularly careful. He could scarcely call her a romantic liar on the slender evidence, scarcely more than intuition, he had built up. Romantic liar? How she would flare up! He would have to make it clear he suspected she was lying, not because she was too conventional or too plain to have a lover, but because he had found her so sweet and wifely during the past few weeks that — yes, this was the line to take! — he supposed the Scot to be her private joke at his expense. Perry began to look on the gloomy side. What if she were not a liar? He wished their talk could be postponed. It would have to be conducted with extraordinary delicacy.

Perry told the waiter to bring some sherry and turned to Mary. 'I'm thinking of resigning from my job.'

'Then we could go back to England? Good.'

'Good?'

Mary removed her white gloves and laid them over her knee. 'Yes, darling, we're going to have a baby. I'd rather be in England for it.'

'What?' Perry was quite as frightened as he would have been if the news were fresh. He stared at Mary, knowing that he had lost colour. 'A baby? That's wonderful!'

'You don't seem very sure.'

'Oh, Mary, I love you so much!' He picked up her hands and kissed them with passion. Pushing the table back with his foot he found he could place his chair so close to Mary's that he could sit with his arm round her waist. 'Is it a boy or a girl?'

Mary began laughing.

'No, I don't mean that! I mean which do you want it to be? I feel quite bowled over. Look, there's the fellow with the sherry!' He jumped up and met the waiter. Putting one glass into Mary's hand he lifted the other, saying, 'To the baby! Long life to her or him! Mary, I'm so excited I don't know what I'm saying. Are you sure you're going to have a baby?'

'Quite sure.'

'That will be twenty piastres, sir,' said the waiter.

Perry gave him a fifty piastre note and told him to keep the change. 'What dreadful sherry! We ought to have champagne. I wonder if they've got any champagne.'

But Mary would not hear of champagne. It would make them conspicuous, she said, and in any case she had something more to say. Perry was scarcely listening. He had become aware that the flower border had perfume, that he wanted to kiss Mary on the lips, that he was very hungry and, after that, he would need a long refreshing sleep.

'I've broken with James, Edgar.' She spoke severely, as though rebuking him for a premature rejoicing. Did he think James a small problem?

'Who's James?'

'You know very well who James is. I've written to end our engagement. Now, Edgar, I want you to understand that our baby is not the main reason. I think we ought to stick together because, when all's said and done, we suit one another. After all, you are my husband.' She gave him an understanding smile. 'And, after all, I do love you. From now on I'm never going to let you be in any doubt about it. None at all. I love you! Do you hear? I love you very much.'

Perry could not go on kissing his wife even in this remote part of the garden. For one thing, they were in full view of the coffee-drinking Egyptian army officers. Nevertheless, he bent down and kissed Mary firmly on the lips, partly because he wanted to and partly because he felt dazed and could think of no better way of covering up.

'What have you done with the gun?' she asked.

'The gun? It's in the desk at home. Locked up.'

'Throw it in the river! Promise me you'll throw it in the

river! After lunch we'll take a taxi, call in at the flat for the gun and drop it off Kasr el-Nil Bridge. It makes me shudder to think of it in the flat. Promise me you'll never, never, do anything so stupid again. You are such a desperate darling!'

'You are desperate, aren't you?' she pressed.

'I — I've never thought of myself like that, I must say.'

'You must promise me that you will never — '

'Of course I promise.'

By some twist of the imagination the landscape of Memphis was conjured up around him; so clearly did he see the alabaster sphinx and the corrugated iron shelter over Rameses that, inevitably, he thought of himself leaving Mary and the students once more to gaze down on the colossal figure with tears running from his eyes. Tears of happiness! He was there, so vividly, at Memphis once again that he could smell the droppings of the donkeys. The corrugated iron ticked like a clock as it expanded in the sun. Above his head the flies hummed at the clustered dates. The familiar tears of happiness pricked at his eyes and he stood up, looking round short-sightedly in the Union garden, repeating, 'Yes, Mary, of course I promise!'

Happiness made him even hungrier. Everything in sight, the green grass, the white Officers' Club, the chocolate trunk of a tree, stirred his appetite. He could have eaten the flowers. He could have gnawed Mary's white gloves. The Union building itself, the walls and roof honey-coloured by the sun, looked edible that morning. Since the picnic he had, now he came to think of it, scarcely eaten anything.

'Well?' He looked at her and raised his eyebrows.

As Mary stood up and took his arm, Perry became aware that Waldo had appeared. Still wearing his tarboosh and *abayeh* he had shot out of the lounge and was now staring round the garden with such obvious agitation he might well have run all the way from the university. Seeing Mary and

Perry he raised an arm in greeting and trotted towards them over the grass. Perry was aware of all this but without conviction. He was sensitive to Waldo's state of mind; he could dismiss a picture of Waldo jogging down the Gizeh road and for it substitute the more likely image of Waldo bouncing impatiently up and down in a taxi. Yet, for all that, Waldo was temporarily less real to Perry than the prostrate Rameses at Memphis; Waldo functioned on a lesser plane of reality. He was there and yet he was not there. Even Mary failed to greet him.

Perry piloted her with extravagant care towards the restaurant. He steered her round a tree and through the scatter of seated members to the path through the flower beds. No one must come in contact with her. She was too fragile. Occasionally she sighed and looked up into his face. They were rapt. Waldo spoke to them but he was unheard. He stood in their path but they walked round him. Still talking, he walked in their rear. He called Perry by his Christian name but even that failed to pierce the magic circle. At the bar the drinkers fell silent. They looked at the curious trio with amazement. The head waiter stood at the restaurant door, plainly wondering whether he ought to admit them.

'Waldo!' At the last moment Perry turned. He spoke with precision for his voice was intended to carry a long way — from what, to him, seemed a higher plane of reality to a lower. 'Waldo! We think you would like to know. We have started a baby.'

As the pair walked into the restaurant and took their seats Waldo remained stiffly where he was. He did not open his eyes until the head waiter spoke to him.

'Good morning, sir. We have excellent shrimp cocktail today.'

'Eh? What? Oh, yes. Well, I'll take a sandwich in the garden.'

He too had the feeling communication had been established between one plane of reality and another; but he would not have put it like that.

The Cypriot hock had an undeniably sobering effect. Towards the end of the meal the head waiter brought a note from Waldo which Perry read quietly and, on the same sheet of paper, wrote a reasonable reply. As soon as the head waiter had retired Mary asked what was happening. Perry explained that in their relations with Waldo they had now reached a point where the most important consideration was reserve. Even formality. Waldo himself appreciated the position. His request for an interview had been couched in the third person. The reply, which had not caused Perry a moment's hesitation, adopted the same style. 'Mr. and Mrs. Perry,' it ran, 'will be pleased if Professor Grimbley joins them for coffee after lunch in the garden.'

The father of Mary's child lit a cigarette and transferred it from his lips to hers. The gesture took them both back to the days of their engagement. It was courtship so blatant that after marriage he had given it up until now; and before walking into the garden they sat smiling at one another through the haze. They could not have remembered what they had eaten or drunk and when they had settled in a couple of basket chairs on the lawn they were unaware of Waldo's presence until he said, 'Well, if you've no objection I'll sit down.'

Perry glanced at him.

'Yes, do, there's a good fellow. You wanted to see me?'

'I hope I don't intrude.' Lowering himself into the chair Waldo sighed and glanced round to make sure that no other members were within earshot. 'I should like to apologize.' Every tremor of his body was made audible by the chair. It complained bitterly if he shifted his weight. It groaned as he leaned forward for a confidential disclosure. 'I should like to apologize for my behaviour this morning,' he whispered and the chair shrieked his embarrassment to all corners of the garden. 'The news was given me so suddenly. It was so shocking I scarcely took it in.'

'That's perfectly all right,' said Perry.

'Think of me as a man. For the moment, at least, don't think of me as the head of your department. I am a man. Now, as man to man is there anything you wish to tell me?'

'What about?'

'What about? All these rumours! Let me make myself clearer. Would you prefer to talk to me alone?'

'I've no secrets from my wife, if that's what you mean.'

'Not secrets. No, of course not. Well then — ' Waldo crossed his legs in agitation — 'put yourself in my position. Now, I ask you. What would you do? What questions would you ask? You see the difficulties. I'm not asking for sympathy, but how would you handle it?'

Coffee arrived. The Sudanese waiter made some ceremony of pouring out and walked back to the kitchen spinning the tray on one finger. Waldo lifted his cup.

'This is a bit confusing,' said Perry. 'Are you asking my advice as a man or as head of the English Department?'

Waldo appeared not to have heard the question. 'You've been here for five years. Good. During all that time — no trouble. Then, in the same month or so, Mrs. Perry arrives, you begin meddling in Egyptian politics — and with what result? Rumours!'

'What rumours?' said Mary.

'Why, about what happened at Sakkara! Now let me make one thing clear.' For the moment he had decided to ignore Perry and address himself to Mary. 'You know very well that the Dean and I were firmly against this picnic. I forbade your husband to carry on with his report. I forbade him to go on the picnic. He ignored me. We'll say no more of that. Do I make myself clear? There is no need to dwell on that aspect of the case because, of course, something very much more important has happened.'

'What's that?' said Perry.

Waldo thrust his head forward and showed the whites of his eyes. 'That is just what I am determined to find out! There are all sorts of rumours flying about and I am determined to get to the bottom of them. Look round this garden? You see? Everyone is watching us and trying to catch what we're saying. There are rumours.'

'Edgar, sweet, I want to go home. I don't want to stay here if everyone is talking about us.'

Perry stood up to check Waldo's observation and found that, in the main, it was true; about forty people were sitting about in the afternoon sun and at least half of them were eyeing him curiously. At the window of the library he could make out the face of one of the secretaries; the Director himself appeared to be watching from his office. The temptation was to shout out some word of defiance but he contented himself with silence when, under his gaze, the faces disappeared from the windows and the members in the garden dropped their eyes. Quite possibly he would be asked to resign.

'Take me home, Edgar.' Mary stood up and looked around with a calm dignity even Waldo must have found admirable, Perry thought, and he signalled to the porter for a cab.

'I'm sure you'll forgive us,' he said to Waldo. 'As to the rumours, if I were head of the department I think I'd forget them. The Dean took it quite gaily this morning, I thought.'

'Forget them! Look here, Perry, you've been damned evasive.' The three of them walked across the grass towards the main gate, Mary erect and silent, Waldo whispering ferociously,

Perry nodding to people he knew and looking about him, at this imitation England in Egypt, the green grass and the beds of flowers, with the suspicion that he was seeing it for the last time.

'Look here,' said Waldo, at the end of his patience. 'Is it true that Muawiya tried to shoot you?'

Mary had already climbed into the cab and gave no sign of having heard Waldo's furtively put question — he had caught Perry by the elbow and actually hissed into his ear. For a moment all movement was arrested. The porter stood smiling, a hand stretched up to a curtain inside the club appeared to pause, a hoopoe in the gravel prepared to fly.

'So that's what the rumour is!' Perry gave the porter an unusually large tip in case he never saw him again. 'Would you like to come along?' he asked Waldo. 'When we get to the flat we're going for a stroll. Perhaps you'd like to come on that too.'

Sarcasm was wasted on Waldo. He climbed into the cab, jerked down the spare seat and crouched in his *abayeh*. 'All I ask is to be treated as a rational human being,' he said as they drove towards Bulaq, 'You'll understand that as head of the department I'm bound to find these rumours peculiarly irritating.'

'What does he mean by "rumours"?' said Mary. 'Surely there can be only one of them.'

Perry held her left hand and looked out of the window. They were crossing the bridge. Upstream he could see the traffic on Kasr el-Nil Bridge and the white bulk of the Semiramis with a hard shadow on its northern face. 'The Professor suggests that I misunderstood what happened at Sakkara. He suggests that Muawiya whipped out a gun — '

'Mrs. Perry, I'm telling you what everyone is saying. There are the wildest rumours. Naturally I must get to the bottom of them. It's my duty. Damn it all!'

' — whipped out a gun, took steady aim and missed, where-upon I claimed I'd fired the gun myself. What d'you mean by everyone?' He looked at Waldo. 'Is that what the Dean thinks? No, of course not. Do you remember what he told you? A very shrewd man!'

'You damn fool!' Waldo's face appeared to distend. He showed an expanse of horse-like teeth. 'Why should you save the skin of a ruffian like Muawiya? Because he got you out of jail? Now look here, Edgar, I know you think I'm an old fool but for once in a while do listen to somebody who knows more about the country than you do. Let's go and see the consul.'

'No,' said Perry. He was aware that Mary had tightened her grip on his hand.

'And another thing!' said Waldo. 'Suicide is a slur! It's a crime. You can be prosecuted for it. Consider your own in-terests for a moment. "Perry? Oh yes, he's the fellow who tried to shoot himself!" That's what people will say. Once a label like that is stuck on you you'll never get rid of it. When you apply for a job in England they'll hear about it.'

'Are you threatening me?'

'I'm trying to save your reputation. A suicide is a coward. He's contemptible. That's an old-fashioned way of talking but dammit, it's valid. You're not a religious man so I can't appeal to you from the religious point of view. You wouldn't under-stand my language.'

'I don't need dissuading from suicide. I haven't the slightest intention. As a matter of fact we're going to throw the gun in the river.'

'My duty,' said Waldo heavily, 'is to tell you what the world will think of you. To protect Muawiya you'll make yourself an academic outcast. I warn you, I won't have you on my staff.'

Perry could feel Mary stiffening and turning away from him.

Ignoring Waldo's presence he placed an arm round her waist and drew her to him.

'And if I understand you rightly,' Waldo shouted, 'you're now going to destroy some valuable evidence.' He made such a noise that pedestrians peered in. 'Unless you charge the fellow no one else can. And what will you feel like if Muawiya really does murder somebody, the Ambassador, say? This is no occasion for sentiment. It's politics. It isn't a personal matter at all.'

They had arrived at the Mixed Courts. Perry ordered the driver to stop because, as he explained, his guest would be able to catch a Shubra bus on the corner.

'That kind of liberalism,' said Waldo, 'is so dead that I'd describe it as intellectually disreputable, the way you're behaving.' He had hesitated about leaving the cab but Perry leaned forward and opened the door. 'Mrs. Perry,' he called from the pavement, 'for God's sake argue some sense into him.' Mary was gazing fixedly out of the opposite window. Because of the traffic, the taxi moved off so slowly that Waldo was able to keep pace with it for perhaps twenty or thirty yards. He did not attempt to speak. There was sufficient wind to flap his cloak and cause him to raise a hand to his tarboosh. He hurried along with his mouth open, his body slightly bent the better to see into the cab. Perry caught a last glimpse of him bumping into people because he was trying to follow the taxi with his eyes as it made the sweeping right turn into Sharia Soleiman Pasha. When they arrived at Bab el-Louk some minutes later Mary had still not spoken. Perry told the cab to wait. Mary made as though to leave but he pushed her gently back on to the seat.

'I won't be a moment, darling.' Because of her bewilderment he kissed her. 'Just lie back in the corner here and think of nothing at all for a few minutes.' She made no protest.

The porter crashed the lift gates and sent him up to the sixth floor. The upward surge gave an unexpected lift of spirit. He was back in the Union garden, hungry enough to think of eating Mary's gloves; he was back in Memphis looking down at a granite statue. Swinging and creaking, the lift took him up towards the dirty glass at the top of the shaft. He shouted to the porter that he was leaving the gate open; he was returning immediately. Shouts, like birds trying to escape, flung about the echoing building and as Perry rushed through Mrs. Curtis's saloon to snatch the gun from the drawer where he had secreted it, they died away in sobbing caricature of Waldo's laugh. Was it possible, even now, for Waldo to interfere? Had he followed? Perry found himself considering the possibility of having to threaten Waldo. The sight of the levelled gun would, perhaps, be enough to make Waldo stand back. But no. He was too illiberal. He would try to rush the gun. Perry rode the lift to the ground considering which of his knees to aim at.

'I thought I heard Waldo.'

Mary looked at him steadily from the back of the cab but made no answer. Her face was as small as a child's under the big hat; and, also like a child's, flowering with a wide-eyed expectancy that touched Perry to the heart. She moved her lips as though preparing for speech. He wanted to say something absurd and extravagant but turned instead to the driver and remarked, 'Take us to the Midan Ismailia.'

They approached the river, then, on foot. Leaving the Midan behind them they walked towards the bridge with the sun staring them in the face. They were quite alone. Waldo was not in sight and Perry's weighted pocket beat against his thigh like a pulse.

'That student tried to kill you,' said Mary as they passed the stone lions.

Perry tucked her hand under his arm and looked ahead. It was the dead hour of siesta and traffic on the bridge was not heavy, a couple of cars travelling in either direction and perhaps half a dozen widely scattered pedestrians. To the south, about Gezireh, the Nile was as broad as a lake and the wind lifted an occasional wave into the sun's glitter.

'What a fool you must think me,' Mary said. 'I'm so ashamed I could throw myself in.'

'It's nothing to worry about, sweetheart. Certainly it's the kind of mistake that could happen to anyone.'

'He seemed so positive and — and you didn't deny it.'

'Put it out of your head. At a time like this you don't want to worry about anything at all.'

At the middle of the central arch Perry stepped to the parapet and tossed the gun into the water. Mary gave a cry. The gun twirled slowly in the air and struck a plume from the current before disappearing, so it seemed, swiftly to the north.

RETIREMENT IN GOOD ORDER

19 Sh. Mohamed Sidki Pasha,
Cairo, December 1st, 1946

Yᴏᴜʀ Exᴄᴇʟʟᴇɴᴄʏ,

I apologize. The university has asked me not to do any more teaching until my case has been finally decided. They say that my presence at Gizeh might start a demonstration. As a consequence I have had leisure to think about the happenings of the past few weeks. It has become clear to me that my conduct, judged from your point of view, has been surprising and even bad. Until you gave orders for me to be turned away from the Palace your bearing towards me has always been most courteous, friendly and generous. Taking everything into consideration I do not regard that unfortunate incident so seriously as I did at the time. It certainly weighs less with me than the many memories I preserve of your various kindnesses; and, of course, those of Her Highness, but I do not presume to write to her. My own conduct has, on the other hand, been impetuous. At our last meeting I spoke hastily. I questioned your integrity and I refused to tell you what thoughts were passing through my head at the moment before pulling the trigger. As stated above, for all this I apologize.

May I set down an extenuating circumstance? As an imaginative and sensitive man, with great experience of the world, please consider the case of someone like myself who, long separated from his wife is at last re-united with her. Because of the war we have been four years apart and only the two months

205

together. Your Excellency will understand, very readily, that for the last two months I have been in an unusually excited state of mind. Naturally it has been a period of happiness. At the same time there have been many anxieties. After six years people can change completely and I must confess that I have been haunted by the dread my wife would think differently about me. But why do I not write frankly? I forget that I am not writing to an Englishman. I was afraid that my wife no longer loved me. Your Excellency will not require me to describe the unnatural tension in which I have been living and working. However, my fears were all without foundation, as no doubt I should have perceived much more quickly than I did. The clouds are dispersed, the sun is shining once more, in spite of my being suspended by the university, and if only we could be assured of Your Excellency's continuing good will, our happiness would be complete and we should leave Egypt at peace with ourselves. Her Highness has always been most gracious, not only to me, but to my wife as well. As explained above, I have not presumed to address Her Highness and you will please use your discretion in mentioning the matter to her.

I must tell you that during the moments before the trigger was pulled my thoughts were taken up by reflections on the way the news of my death would be received by various people who know me; strangely enough, they were all people — one in particular — who would not allow the news to perturb them a great deal. Of Your Excellency and Her Highness I did not think at all. They are, I know I can assure myself, too charitable.

Yours sincerely,

EDGAR PERRY

The suggestion that he should write an apologetically-toned letter to the Palace had been made by Mary, possibly with the idea of providing him with something to do now that he no longer had to put in an appearance at the Faculty; yet when he read the letter aloud he could see at once it was not the kind she had expected. Her mouth was open sufficient for him to see the tips of her teeth. She looked straight ahead and her right nostril quivered delicately. 'I had no idea you were so fond of me, Edgar,' she said in a worried tone. 'Not even when I thought it was suicide.'

Perry's inclination, when she had first suggested the letter, was to postpone it until they had finally decided, or had been forced by circumstances, to leave for England; ideally, one would want to post it at Alexandria before embarking. Unless the Palace understood that the Perrys had left Egypt for good any cordial approach would, in Perry's view, be treated as toadying. They had, he and Mary, discussed the matter thoroughly; Perry's last encounter with the Pasha was set in the balance with an edited version of Mary's last reception by the Princess. Would the Palace's attitude be governed by the bitterness of the one or the mildness of the other? If the Pasha was so offended that he had won the Princess's sympathy there would be no point in writing a letter of apology. If, out of interest in Mary, the Princess had tempered the Pasha's anger such a letter might be well received. Perry was confused by all the factors that had to be considered. Eventually he decided to follow his instinct and abandon thought for the consequences. He sat down and wrote an honest letter to a man he liked.

'He's not such a fool as you might think,' he told Mary, 'and when all's said and done I was rude to the chap. He's never been rude to me.'

As the sentences flowed from the end of his nib Perry was convinced that he was writing a noble and affecting letter. He had no object but the demonstration of a sincere regard. And he hoped, too, that Tureiya would forgive him. Who, reading this confession of love, could keep up any ill-feeling for the writer? Tureiya would, surely, be captivated. Perry was so happy in the composition of his letter that the words seemed to come with no effort on his part, even though he wrote in French. Only when he read the letter aloud, translating as he went, and saw the expression on Mary's face did he realize he had built better than he knew, that he had written no more than the simple truth! His wildness of the past few weeks had been due to Mary! He had been tossed on a wide sea without knowing it was the sea of love. Now that an uncertain journey was over he had been granted, in a quite unexpected way, a revelation. A profound revelation! he thought, gazing at her with a mild incredulity that the revelation had been so long in coming. He did not consider himself an obtuse or inobservant man. Now, for example, he could see that Mary was both surprised and moved by the letter.

'I have something to tell you, Edgar.' She spoke after considerable hesitation.

Not only did Perry understand how the letter had affected her; he could see that remorse was driving her to the most painful confession of all; that her Scots lover had never existed. And he knew it was his duty as a man of honour to spare her such a humiliation. But how? He could not forbid her to tell him. He could not put fingers to his ears. He could not pretend deafness. He could not rush from the room.

'Something to tell me?' He sounded surprised. 'Sweetheart, d'you mind? I simply must catch the mid-morning post.'

'But this is important, Edgar.'

'Then there is only one thing for it. You must put on that floppy-brimmed hat which makes you look so nice and come out to post with me. The exercise will do us good. It's a splendid morning. No, I won't take a refusal! You put a hat on and I'll find a tie. I particularly want the Pasha to have this letter by the last delivery this afternoon.'

He talked, bustled about, and was so impatient to reach the street once they were ready that he would not wait for the lift. He insisted on walking down the six flights of stairs, turning at every landing to call up to Mary encouragingly. She followed without a word. She clearly thought Edgar's behaviour baffling and would have liked to call him to account there and then. But the old certitude was ruinously undermined and, frankly, she doubted whether she would ever be able to call him to account again. So she pretended to find the descent exhausting. Perry, pale with concern, had the lift brought to the floor where she stood and supported her into its creaking, swaying cabin, with murmurs of apology for his thoughtlessness. The cabin fell the remainder of the shaft like the gondola of a rapidly deflating aeronautical balloon.

Although Perry had recently escaped assassination he could not believe that he stood in any danger. Muawiya had acted, presumably, for some obscure political reason but there were a number of personal issues (supposed ingratitude, for example) which seemed to indicate that the Sakkara incident was a freak. Perry was simply not important enough to figure on anybody's assassination list. Even so, he paused uncertainly with a hand on Mary's arm when they came out of the hall. A boy with a neatly cropped head had started up from the opposite pavement and hurried to the café on the corner. The boy had obviously been on watch and now he was reporting to a man who sat at a kerbside table.

'Get back inside.' Perry spoke so fiercely that Mary obeyed.

He stood with the sun in his face watching the boy and the man who were were now openly looking at him. The café was about thirty yards along the street, on the corner facing into Bab el-Louk Square, so when the man stood up and began walking with soft-footed precision in Perry's direction there was ample time to observe him. Perry could see that the fellow had an ostentatious respectability, like a lawyer. He was about thirty years of age, wore a black, well-tailored coat and grey trousers, a tarboosh of rich plum and winking shoes; and a heavy, square-ended moustache gave an uncompromising look to his broad face. He stood on the opposite pavement studying Perry as boldly as Perry studied him. When he spoke it was in excellent English.

'Professor Perry? Forgive this approach by a stranger, but may I have a word with you?'

There were remarkably few people about and the gummy Egyptian voice set up an echo. The buildings were tall and echoed the voice like rock. He crossed the street with eyes that never left Perry's face. His mouth was softening into a smile and when he took up position immediately in front of Perry his jacket fell open and revealed that he was wearing a gold watch chain like a Victorian statesmen. 'Muawiya Khaslat is a friend of mine and it is about this young man I should like to speak.'

Perry turned and called for Mary to come out. The mention of his would-be assassin should have alarmed him. On the contrary, he was reassured. 'You're welcome to walk down to the post office with us. What can I do for you, Mr. — '

But the Egyptian did not give his name. 'Perhaps you and Madame would take coffee with me.'

Perry disliked the man's methods: the boy on watch, the wait at the café, the cool almost impudent calling across the street. Why had he not come up to the flat or telephoned? Perry set off in a direction opposite to the one originally intended, saying that his wife and he had only recently breakfasted. He decided the man was definitely a lawyer and not to be treated with much ceremony.

'I don't suppose you have the gun with you, Professor Perry,' said the man unexpectedly.

Following the broad pavement north they walked into the shadow cast by the building the Perrys had just left. The smell of steam and scorched cloth rose from basement laundries. At the stall on the waste ground the salesman was displaying the pink flesh of a cleft water melon. Perry steered Mary in the direction of the Ministry of Waqfs and wondered if the fellow could possibly be from the police.

'What gun?' he asked.

The Egyptian pulled a white handkerchief from his sleeve and trumpeted. The air immediately changed its nature. Instead of bearing the customary goat-like reek of a Cairo side street it was charged with jasmine. The handkerchief was so impregnated with the cheap scent that when the Egyptian lifted his head Perry could see that his eyes smarted. 'The gun you took from Muawiya Khaslat, of course. With your permission, I should like it back. It is not his property and it is an article of some value. Apart from financial considerations, though, it is a matter of honour.'

'Honour?' Perry was surprised and came to a halt.

'Certainly. The honour of a patriotic brotherhood. Look at the matter from our point of view. A brother goes on a mission. He fails. Well, bad luck! But he returns without his weapon. This is disgraceful. One is exposed to ridicule.' The Egyptian presented an unusually large hand, palm uppermost. 'You will give me the gun or it will be the worse for everyone.'

Perry slowly raised his eyes from the hand to the smile curling away behind the big moustache. At close quarters the Egyptian did not appear quite so respectable. His nose was fleshy and the cheeks were beginning to hang. Were he an Englishman one would have known him for a heavy beer drinker. But although the smile was there, and growing larger, there was no humour in the expression. The man was not joking. He made his preposterous request in the light tone of one whose wishes are normally met.

'Edgar! I insist that you call a policeman.'

'It's *all right*, dear!' Perry patted her hand absently. 'I suppose you're one of these Moslem Brothers?' he said to the man, who shrugged wearily and wound a finger into his watch chain. The street was still residential at that point but there were plenty of people about. To them, no doubt, the Perrys and the Egyptian appeared to be holding quite an ordinary conversation. Women appeared on a balcony and began draping carpets over the ironwork railings.

'I really think,' said Perry, 'that if I had the gun here I should pull it out of my pocket and shoot you in the foot. If I understand you properly you sent one of the gang out to shoot me. He didn't and left his gun behind. Now you want it back to have another go.'

'No, no, Professor, sir. Don't misunderstand me. We demand the gun back — we are only asking for what is our own property — and in return I do not think there will be more attacks on you. Is this not a good bargain?'

Perry gave Mary's hand a firm slap to silence her interruptions. 'I wouldn't make any bargain with a cut-throat like you. Anyway, I threw the gun in the Nile two days ago.'

The smile disappeared. Under the black moustache the lips puckered into a bud of dismay. The eyes became enormous. 'You have thrown it in the Nile? But it was a most excellent weapon! Really, it was like drowning a kitten!'

Perry took Mary's hand and raised it to his lips in apology. 'I must find out what this chap's up to. You see, he likes guns.' He turned to the man. 'If you want to accompany us we are still going to the post office.'

They turned into a street where tramcars appeared out of a

remote asiatic distance. Barbers' shops and laundries alternated on either side, blankets and carpets hung from the balconies above and, where the sun fell, the shuttered windows creaked in the sandy wind. They walked three abreast, Mary on the inside and Perry in the middle. He was thinking how effectively the Egyptian must have taken Mary's mind off the need for confession.

'So you sent Muawiya to kill me?'

'That's right, sir.' Sorrow appeared to have made the man eager to please and he spoke politely. Perry imagined he was the leader of some 'cell' in the Brotherhood which took special pride in the preservation of their weapons. 'But you understand, of course, that there is nothing personal in it.'

'I don't understand.'

'It is not that we do not like you. We kill you because we are opposed to your country's policy. Personal feelings do not come into the matter. Some Egyptians believe that they can like individual Englishmen and hate England. Now we, in the Brotherhood, do not believe that. For this reason Muawiya was to shoot you.'

He had lost real interest in the Perrys now that the gun could not be recovered; he gave the impression that but for appearing discourteous he would have left them. 'We observed,' he explained further, 'that Muawiya had formed a liking for you. It was genuine and dangerous. He was told to shoot you and he failed. He will be punished.'

'Do you know Professor Grimbley?'

'I have never met him. I know who he is, of course.'

'He'd see your point of view.'

The Egyptian laid a gentle hand on Perry's arm. His cheeks drooped; there were lines of pain at the nostrils and mouth; his voice rose from a pit of suffering. 'Professor Perry, you were not serious when you said you had thrown the gun in the river?'

'Indeed I was.'

'It was a most excellent Colt automatic.'

'I'm sure I don't know what it was. I don't know anything about guns.'

'It was a handsome weapon. A Colt automatic, point three two.' He was unmanned by the loss. The black eyebrows thrust forward to indicate his aspiration for the outburst of anger proper to the circumstances; but more natural feelings were too strong for him. Sorrow brought a dewy flush to his face. 'I should not have minded so much if he had taken the Mauser. The Colt, you understand, was a weapon I had used myself. It is no good speaking to you, Professor Perry. You do not understand these matters. They are too military. To throw a fine gun into the river like that! It is not reasonable! Where did you throw it? A good swimmer might get it back. Or a fisherman with a net.'

He was so preoccupied that Perry had to grab his arm to save him from walking under a bus. On a traffic island in Opera Square they stood indecisively while the American limousines, the ancient British taxis, the infirm Italian buses and the Hungarian tramcars raged about them. Since Sakkara Perry had neither set eyes on Muawiya nor heard news of him. What was this punishment the gun-lover spoke of? As they plunged for the pavement Perry discarded the notion of offering to replace the gun in the hope of saving Muawiya's skin. He discarded it with shame.

'Where is Muawiya now?'

They walked north under the shadow of some governmental building. Mary pressed his hand tightly, obviously signalling that he must get rid of the Egyptian as quickly as possible. But the man stuck close, conveying by an occasional sideways glance that even now he had not given up all hope. Even now Perry might produce the Colt from an inner pocket.

'Muawiya Khaslat is in a secret place.'

'Why are you punishing him? Is it because he failed to shoot me or because he didn't bring the gun back?'

'Well, of course, both. To be a good patriot one must be realistic. He is not realistic. He is sentimental.' The man would never have spoken so freely had his tongue not been loosened by shock. 'His mission to kill you was a test. He failed. He does not understand the twentieth century.'

'For God's sake!' said Perry. 'Will you tell me what you mean? Punishment! What sort of punishment?'

The man appeared not to have heard the question but when he saw that Perry wished to buy stamps and that there were crowds before the grille in the post office wall through which they were sold, he pushed forward and shouted in Arabic, 'Make way there! Stand back!' In twenty seconds he had cleared a path to the grille and Perry was saved a wait of ten minutes. He felt guilty about jumping the queue in this way but even more apprehensive of the embarrassment he would cause if he declined the fellow's good offices.

'These people are cattle,' said the man when Perry had posted his letter of apology and explanation to the Pasha. 'In the new, independent Egypt they will not smell. As a patriot I should have been ashamed for you to take your place among them. Professor Perry,' he said in a low voice, 'never throw guns away! All my life I shall think of the Colt rusting on the bed of the Nile. Clean a gun regularly, keep it oiled. It will always be your beautiful friend. Take my advice, Professor Perry, find out all you can about guns.'

At long last anger was beginning to break through.

'Even buy a gun,' he hissed, staring at the ground. 'Because if you and the lady stay in Egypt you will certainly need one.'

Perry held Mary tightly by the arm as they watched the black-coated figure pace firmly away in the direction of Ezbekieh Gardens. He was tempted to run after him — tempted even to suggest the fellow came and had lunch with them one day when it could be arranged for Waldo to be present too. Men having so much in common would surely like to meet. But the Egyptian had gone. Without so much as a glance behind he had reached the pavement and was following the railings in a direction that would bring him to one of the bazaar quarters.

Mary appeared quite dazed. 'I've never heard such effrontery! He must be mad. Surely he's crazy, Edgar?'

Perry looked at her and smiled. He kissed her cheek. Thank God her compulsion to confess had apparently passed! With a little luck he might be able to stave the confession off for ever.

'Crazy?' he said. 'Oh, I don't know. In the opinion of most people not so crazy as me. Or Muawiya.'

'Muawiya?'

He nodded. 'For having ridiculous scruples about killing people. I wonder where he is now.'

The siesta is an art. It is only secondarily a matter of going to sleep. One lies on a bed that is not too soft, one curls and uncurls one's toes; one asks, 'Is that leg at rest? Is it doing any work the bed itself should be doing? And now the other leg. Is it relaxed? Is there any tension along the line of the spine? If one were suddenly dead would one's body take up a position even slightly different from the one it now holds?' If so, the siesta was not being practised skilfully.

All this had been explained to Mary by the doctor at the Anglo-American hospital. Initiation into the art of siesta, he said, required that one must even *fight* against sleep! Watch the finger of sunlight moving through the shutter, fight against somnolence and meditate on the state of one's body if all the bones, even down to the very tiniest, were suddenly removed.

In this relaxed state *give* oneself to sleep for, say, half an hour. No more. At the end of that time one will be refreshed and alert. But Mary, in spite of the best intentions, fell asleep as soon as she was stretched on the bed. For two hours she lay in profound slumber and woke, at four o'clock, feeling drugged. It was not a siesta at all, it was damned laziness, and she excused herself by remembering she was a humiliated woman. How could a humiliated woman keep awake to meditate on the different parts of her body?

Perry sat on the balcony with a carpet-beater in his hand in case a kite suddenly swooped. There was little likelihood of this happening unless Hassan put food out — which he had not — and Perry would readily have admitted his fear of the birds was becoming morbid. Nevertheless, he sat there in the two o'clock sun, very much on the alert. After the encounter with the gun-lover Perry had telephoned the Faculty Secretary for confirmation that Muawiya had not put in an appearance for the last few days and, while they were on the subject, asked for Muawiya's Gizeh address. The Secretary innocently read the address out in his high-pitched voice and Perry wrote it into his diary. It was unlikely that Muawiya would be there. The gun-lover had spoken of 'a secret place' but there was, Perry hopefully supposed, just the barest possibility that he was lying.

At a quarter past two Perry rose as silently as the basket chair would allow him and walked into the bedroom. Mary was soundly asleep on her bed, curled up like a child and when he kissed her on the brow she did not even stir. He closed the door gently behind him, looked into the kitchen on his way out to tell Hassan he would be away for an hour or so, and walked the six flights of stairs to the ground floor to avoid using the lift. The clash of the gates might have wakened Mary. This afternoon there was no watching boy on the opposite pavement. When Perry caught himself glancing up and down the street he managed to persuade himself he was looking for a taxi and, indeed, by the time he reached Midan Ismailia, was twisting his head about for just this purpose. He sat back with his eyes closed while the 1932 Morris creaked over the long bridges.

The house turned out to be a three-storey building over-looking the railway line on the southern limits of Gizeh. Perry told the driver to wait and called for the house-porter who was usually to be found asleep on a bench in the hall; but no one came in answer. He climbed the stairs slowly and paused at the first landing to look, through the unglazed window, at a camel loaded with berseem being whacked over a level crossing. Beyond a fence were the level fields and, away in the distance, a white villa surrounded by Lombardy poplars.

'Please! I invite you. Come and eat,' said a gentle voice.

Perry turned and saw, through an open door, a youth seated at a table dipping flaps of bread into a basin of soft cheese.

'Does Muawiya Khaslat live here? Do you know him?'

'Please,' smiled the youth. 'Eat and be welcome.'

'You are very kind. I have already eaten.'

The youth had something of the Abyssinian in his long, toffee-coloured face. Continuing to dip his bread into the cheese he explained that Muawiya occupied the room across the landing but had not been at home for at least — the youth paused, frowning, with bread poised — for at least five days. The door was locked fast. Perry was advised to try it. 'He is not someone I know well. He owes me fifty piastres. I wish he would come back and pay me.'

'Has he any friends, d'you know, who live hereabouts?'

'It is not possible for such a man to have friends.'

'Why not?'

The youth shrugged delicately. He was slender, like a girl, and as he moved his jaw the skin over his cheekbone glistened and dulled. 'He is old. How can a man like Muawiya have friends among students? But you are a friend, perhaps. You are a man. Indeed, you are an old man.' The youth said he came from Suakkin and was not happy in Egypt because it was a country of vice and irreligion. When Perry descended the stairs he was still scooping up the soft white cheese and, as though Perry's appearance had cheered him up, wailing out a barbaric song.

The porter appeared from behind the house wiping his beard with a towel which he then hung round his neck like a scarf. No, Muawiya was not at home, he confirmed, but there was never any knowing when a fine gentleman like that would turn up. He was a very smart gentleman! He was of the nobility! He was Muawiya Bey! Even a Pasha! The porter was a Berber and spoke Arabic with such a thick accent it was difficult to understand him. He touched his white headdress and smiled. No doubt Muawiya Pasha was visiting his country estate and would soon return, riding on a fine horse. He would throw money to the ground for all to scramble for. He would give cloth to the poor. 'No,' said the porter, 'Muawiya is not at home.' Only when he opened his mouth and began to laugh did Perry realize the old fellow had been indulging his sense of humour. Laughter shook all the breath out of his body. He leaned against the wall of the house gasping. 'When Muawiya comes back,' he eventually managed to say in a choked voice, 'he will ride a white horse.'

Perry gave him ten piastres, woke up the taxi driver, and gave orders to drive back to Cairo. The journey had not been entirely in vain. It would have been foolish to accept the gun-lover's story without checking; Muawiya was definitely away from his usual quarters. But the question remained. Where? How secret was his secret hiding place? Could it be located before Mary woke from her two-hour siesta? Or, if not located, at least some clue uncovered? He looked at his watch. The time was already three o'clock.

At the Abdin Police Station silence was broken only by the remote tapping of a typewriter. Having finally dismissed his taxi, Perry climbed the steps and entered the bare-walled waiting-room where two old men sat asleep on a bench. A policeman was busy prising a nail out of his boot with, apparently, an ordinary pen; but hearing Perry's footsteps he looked up with a sly expression on his face, as though expecting a complaint to which he was determined to attach no importance. He put his boot to the ground with a smack.

'I should like to see Captain Asfur.'

'Captain?'

'Captain Asfur.'

'Not here.' The pen was clearly a general purpose tool for the policeman now used it to scrawl some numbers in a book which lay open on the desk in front of him. He paused while a tramcar clanged its way down the street; the noise, he implied, was a distraction too great for a man like him to bear patiently. When he realized that Perry was still with him he looked sullen. 'What do you want?'

'Captain Asfur.'

'Why do you want to see Captain Asfur?' (They both spoke in Arabic.)

'He is a friend of mine. This is not a police matter.'

Finding still another use for his pen the policeman used it to indicate the door which, as Perry well knew, led to the hall of cages. 'Go through there.'

The sergeant with the enormous chevrons, the man who dealt on occasion with Perry's ration cards, stood before one of the cages talking to a plump, smiling prisoner in a *gallabieh*. Hearing Perry's footsteps on the stone floor the sergeant swung round and recognized him immediately. His jaw hung in a carnivorous smile and he pressed Perry's hand convulsively as though it were an old-fashioned motor horn. 'Es-selám 'aley-kum. Thou hast made us desolate by thy absence. Alas! It is not possible to increase your ration of cooking fat. The Minister is severe. Alas! What abundance there was when I was a young man.'

'It is not a matter of cooking fat,' said Perry. 'I should like to see Captain Asfur.'

'Certainly, certainly.' The sergeant was delighted. He turned to the prisoner. 'Please to excuse me. And you, sir — ' to Perry ' — come at once to the Police Captain Asfur, without the slightest delay.'

By the light of day the building appeared smaller but dirtier. The higher temperature brought out the smell of unwashed bodies. But compared with Perry's impression of his last visit the police station now struck him as silent and deserted. The sergeant opened Asfur's door with ceremony and Asfur, who was seated behind a desk immediately facing it, looked up without surprise. His tarboosh stood on a shelf behind him. The grey, almost white curls, which clung so close to his skull, made Perry think — momentarily — of Uncle Remus. He was still very tired. The blood-flecked eyes moved, sluggish with weariness. And he did not speak.

Perry entered the room and closed the door behind him.

'Where is Muawiya?'

For a while Asfur stared vacantly and they both listened to the sergeant shuffling about on the other side of the door. The noise seemed to irritate Asfur. He shouted and the sergeant's footsteps were heard retiring down the passage.

'Who is Muawiya?' said Asfur. He picked up a leather fly-swat and sighted it through the window like a gun. Pang! said the thick lips noiselessly as the finger curled on the imaginary trigger. He appeared quite indifferent to Perry's presence.

Perry did not think the mime made any reference to the incident at Sakkara; Asfur was merely behaving as though he were alone.

'You know very well who Muawiya is?'

Asfur yawned, reversed the fly-swat and struck the top of his desk with it. 'I do not know anyone by the name of Muawiya. Why should I? You come into my office and make these accusations. Can't you see that I am busy?'

'I suppose you'll say you've never seen me before.'

'Certainly,' said Asfur comfortably. 'I have never, at any time, here or in other places, seen you before.' Tilting his chair back until he could look at the ceiling with comfort, he added, 'Now please go.'

'Not until you tell me where Muawiya is. Or at least give me some news of him. I mean it! You'll have to remove me by force!'

Asfur clapped his hands and a mouse-like policeman appeared through the very door by which Muawiya had conducted Perry to freedom. The mouse was instructed to make coffee. He went into an ante-room with a bob and a run. For some moments Asfur sat listening to the pumping up of the primus stove and then remarked, 'We Egyptians are taking up all sport successfully. We have the best swimmers. We swim your English Channel. Soon we shall beat England at football.' He sighted the fly-swat on a distant fly. Pang! said the noiseless lips again.

'Really!' Perry was incensed. It was already half past three and Mary would soon be waking. 'I think I deserve a bit more consideration. A gang of political fanatics order one of their number to assassinate a harmless foreigner because he likes him! It doesn't matter to you that he is harmless, or has a wife and is about to become a father — ' Perry was so angry that he spoke more freely than he had intended.

'I have eight children,' said Asfur. 'Only two of them are

boys! Eight children and I am a captain of police! Does it occur to you that I am the only honest captain of police in Cairo? I am honest and yet I have eight children!' He slew a fly on the back of his hand. 'I do not know what you are talking about. Have you come to report an assassination? Who is dead?'

The mouse brought coffee and water, saluted absent-mindedly with his left hand and retired. Asfur dropped his head with some gravity and appeared to sniff the coffee up his nostrils. Perry ignored the cup which had been placed before him. Although he saw perfectly well that he was going to winkle no information out of Asfur he could not bring himself to admit defeat. 'Honest? I wouldn't call you honest! When you had me in custody you let Muawiya bring some sort of pressure to bear to let me out. You're as corrupt as the rest of them!'

'Then there is no assassination? There is no one dead?'

'That was not Muawiya's fault.'

'I do not know this Muawiya. So let us call him Abdul. Abdul I know. Why was it not Abdul's fault there was no one dead?'

Perry changed his mind about the coffee and sucked it between his lips to keep out the sediment. 'Abdul if you like. He had bad luck. He slipped. He slipped, I tell you. He stood on some rubble and slipped. It was beyond any man's calculation. Who should know better than me? You're a religious man. It was God's will. I jumped,' said Perry, shouting to make his story more convincing, 'I jumped on his back and took him quite by surprise. But on the whole I don't bear him ill will. My wife and I are going back to England to have this baby — it's nothing to do with this other business — and if Muawiya —

'Abdul.'

' — Abdul wants any reference from me I'd say he was a damn good assassin and I don't bear him any ill will.'

223

'This child of yours,' said Asfur, as he lethargically rose to his feet and revealed a red stripe down each trouser leg, 'Is it the first?'

For the second time Perry found himself walking down the passage which communicated directly from the police captain's office to the street; but on this occasion he was accompanied by Asfur himself who yawned, sighed, excused the quality of the coffee, gave advice on the upbringing of children, asked Perry his name as though he were not already well aware of it, and finally shook hands with the cordial promise that if ever he came to England he would certainly call. But that would be after the revolution!

'What revolution?' said Perry.

'After the revolution I shall be ambassador in London,' said Asfur gravely. 'It is the only way for a man with eight children to travel.'

Perry had not made good his threat. He had not been told where Muawiya was; neither had he been given news of him. But he had walked down that passage, listening to Asfur, with a willingness he did not properly understand. Perhaps there was something in Asfur's bearing that encouraged Perry to believe he had not been so inconsistent as appearances seemed to suggest. At any rate, he went home in a cheerful frame of mind and was not greatly surprised when, at nine o'clock that night, he answered the door bell to find Muawiya himself on the landing outside — Muawiya dressed in a native *gallabieh* and wearing an unmistakable black eye.

Mrs. Curtis had been drinking. After dinner she had shut herself up in her room 'to write a long letter home'; normally she would not have appeared until the following morning but the door bell roused her like a conscience. Wearing slippers and a blue wrap she suddenly appeared in the 'saloon' to demand,

'Did you say something? What was that you said, eh?' She tried to moisten her lips with her tongue. 'Hassan!' she cried, mistaking Muawiya at the open door for her servant, 'Come in at once! Whatever are you thinking of? Hassan! You've been fighting! Come here at once! Let me look at you! Ah! what a lovely black eye, dear! It isn't Hassan though. Speak up, young man! What was that you said?'

Perry closed the door and explained who the visitor was. At the first sight of Muawiya he could have shouted aloud with triumph; but the unsmiling, wounded face looked at him so steadily he was dismayed and could say nothing. He could not have pronounced Muawiya's name if Mrs. Curtis's mistake had not surprised it out of him. He did not need to invite Muawiya in because the student shuffled forward to stand with the poised expectancy of a blind man in front of Mrs. Curtis. She nodded at him. All the stiff iron-grey curls of her head nodded. Her face filled with compassion. She put out a hand and touched Muawiya's left cheek. 'One of the finest black eyes I've ever seen! I used to be a nurse. Did you know that now? Come into the kitchen. We'll put a slice of fresh liver on it.'

'Edgar!' Mary emerged from the dining-room and all three turned towards her. 'What's that man doing here?'

'I'm going to treat his bad eye, dear,' said Mrs. Curtis.

'I wanted to see him, Mary. It's perfectly all right.'

'It *isn't* perfectly all right!' She had lost colour and was plainly shaken. 'How dare he come here!'

Perry was going to have to take a risk. Mary was shaken but she was not frightened; she did not believe that Muawiya had another weapon under his *gallabieh* and had come along to complete the job he had muffed at Sakkara. She was shaken because for the first time in her life she had met someone she could hate with all her heart. There was no torture she would have spared him. The situation was all the more dangerous because her hate seemed well justified. What woman would not hate her husband's murderer? Or even the man who had just failed to be her husband's murderer? But Mary, unexpectedly confronted by Muawiya, hated him principally because she had once believed him: when he had tossed the gun out of the excavation and claimed he had saved Edgar from suicide. It was the turning point in her life. She hated him so much she almost fainted; and then recovered strength at the thought of attacking him there and then. She could claw his face. The risk Perry was having to take was that of ushering Mary from the room and calming her down while Muawiya was left to the care of Mrs. Curtis. But what else could he do? Mary was becoming hysterical.

He said to Mrs. Curtis that the slice of cold fresh liver was a splendid suggestion and that he himself would be back just as soon as Mrs. Perry was comfortable. He took Mary by the arm and hurried her into their bedroom where he placed her gently, unresisting, into a chair and said, 'You know the doctor said you mustn't excite yourself.'

'He didn't.'

'Well, it's common sense anyway. Look here, darling, why don't you go to bed and have a good rest? I must talk with this man, don't you see?'

'I want to kill him. The beast! The beast! What's he doing here?'

When he put an arm round her shoulders and pressed his lips to her forehead she was, he discovered, trembling. 'For God's sake, Mary. Take a grip on yourself.'

'I can't help it! I hate him!'

'Now listen! If you don't stop talking this nonsense I shall have to lock the door behind me when I go. Can't you see the fellow has had his lesson? He's probably been beaten up by those thugs he's been working with and, I dare say, changed his mind about all that nonsense. That's probably what he's come here for; to say he's left the Moslem Brotherhood.'

No sound came from the rest of the flat. Hassan had gone home immediately after dinner so the slightly drunk Mrs. Curtis was alone with Muawiya. The lack of noise worried Perry. The flat was so small that conversation carried on in one room could normally be heard in all the others. But Perry could hear nothing but Mary's breathing.

'Will you be all right now, dear?'

When he repeated the question she nodded. 'You're not to leave me here alone.'

'But I've got to talk with this man!'

'I'm coming with you. I can't bear the thought of his being in the flat when I can't see him.'

Short of carrying out his threat of locking the door Perry could think of no way of dissuading her.

'Then promise me you'll behave.'

'No, I can't Edgar! Don't make me promise!'

He turned abruptly, wrenched open the door, and walked through the 'saloon' to the kitchen, where he could see a light burning. The top of the ice box was flung back and a piece of gamoose liver, together with a large butcher's knife, lay on a marble slab. The air was sweet with the smell of blood.

'They're in Mrs. Curtis's bedroom,' Mary called from the doorway.

Perry rushed past her. Mrs. Curtis's bedroom lay next to their own so, in making for the kitchen across the circular 'saloon' he had not looked back to see the spectacle which now met his eyes: Muawiya still wearing his tarboosh and lying back on Mrs. Curtis's white pillows with a bloody bandage holding a flap of liver to his left eye. Mrs. Curtis looked down upon him thoughtfully swilling round a glass what was probably a dose of home-made fruit liqueur.

'Mr. Perry,' she said when he came in, 'he'll do nicely now but if he's a friend of yours he's not what I'd call a strong young man. Wants a shave bad, too.'

Perry felt that he could not appreciate all the implications of this scene; his mind docketed as much information as possible. Why should Mrs. Curtis, the woman who sometimes spoke of the Egyptians as 'wogs', who despised them as dishonest and immoral, why should she pop Muawiya into her own bed? Even if she were a little drunk. Muawiya lay there quite calmly while Mrs. Curtis drank and chattered. The information was filed in Perry's mind. Later it would be classified and pondered upon.

'How does it feel now, Muawiya?'

The student was lying on top of the bedclothes. He swivelled one eye and looked at Perry, 'You wanted to see Abdul?'

'So Asfur told you.' Perry was aware that Mary was standing behind him. 'What have they been doing to you?'

'I jumped from the window.' He picked the English words out carefully. There was an unmistakably hostile gleam in the one eye which said, 'I am speaking a foreign language.' Suddenly he sat up. The piece of liver looked black in the electric light. He knocked away the flies and spoke with a set jaw. 'You will not let me rest! You will not let me forget! You will not let me die! All the time you chase me. You have no mercy. You hate me so much that you will not let me rest.'

'What the devil are you talking about?' Perry was angry because Muawiya was putting Mary in the right.

Muawiya set his feet to the floor — for the first time Perry noticed that his feet were bare — and extended his right hand like an orator. 'Consider our relations! You insult me rudely over Shakespeare's *Othello*! You are not glad I save your life from a mob! You go to Sakkara with *other* students. Then, when I do not succeed in killing you you tell my friends I am a good assassin! You mock me too much. Now, I hate you, Englishman!'

'It is very naughty to speak like that,' said Mrs. Curtis. 'Only the other day poor Mr. Perry got so worried about you Egyptians he tried to shoot himself. Now, what d'you think of that, young man?'

Muawiya had begun to shout. 'Not true! I — ' he struck himself on the chest — 'I nearly shot him! Not suicide!'

'I don't believe you,' said Mrs. Curtis. 'Sorry!'

'Do you seriously mean to say,' said Perry slowly, 'that you're stupid enough to take offence because I told Asfur you were a good assassin?'

'They all laughed at me!'

'You idiot!'

Muawiya jumped up and the two men stood breast to breast, shouting at one another. Perry pushed Muawiya in the chest, the student sat on the bed only to jump up again. Mrs. Curtis rocked about the room, laughing and crying, 'Oh dear!' Mary (Perry sensed) was manœuvring for a shrewd blow at Muawiya and he was tempted to step aside and give her a clear field. He was bitterly disappointed. Muawiya's arrival in the flat had seemed a clear victory over the Waldos and Moslem gun-lovers of this world. Perry had boasted of it to Mary. Muawiya would leave the Moslem Brotherhood! One more creature would be saved from the twentieth-century arena! It would have been a triumph sufficient to reconcile him even to the failure of his scheme for the students' hostels at Gizeh. But Muawiya had broken out of his jail merely because he had been mocked. After a while Perry was less angry. He grieved.

'Edgar!' said Mary. 'How can you have taken it on yourself to tell anyone he was a good assassin? It wasn't for you to give him a testimonial. Really, I don't understand men! Can't you see how humiliating all this is for me? You — actually — told —

someone — ' Mary drew near and spoke each word as though it were a sentence — 'he — was — a — good — assassin? It's dishonest! It isn't true. You talk as if he were a butler or something. Edgar!' Her voice deepened and he thought of the smell of blood in the kitchen. 'I tell you I *hate* this man.'

Muawiya had been cracking the finger joints of his right hand in agitation. At Mary's words he stopped. Perry was watching him and saw the signs of a transformation. The one eye showed less white; the shoulders hung more slackly, the corners of the mouth began to rise. Muawiya turned slowly until he was looking in Mary's direction; and, as he did so, conveyed to Perry the impression of blossom unfolding in the sun. He was like a man in a foreign country, not speaking the language and very lonely, who suddenly hears his own tongue in a crowded street. Muawiya breathed deeply, he lifted his chin, he glowed. Extending his right hand towards Mary, he brought the tips of his fingers together and carried them to his lips.

'What did you say, Mrs. Perry, please?'

Mary hesitated. The odd behaviour frightened her in spite of her anger. 'I said I hate you!'

'Then may God bless you!' Muawiya touched his forehead with his right hand. 'You show me my path. But you are only a little light. With God's help ask Professor Perry to say the same.'

'You irritate me,' said Perry. 'I will say that. You irritate me like hell. But I'm not going to let you dramatize the situation. Now that I can see you're in reasonably good shape I'm satisfied. No, of course I don't hate you. Neither does my wife for that matter. She's a bit cross with you and I think she's every justification. But don't make any more of it than that. We just feel very sorry for you indeed.'

Muawiya would have none of this. He tore the bandage from his head and looked about the room as though for somewhere to put the liver. Glazed doors, he saw, opened on to the balcony. Before anyone could interfere he had swung them back and stepped into the cool night. His right arm moved across the stars and the lights of the city; when he turned to the room once more he was empty handed and, in his theatrical setting, larger than life with triumph. Mrs. Curtis's reading lamp threw light on his face; spots, flecks, scars of brilliance trembled out of the immense night distances behind him.

'Confess you are my enemy,' he said to Perry.

'No, don't move, Mrs. Curtis, please.' Perry grabbed her arm. Muawiya's aggressive bearing after the excellent first-aid treatment he had received at her hands shocked Mrs. Curtis a great deal. She had lifted her father's Bucks Constabulary truncheon off its hook at the side of her bed and was now making a threatening move towards the veranda. Perry held her firmly because he feared the least bit of extra excitement might cause Muawiya to throw himself to the street eighty feet below.

'Come back into the room, Muawiya, for heaven's sake and get those doors shut. It's cold.'

'Confess that we are enemies.'

Perry stared into the dark face thoughtfully. For the second time in his experience of Muawiya he found himself wondering whether the fellow had taken hashish. Muawiya was touched with exaltation; but it was a dim, obscure exaltation, as though he were only partly present. There was a chance that the real Muawiya was elsewhere, waiting to make his presence felt. Perry looked beyond him at the night sky, shifting his gaze from star to star and frowning in his effort to understand. Why should Muawiya want hatred from him? Did friendship with an Englishman make life impossibly difficult? Did it cloud his allegiances? Did it confuse motives? Did it make too difficult the path of the patriot? In that case why had Muawiya taken the initiative in friendship? Perry had made no gesture comparable to the way Muawiya had rescued him from the Azhar mob or helped him out of prison. At this very moment, possibly, Muawiya was asking for reassurances not of Perry's implacable enmity but of his own.

'Did you know that Mrs. Perry and I are going back to England?'

'You are leaving Egypt?'

'Yes.'

Perry had given Muawiya the information primarily to show how stupid they were to stand talking about personal enmity when, after a little while, they would probably never set eyes on each other again. Muawiya's kind of enmity demanded years of application; these it was not going to have. More likely they would forget one another. Yet Muawiya jumped into the room and laughed. Throwing his shoulders back he swaggered up and down, slapping his bare feet on the parquet, considering the news that his 'enemy' was leaving Egypt. He did not seem the same man who had crept into the flat half an hour earlier. His nostrils dilated with passion and he looked more negroid, more African, than Perry had ever noticed before. It was a cool night but Muawiya's cheeks and forehead were touched with a moist gleam. Speaking in Arabic he said that Professor Perry was leaving Egypt and the rest of the English would leave in the same way, driven from the country by the resolution, courage, and blood of patriots; blood that was gladly shed for freedom.

He stopped. The absurdly delicate, almost feminine, fastenings at the front of his *gallabieh* had come undone, exposing tiny black curls on his chest. His body gave off a dry, not unpleasing reek. 'Sir, you go back to England. It is your own country. It is impossible for you to stay. The sun fights against you. The Nile fights against you. It is not possible for you to

resist. Is it? You admit that? The sun and the Nile and Muawiya Khaslat drive you out? Yes? While you are here I have
no rest. While you are here you have no rest. To go is better
than to die.'

Muawiya was rapt. The words came singing out into the
room which seemed too small to contain them. He played with
the words as sounds. An Arabic phrase was thrown in reson-
antly. It was verbal dance, it was rejoicing, it was intoxication.
The words rose like a fountain. With lips apart he gazed at the
ceiling and the words bubbled past them. 'Let God be praised!
We have driven the English to the sea!'

Neither of the women was impressed. Mrs. Curtis shook her
truncheon and said she had lived in Egypt longer than Muawiya, a good thirty years, that it was as much her country as
it was his, that she was perfectly happy there, thank you, provided she had her occasional holiday in Europe to freshen her
up; and as for being driven into the sea — well, she was ready
for Pharaoh and all his chariots! She said that the trouble with
Egyptians was ingratitude. Mary, more to the point, said they
were not being driven out of Egypt. She and her husband
were leaving because they were fed up with the place.

'Down with all imperialists!' shouted Muawiya. 'Now are
we masters in our own land. The English are going. We are
driving them, even from the Canal Zone!'

'You can't hold a political meeting here.' Perry did not want
to argue. He had only to consider explaining why he and Mary
were leaving Egypt to discover the reasons sprouting like fungi
and proliferating through the whole tissue of what could be
called his Egyptian experience. He had lost his job but could
probably get it back again by some gesture of surrender. Mary
insisted on having the baby in England but they would be
there on holiday anyway, in the late summer, when it was
expected. It was unlikely that the Pasha would want any more

English lessons but there were other pupils, equally profitable. Reason and objection were so well balanced. Yet there was no doubt in Perry's mind that Mary and he were leaving. He saw with surprising clarity the view of Alexandria as the boat made out of harbour. It was so certain that they were leaving, and Muawiya so positive he knew why, that all further reflection appeared a waste of time. Perry could not think. He saw confused pictures: dark faces called out of the sun at his own small child; Rameses fell back heavily, splintering the palm trees; the thick legs of girls walked up hill to the tombs; the blue gun glinted, then mewed in a foot of mud. Perhaps Muawiya was not so very wide of the mark after all. Perhaps he really was the force that drove Perry all the way back to England. But it was not intimidation. It was deep regard, shot through with jealousy; an abortive love affair.

'I must go,' said Muawiya.

'Where to?'

'To my friends.'

'The Brotherhood? Won't you get into trouble for coming here tonight?'

'They are my friends. You do not understand. They are my countrymen. It is good for a patriot to be beaten by other patriots.'

'Well, take my advice — '

'Yes?'

'Don't tell 'em you've driven the English into the sea or this time they'll give you such a damn good hiding you won't get over it.'

Muawiya smiled and stared. He had been so carried away even now he could scarcely tell which was dream and which reality. 'You cannot advise me what to say to Egyptians. We talk wonderful things and we understand them. We have more sense of humour and more imagination than other people.

Every day we say the English are gone! One day, who knows, they will be!'

'Tais toi! Méchant!' The blue hound moved threateningly in Perry's direction and the Pasha, who had seized the beast's collar, was dragged after him. 'He would not have hurt you,' said the Pasha after Afifi and Swain between them had succeeded in hauling the animal, snarling and stiff-legged, into the next room. 'Poor boy! His eyes are not good. He has to smell you to know who you are.'

Perry surreptitiously released his grip of the Japanese bronze (a deer of some kind with a bush of sharp horns) which he had planned to thrust into the dog's face if the Pasha failed to restrain him.

'And now,' said Tureiya pressing Perry's hand, 'you will go home and forget all about us. You will forget Egypt. You will never think of your friend, the Pasha! What a dreadful thing life is! Nothing but partings! For me it is heartbreaking! M. Perry, do not abandon us completely. Egypt has need of friends.'

Perry looked at the Pasha's full, moist lips and at his full, moist eyes; he noted the suffusion of countenance which only strong feeling could have brought about. Was it, he wondered, sentimental and insincere? Or was it innocence?

'One way or another I shall be doing a lot of writing about Egypt. So it isn't likely I shall forget, is it?'

'Writing? What sort of writing?'

'Newspapers, magazines perhaps. That sort of thing. I want to write up something about the students. My report on their living conditions, you know.'

Perry had decided he liked the Pasha very, very much and spoke more with the idea of reassuring him than anticipating the future. What paper would ever publish his views on Egyptian students?

'Excellent,' said the Pasha. 'You must tell the truth about this country. Hide nothing. You must, of course, pay full tribute to the work of Her Highness. There is no one like her.'

'*Chérie!*' the Pasha called as he opened a door and walked into the more spacious room beyond, '*Chérie!* M. Perry is going to write articles about you in the English newspapers!' He turned, his face radiant with happiness, and beckoned Perry to follow. 'Mme Perry, your husband and I have been enjoying a good talk. It is so sad that you are both leaving our country, but your husband will keep in touch.'

Mary had stood up on Tureiya's entry but the Princess waved her back to her seat. 'What is this you are going to write about me in the English papers, M. Perry? Be honest now! Are you going to attack me?'

Tureiya's eyes were large with horror. The Princess smiled, looking up at Perry with hers almost closed. He studied the chalky folds of her eyelids and wondered whether it was really true; that this was the last time he would see her. She wore dark blue trousers which were bright with birds and flowers in gold thread. The bracelets jangled on her thin arms. Perry was struck by the contrast between her old face and her young woman's costume. But she was beautiful! He would have liked to touch the lined cheek, see the eyelids rise and the bold brown eyes looking at him.

'Of course M. Perry is not going to attack you,' said Tureiya.

'In any case I don't care,' said the Princess. 'Don't write in the newspapers, though.'

Perry began seriously to wonder what his chances were of selling an article. 'Your Highness, I was thinking more of the weekly papers. The magazines. Or the quarterlies.'

'There was once a bad article on my great-grandfather, a great man, in the *Edinburgh Review*. No, it is much better to follow my example and say what you have to say in the novel.'

'Write a novel? About Egypt? Oh but I couldn't do that. I mean, to write a novel you have to have — '

'Well, what?' said Her Highness, with the calm of one who has written many novels and whose most recent work, the story of the pathetic concubine, was even then in the hands of the printers.

'Imagination, I suppose.'

The Princess turned to Mary who was sitting demurely at her side; she patted Mary's hand and began laughing with a boisterous violence that reminded Mary of the night Edgar was in prison; having pretended not to know where Edgar was the Princess shook with laughter when the Pasha gave the game away; as she laughed now, with a tear on her powdered cheek.

'M. Perry,' said the Princess, 'Imagination? Your dear, pretty wife will supply you with all the imagination you will ever need.'

'Stand back there! Make way! Perry! For heaven's sake! Perry!'

At last Perry, leaning from the carriage window, heard Waldo's shout above the chanting of the students. He saw Waldo's red, angry face and the raised hand with the white envelope.

'Perhaps it's a farewell cheque,' said Mary.

'Let Professor Grimbley get through!' The students took no notice of Perry's plea. They continued to shake his hand and Mary's hand. Perhaps there were as many as fifty, mostly from the English section. Even the two Saudi Arabian students had turned up.

'Please! Please! Let Professor Grimbley pass!'

A bell rang. Within two minutes the train would be leaving.

'It's no good Waldo, you'll have to fight for it.'

And Waldo could be seen, clawing at shoulders and shouting.

'It's your testimonial. You can't leave without it. Dammit, where's the station master?'

'Post it! Post it to me in England,' Perry called.

Waldo had now forced his way sufficiently near to pass the envelope to Perry if they both reached as far as they could. But the students had realized the train was moving and tried to draw away. Suddenly unsupported Waldo staggered forward, caught at the carriage door, placed a foot on the running board and began to move sideways down the platform at an increasing speed. He had already lost his tarboosh.

'An excellent testimonial. Couldn't be better. Read it at your leisure. Fully explains all circumstances. I've taken the broad view. After all it isn't everyone who can adapt himself to life in a foreign country.'

'Get off!' Mary was screaming and picking at his hands. 'Jump off, you fool, or you'll get hurt.'

'What d'you mean,' said Perry, 'it isn't everyone . . . ?'

'You've got to be adaptable,' said Waldo. 'See the other fellow's point of view, listen to him, but never forget you're British.'

'Jump!' said Mary.

'No, climb in,' said Perry. 'You'll break your neck.'

'Nonsense!' said Waldo. The train was travelling at about ten miles an hour. He put out his left leg and jumped. 'Goodbye! God bless!' For a while he ran after the train, dodging porters and piles of luggage, and the last they saw of him he was standing with the students all round him, everyone waving.

Perry turned back into the compartment and showed Mary the envelope. But for her he would have torn it into pieces but she caught him just in time. 'No, Edgar, there's a limit to foolishness,' she said firmly and put the envelope in her handbag.

They had the first class compartment to themselves for, perhaps, the first five minutes of the journey to Alexandria. The door from the corridor opened and Muawiya appeared, wearing a smart new suit and carrying a heavy basket. Without a word of greeting he removed the lid of the basket and spread a white cloth on one of the seats. He produced roast chicken, hard-boiled eggs, butter, bread, grapes, dates and bottled beer.

Mary stood up, but Perry laid a hand on her wrist.

'What's the meaning of this, Muawiya?'

He smiled. All signs of his recent beating had disappeared. His eye was back to normal. Mary sat in a corner of the compartment watching him. For her Muawiya had a special smile. He handed her table-napkin, knife, fork and plate. When he saw that she was no longer watching him but was, instead, running a hungry eye over the display of food, he turned to Perry and remarked, 'I worked on the railway. It is my policy to keep in touch. All are my friends: station-masters, guards, drivers. How else do you think you have a first class compartment to yourselves? Now, I leave you. And good appetite.'

'But aren't you going to eat with us?' said Mary.

'Not unless you wish it.'

They were, all three of them, very hungry and ate from the outskirts of Cairo to Benha and beyond.